# NOT HONOUR MORE

*Not Honour More* concludes the trio of novels — begun with *Prisoner of Grace* (UL-125) and *Except the Lord* (UL-141) — that James Stern, in a *New York Times* review called "the richest, most fascinating saga in modern English literature."

The novel's central figure is, again, the Liberal politician Chester Nimmo, a "dynamic little man trailing wisps of glory and shreds of innocence through a lifetime of expediency." Earlier, Mr. Cary explored Nimmo and his world as they appeared to his wife Nina and to himself. Here we see Nimmo from the point of view of a character who has hitherto been silent: Captain Jim Latter, Nina's first love and second husband, the third point of the triangle that has endured for thirty years. Surely there was never a more dramatic domestic situation than this: comic, ludicrous, tragic.

In the course of his narrative, Mr. Cary brilliantly recreates the great political events of the first quarter of our century, concluding with the bewildering days of England's General Strike. For he has set himself to reveal a world in action, and having given us his consummate portrait of the democratic politician, now produces, through his soldier-spokesman, the most penetrating attack on all that democracy involves. Democracy for Nimmo, is, despite its compromises, the only possible government for free men, while for Latter, it is a racket, a skin game manipulated by power-merchants, a corruption destroying the very soul of modern civilization.

The unpredictability of Joyce Cary is one of his great charms as a novelist — that and his eager acceptance of life, his boundless pleasure in people. *Not Honour More* is unquestionably one of his most surprising creations. Many readers are certain to consider it one of his best.

JOYCE CARY

# Not Honour More

THE UNIVERSAL LIBRARY
GROSSET & DUNLAP
NEW YORK

*Library of Congress Catalog Card Number: 55-6570*

UNIVERSAL LIBRARY EDITION, 1963

BY ARRANGEMENT WITH HARPER & ROW, PUBLISHERS

PRINTED IN THE UNITED STATES OF AMERICA

To My
Godchildren
*Courtenay, Laura, Sophie,*
*Anna, Delia, Brigid*

# NOT HONOUR MORE

# 1

THIS is my statement, so help me God, as I hope to be hung. My name is Latter, James Vandeleur, late Captain 21st Hussars and District Officer Nigerian Political Service, retired, resident at Palm Cottage near Tarbiton, Devonshire, England, with wife and one child; also a visitor, Lord Nimmo, who occupied one room on ground floor.

I had lately received certain anonymous letters suggesting something between Lord Nimmo and my wife. I have always considered such communications as beneath contempt. I handed them to Lord Nimmo who was highly indignant and pointed out they were due to political spite against himself, due to his speeches against Communism, Fascism and Socialism. He thanked me for my confidence in him and assured me of his high regard for my fair dealing with him on all occasions. His exact

1

words were as follow: "Forgive me, my dear Jim, if I use language which may seem to you a trifle old-fashioned and high-flown, but let me say that I know how to value your high sense of honour, none better. For in my long and stormy political life, and especially in recent years, I have had too much to do with the other sort."

It was true Lord Nimmo had lately been engaged in political arguments with all the parties mentioned. In view of the labour trouble of this year, unemployment and the threat of a general strike, he had written to *The Times* and suggested a national all-party committee to deal with emergency, in which experience of Mr. Lloyd George and himself, as Ministers in late War Cabinet, would be at disposal of the Prime Minister. He was also speaking at meetings all over the country, demanding a plan of action.

On May 1st, Labour Day, he was engaged to speak at Shagbrook on the Moor. At 9.10 that morning, I received a phone call in a man's voice who said, "This is a personal call to Captain James Latter." I said I was Captain Latter. He then continued in these words, "I see Nimmo's billed to give his second address at Shagbrook to-day. Perhaps you don't know it, but the idea is to get your wife alone with him in a nice quiet spot on the moor. That's why he picked on Shagbrook for his preachings. Last time he handed it out about God's work in the political world, he took her in Shagbrook wood for a tickle before and after."

This fellow was referring to the second of the so-called Shagbrook addresses on God in Politics, due for that day, and it is

2

well known Shagbrook is an out-of-the-way spot. A lot of people had wondered why Lord Nimmo picked it for his come-back talks. But I fully believed his tale that he picked it because his father had been a preacher there and his parents and sister buried there. It was just his touch.

Fellow on phone now went on to tell me these people had seen Nimmo with my wife in the wood; one with strong field-glasses, and there was no doubt about the criminal nature of this connection.

I told him I had heard such stuff before and didn't like his dirty mind or games with field-glasses, typical of such miserable spies. I happened to know Lord Nimmo had very good reasons to pick Shagbrook which were nothing to do with my wife, and clapped on the receiver and said nothing to my wife or Nimmo. In fact my wife told me voluntarily she would not go to Shagbrook that day because it looked like rain. She hoped also Lord Nimmo would put off meeting because of weather which was bad for his chest. The Shagbrook meetings being in the open air, because of the crowds, the chapel being small.

As the rain came on, I expected meeting to be off, but at three o'clock saw Lord Nimmo's Daimler with chauffeur leave the gate. I was then in road and stood aside to let it pass but he stopped the car to tell me he was going to Shagbrook in spite of the weather because of importance of the day. On account of the labour unrest, this was a critical Labour Day for the whole nation. He asked me what I was doing with a gun in this month and I said that it was not a gun but a rifle, my Winchester 22, and I was going to shoot rats in Potter's boat-yard with my friend Sergeant Varney.

He said then, "Shall you be back to dinner?" I said, "Probably, but not before seven." He then said, in that case he would not hurry back but would return only at half-past seven. Lord Nimmo always affected great politeness towards me as his host. From my position on the bank beside the road, I had already noticed my wife was not in the car. It is not true I placed myself on the bank for this purpose. Nor is it true I returned early from shooting because of any suspicion or doubt of Nimmo's statement to me he would not be back till seven-thirty.

I returned at six because of a disturbance at Potter's yard, where agitators were attempting to bring out the men. I was much surprised to see Nimmo's large car in the drive, and it was by pure chance I did not enter the house by the hall door. Having much river-mud on my boots I made for the gun-room direct by the back door, and so was obliged to pass the back drawing-room windows. It was also a chance I looked in, to see if my wife was there, and that I saw him, this old swine over seventy years of age, interfering with my wife.

I returned at once to go in by front door and entered the room and said, "Now I've got you, you damn swine." I then took aim, but my wife, Nina Slapton Latter, jumped in the way. I pushed her on one side and fired three times, but Nimmo was backing up against the window, and as I fired he took a back somersault through glass and disappeared over sill. I thought I had killed him, not expecting him to be capable of a trick as he always held himself out to be in bad health. Nevertheless I

4

then advanced to the window to make sure, when my wife caught hold of the rifle and before I could break her hold off the barrel, Nimmo's bodyguard, Sergeant Grant, came running into the room, who hit me on the jaw and knocked me black.

I should like to state here and I can call witnesses to prove I had always objected to Lord Nimmo's presence in my house as I considered him a faker and hypocrite. Neither was this a new idea with me due to personal feeling, as has been charged, as I can prove from my book *The Lugas and British African Policy. The Great Betrayal.*

I wrote this book ten years ago when I was hounded out of the African Service for trying to protect my people, the Lugas, from the government policy of what they called civilization but is really materialism and general European degeneracy.

I say my Lugas were better Christians in every way, and better men than any in Whitehall. They were truly nature's gentlemen and the finest I ever knew. But since then entirely ruined and destroyed as a people by European so-called progress. See page 67, last paragraph; "England has lost her honour and her soul due to the Whitehall policy of buying off every kind of grabber and smart Alec all over the world by handing over simple tribesmen and helpless poor people to be exploited by so-called nationalists, otherwise local political crooks."

The only reason why this evil man Nimmo was permitted in my house was my wife who was under the belief that he was a great man who had saved the country and spent his life in the service of the people. I say he spent his life destroying the country and selling the people. I say he corrupted everything

5

and everybody that came near him and stole this woman, my wife, from me when she was little more than a child and set to work to destroy her body and soul. He wanted her money to get into what he called politics, which was stirring up hatred and envy and making promises he knew would never be fulfilled, and when he caught her he proceeded to rob her and terrify her into his slave. I say if a murderer should be hung, which I agree to, then men like Nimmo should be hung twice over because they don't only murder people's bodies but their souls. I say it's the Nimmo gang who have destroyed all truth and honour in the country, including the sanctity of the home and marriage so that it is nothing but a jobber's match of gimme and what do I get out of it. No confidence or faith in any man and divorces running at fifty thousand a year.

That's why I say I meant to kill this old evil man and should certainly have completed the execution of my act at that time if Nimmo's paid bodyguard had not intervened.

When I came to I was in my bed on first floor, and two men on guard, Sergeant Grant and Wilkins, my own gardener. It was then quite dark at the windows and when I asked Wilkins what time it was, he said past ten o'clock and I had been blacked-out over four hours. The doctor had given me an injection and ordered me to be kept quiet.

As I heard voices outside I asked if police had arrived, and they told me yes. But noises were cars coming and crowds of people from Tarbiton and all round on account of report Lord Nimmo had been murdered.

I then said I was quite ready to go to prison at once and they could hang me as soon as they liked. Life was over for me but at least I'd made a good job of it at the end.

Sergeant Grant made no answer to this. He's an ex-policeman. You couldn't expect him to take my view. But I may say that when Sergeant Grant went out of the room for a moment to answer the telephone, Wilkins wrung my hand and said, "You did right, sir. Everybody says so, God bless you, sir." This tribute was a great encouragement and brought the tears to my eyes. Wilkins is an old sailor and a decent fellow, but I had not thought he cared for me in that way, or had such loyalty. Neither had I thought my action would receive popular approval. It showed there is still honourable feeling in the English people. Sergeant Grant now returned to inform me the Chief Constable himself was on his way to the spot. I said, so much the better.

# 2

MY wife entered the room a few minutes later and asked the men to leave us alone. She was greatly distressed and the men duly went, Sergeant Grant, however, locking the doors into corridor and dressing-room. My wife, who was crying, then knelt down and took my hand and kissed it and asked me how I could do such a terrible thing and if I had not thought of Robert.

Robert is my son, aged four that year. I answered of course I had thought of Robert. He was always in my thoughts and I had to think of the kind of home he was living in.

My wife's great agitation affected me very much. I am not ashamed to say I was also in tears. When she saw this, she threw herself into my arms and for some time we could not speak. But when I could do so, I said I ought to go on my knees

8

to her for dragging her name in the papers and courts. But it was because I loved her so much. I couldn't have done anything else in the circumstances, and I'm sure she would agree with me. And all decent people would understand. I said even juries sometimes understood for they sometimes acquitted men for my action. But if I had to die then I would die happy and thanking God for her, the only joy of my life. And I said I had a confession to make. For I said, "I will admit I have had suspicions of you with Nimmo, but I'm ashamed of them now and I ask you to forgive me. For when I looked in the window your back was turned so you couldn't see me and I saw you struggle with him and try to push him away. Thank God," I said, "for that lucky thing, because I might have done a fearful wrong and gone to my death with it on my head."

"But Jim," she said, "it is a wrong you have done, a most fearful wrong. And I can't believe how you could be so cruel to that poor helpless old man—how could you be jealous of him?" I said I was not jealous and if I had been jealous, I would have shown it before. She had given me cause, even from the beginning.

Then she was still more agitated and said this was a cruel charge, though she supposed it was her own fault. But all the same it was cruel of me to bring it up against her. I was the last person.

This was an old argument between us which my wife always brought up at such times, saying it was all due to her having given herself to me. "And God knows," she said now, "I only did it because you said it was what you wanted or I should never have done such a wrong thing—and worse than wrong, it was stupid."

In view of questions asked, I am not attempting to hide I was guilty to this woman. I say I behaved like a brute to her, in this respect. Even if due to my great love. For we were brought up together as children, being cousins, and I loved her most passionately from a boy of ten. My mother being dead and my father abroad and not interested, she was all I had in the world. And she being an orphan, she also loved me and gave me all my happiness. So when she was seventeen and I was twenty-one, in my first regiment, our aunt May Latter, who had brought her up and done so much for me too, was afraid we would get married and ruin my career. Because in my Hussar regiment no one was allowed to marry under captain. So I was afraid to lose my darling if she would not wait for me, and many were interested in her, being so pretty and having money, and one day when we were in Lilmouth, I said she must be my wife for ever, and she said, yes, and I said, but words were not enough, and she said what did I mean, and I said she knew what I meant but it was no good saying anything because she did not really love me, she did not love anybody or anything but her own amusement.

So then she said, what a time to start on that old argument on a day when there was this special concert on the pier. Because in fact there was a special concert that day with some fiddler she was mad about.

I said that was a proof of what I was saying, her music and her damned fiddler were more to her than all my love. So then

10

she said, for God's sake tell her what I wanted. And when I said again she knew very well, she said no, how could she know, when I had never told her in so many words. But I was afraid to tell her. I said then, like any young brute, I was not afraid, it was her who would be afraid to prove her love. And I said so because I was not sure of her love. So she said, "Is that a dare?" and I said, no, it was because I loved her so much more than she loved me.

So then she said she was not afraid of anything I could do to her and as for loving me, she loved me much more than I loved her, but if I spoilt this concert, she would never forgive me. And there was the Blue Lion Hotel opposite where we were known and we could take two rooms at once and if I really meant what I said, for heaven's sake let us get over the agony and have some peace. So we went in and did what she suggested. But we were angry with each other and I accused her of spite against me and spoiling something that should have crowned our great love, and she said I was cruel and tried to make it a punishment to her. We had a great quarrel and the day was spoilt. And this has always been a cause for anger between us.

But now at this terrible time, seeing her in such great agony of mind, I took my wife's hand and said to her we must not quarrel any more. I said for all the evil I had ever done to her I begged for her forgiveness. "Perhaps," I said, "I shall never be able to speak to you again without witnesses, before they hang me, and so I want to thank you for your great true faithful love, as I saw it proved this afternoon. And as for that time at Lilmouth, it was my fault. I was a brute to you, but it was because of my love. I was afraid to lose you. And you behaved nobly and like the sweet true-hearted girl you were, proud and generous."

And when I remembered how she came to me and threw off her clothes and said, "Here you are—do what you like to me. And then I hope you'll believe me and not say I'm only amusing myself with you—" When I remembered this, I took her in my arms and said she was the light of my life and I saw now how wrong my suspicions had been. Because it was simply because of her generous nature she had fallen into Nimmo's trap.

She answered then there was no trap and I did not understand Nimmo nor the fearful situation I had started. The police were here, and not only the police but reporters were coming all the time. And what were we going to tell them?

"The truth," I said. "Do you think I'm going to play any more of the wangling game?" For I saw her mind was on the political effects. "This is something bigger than politics," I said, "when a man has to defend his home and his honour against a canting crook, the lowest of them all. My darling," I said, "I know I haven't done much good in my life and now I've thrown away my only joy and comfort just when I'd found it again— which is your love and loyalty. But at least I've done some good at the end in killing that old swine and stopping some of the rottenness."

She answered, thank God, Nimmo was not dead. Though he was nearly unconscious and under oxygen the doctors had not given up hope.

This was a big shock to me, and I said so. I said the doctors

12

might hope to save him but there was no hope for the country if they did. But she answered all this was simply my blind jealousy and hatred. That was why it was so terribly important for me to think carefully over what I was going to say to the police.

I asked her if she wanted me to commit perjury.

"I don't want you to do a really wicked thing—cruel and spiteful."

"How can I explain shooting him if I don't tell the truth? Unless I say I was mad and they can shut me up."

"You were mad and now you want to ruin him—and us too."

"He's ruined me already—he's ruined both our lives—what's left for us now, after the courts have mauled us over."

"It could be all right again if only you're careful what you say now. If you say it was an accident, and so it was. It was all such a misunderstanding. Jim, I implore you—if you really do care the least little bit for me or Robert. That poor old man, think what he's been and what he can be still." And she went on to a long excited speech about Nimmo's being the only hope of the country. What's more, he was a good man—in his heart he was a true, good man, and in my heart I knew it quite as well as she did.

"Good man," I said, absolutely amazed. "After what happened to-day. I think you must be the mad one."

# 3

I SAY I got a surprise when my wife, after all I had seen, went on trying to defend Nimmo. I called her mad, and I meant it. What could be madder than to call Nimmo good. A known crook and wangler. But I had no right to be surprised. He'd always worked the religious game on her, prayed over her frivolity and frightened her with the idea she was no better than a social parasite. And now she might well be madder because they all were. What could be madder than to call him the hope of the country when everyone had seen his game. Not a week before I'd been at the Town Hall, when Nimmo made his big move to get control in Tarbiton area and wangled himself into the chairmanship of the Emergency Committee. My old friend Pickett had been working on this committee for five months, recruiting specials, organizing services. Doing honest careful

14

work. Pickett doesn't know how to wangle, how to promise what can't or won't be done. Then emergency comes along and Nimmo jumps in and snatches the top job. And Pickett resigns. That is, he is pushed out.

How was it worked by this good, true man, his lordship? First you write to the papers, address hunger marchers, saying present government won't do anything for 'em. Telling 'em their treatment a disgrace to civilization. Encouraging 'em to make trouble. Result. Meetings all over place and lots of violent trouble. Finally, mass meeting in town square. Including solid block Communists complete with banners under Mr. Bill Pincomb, Chief Commissar for the county. Crowd getting bigger all the time. Some come to see banners, some fun. A lot more to work off general feeling life wasn't good enough on half-time, or dole. Police reserve in basement on toes. S.O.S. for specials to come in quietly one by one.

I got in about half-past three. Square pretty well jammed. Traffic stopped. A lot of noise all the time like wolves and hyenas. A lot of nasty feeling getting worse all the time. Due to nasty noise. One barking dog starts another. And then they all want to bite. Out of nerves—nerves inside too. Local politicos, having been talking for three years about hard times, misery in the town, and done nothing, find talk won't wash any more. Two of 'em have been shouted down already. What a fearful situation! Unemployed won't swallow any more wind. Want bread. Councillors running about like hens in a thunderstorm, with faces spreading alarm and despondency. Telling each other, "I told you so. It's all so-and-so's fault, for not talk-

15

ing the right slush." Lady secretaries making tea like mad. Four members of Watch Committee arguing with Chief Constable. Time for truncheons, or too late? About four, mob gets on move. Sends in demands—special relief—new works to be started—resignation three councillors who'd opposed works and said something rude about Mr. Pincomb. Deputation to be received at once. Mayor says no. Councillor X says yes. Councillor Y says, let 'em in and the mob will storm the Hall. Chief Constable says fatal to give way to force. Councillor Y says fatal not to. Four members Emergency Committee equally divided.

Mayor goes out to address crowd and is received by noise like fourteen lunatic asylums. General rush at the doors. Crowd push 'em in. Police push 'em to. Diversion down far end by Slapton Arms. Somebody talking from first-floor window. Somebody says it's old Nimmo. General indignation. Councillor Y says Nimmo at bottom of whole disgraceful trouble. He's responsible letters and speeches encouraging worst elements. Truth is he doesn't care what happens country so long as he gets limelight.

Councillor Y speaks truth, and everyone knows it's truth. All agree. Great outbreak of fury from all local talky boys against Nimmo, for talking out of turn. Mayor says he'll have him arrested. Never mind him being great Nimmo, champion talky boy. He'll be treated like every other disturber of peace.

Diversion getting bigger. Cheers heard from crowd Slapton Arms. Mob looking that way. Nimmo in back of car coming towards Hall. Crowd separating in front. Meeting in mid square

16

with Trade Union leader, unemployed March-leader and Bill Pincomb. Great talk and hand-shaking. They walk on together towards Hall talking, followed by car.

Councillors in consternation. Does he mean to come into Hall? Does he think he's going to talk from Hall? What audacity. Mayor says can't come in, not on any account. Nimmo says very well, he'll go back to car. Talk from car—explain why excluded from Town Hall. Because council against works and special relief. Councillors surround Mayor, talking. Chief Constable says inadvisable keep Nimmo out. Councillor X says inadvisable let him in. Impossible let him talk from Hall reserved for councillors' talk.

Crowd makes ugly rush. Mayor says admit Nimmo but no one else. Nimmo says not without his friends. Crowd breaks three windows in side lane. Mayor says let Nimmo in with two persons only, March-leader, Trade Union Secretary. Doors opened, crowd push and Nimmo comes upstairs on wave into council chamber on second floor, grinning all over face, skipping like sparrow. Followed by three labour men, four or five Communists, and about twenty-five Tarbiton riff-raff, unemployed, unemployable, or just dock side toughs; two political agents, three Press men, four young lady secretaries, one countess and my wife. Countess and wife in smartest new spring frocks. Bought for occasion, i.e., for any revolution on any side. Both smiling all round. Flushed with joy. Pushing out bosoms. Giving love call, "Let us come together in the name of our dear lord. Let us adore him, the prophet of love."

Nimmo goes balcony with unemployed leader and Pincomb.

17

Received with mixed noises like a dog fight. A lot of crowd are saying, "To hell with the old wangler."

Poor aren't so mad. They've had a lot of talk before; they don't love the talky boys. And when he begins to speak, noise gets worse. No one can hear a word. In fact there aren't any. He just moves his mouth, saving celebrated voice. Smiles celebrated smile, waves celebrated arms. Yells of, "Get out, Ches." But not so many yells. And some people near bawling for silence. See his celebrated mouth moving, see him grinning, think they're missing something.

In five minutes, a lot of them can hear word or two. "Time for talk is past—the crisis is upon us. What's needed is action —at once—on largest most courageous lines. National works. To rebuild England. Money is there—only will wanting. And leadership. Let us go straight forward, with God's blessing." He's promising the earth and they begin to lap it up. Fellows in middle distance straining their ears. Chap out there calls again, "Get out, Nimmo," and they nearly lynch him. In ten minutes not a sound, not a cough. The ones at the back who can't hear a word are popping their eyes at celebrated saviour.

Inside all smiles. Councillor X shaking his head, "All the same, what a gift—what an artist." Councillor Y, "His voice is as strong as ever." Countess and wife working their charms on councillors, committee, the whole lot. "No one like him—and they said he was finished."

My wife up by window talking to three young Bolshy toughs as if greatest privilege of her life. Asking after conditions in their homes. Making big eyes in sympathy. Shaking head in deep grief for bad times. Putting out all her chest. Quite a Leicester Square turn. Nimmo will save them. Nimmo is only man with a plan, with courage to act.

I go up and say, "Hullo." She blinks and turn red. Didn't know I was there. I say, "Busy afternoon—nice frock." She says, "Isn't it exciting—isn't he quite wonderful."

But crossing her fingers and watching me like a cat on a wall. She says, "I thought I'd better be at hand," and shows me a little bottle in her bag, Nimmo's heart medicine.

I say it's a good ramp. "First you get the unemployed and Communists to demand the earth knowing all the time it isn't there to give. And then you come along and promise it to them."

She looks at me with a smile. Takes a bit of fluff off my lapel, which wasn't there. Charming gesture. Thoughtful wife. But her eyes are trying to see what's going on in funny old Jim. Who doesn't understand politics.

"They tried to keep him out—but they couldn't. They'll have to have him back now. He's the only man who knows what to do. He's doing everything already."

"Stealing everything."

"His name alone—" she says.

"That's all he is."

"Oh, no, Jim—such a wonderful speech. Thank goodness he got over that cold he caught at Shagbrook. If it had been last week, he would have been too hoarse, and his voice is half the battle. Oh, dear, what's that?"

Nimmo has stopped. She makes a run to look out on balcony, bottle in hand. Quite pale with fright in case great man has

19

fainted, or worse, lost his precious voice. But he's only doing one of his famous gestures, hands in the air—groping for image. Which he has had ready since last week. Out it comes. The crowd cheers. Mrs. Jim Latter comes back pink with relief. And gazes at her husband as if he had dropped in through the roof. Sighs and recovers herself. Turns on charm. Takes another bit of fluff off same lapel. Which isn't there. Says "Poor boy, what a bore for you all these politics. I really hate it more than you do. But it'll soon be over. This crisis can't go on much longer. And it is so exciting to see poor old Chester coming to the front again. It really does rather restore one's faith in human nature. It was so horribly cruel the way he was treated after the war."

And then the big cheers. Nimmo has finished. He steps into the room. She runs to congratulate him. The countess takes his other hand. All the ladies would like to kiss him. Mayor, Councillors, etc., come round, each trying to get a word in first. Because it's obvious to every talky boy in the place that, for talking, Nimmo is top boy. That he's talked himself into top job. That he'll run the show. Give out the jobs. Perhaps he's going to be Prime Minister. And dish out the real big stuff. Knighthoods, gongs. You never can tell, and congratulations cost nothing. Only a bit of talk.

And it was just as I said—only sooner and worse. Same evening a special meeting of the council and Nimmo asked to be chairman of the Tarbiton Committee. In three days, he was chairman of the County Committee. And handing out the jobs. One of them was Pickett's. The committee was non-party but

Pickett was a Tory and Nimmo suddenly found he had no confidence in him. And everyone agreed Pickett had no imagination. He hadn't promised the earth. For now the Nimmo fever was well on. My house was full of ladies sizzling in the dream of his glory like apple fritters. Especially my wife. For her, it was an act of God. She bought another new frock for the next political crisis. And no one thought it funny. No one said, "This is a bit queer. The talky boy talks about the evil of talk and gets the job, over the men who have been doing the job and saying nothing about it." No one was even surprised at this conjuring trick.

I say this is madness, when a whole lot of lunatics say to each other of a crook, "At last a man who knows how to do things." When a whole nation puts straw in its hair and says, "The only way to keep a country straight is by lies and wangle, crookery and the Piccadilly smile. And anyone who says it isn't is simply a fool and not worth talking to."

# 4

HERE was my wife who was supposed to be a clever woman, weeping and clutching at me because I might tell a little bit of truth about this liar and welsher Nimmo. "You call me mad," I said, "but what are you? Why is Nimmo a great man—because he's got away with every kind of dirty work? Why is he good—because he talked about God at Shagbrook, cashing in on his sister's grave?"

Because Nimmo had made a big thing of his dead sister, saying she had been the great influence of his early life. All I know of this girl was she jilted a poor chap who cut his throat and the Shagbrook people say she was possessed with seven devils and still walks the moor because Hell wouldn't take her in. But that wouldn't stop Nimmo from making up a yarn if it served his political turn.

And his tale was she brought him back to God and a true idea of freedom which was to know good and willingly do it.

"To know and do good," I said. "My God, that hypocrite and devil. It would make a cat laugh. And to-day proved it."

But she would not listen to me. "And you know he's devoted to you. This is the most terrible blow to him."

"Of course, that's what he would say. He's got to strike an attitude."

But she answered he meant it, he had always admired and respected me. And then she brought up an argument that surprised me even more. "Oh, Jim, don't you see that if he gets back into office, he'll go away from here and we'll have peace again."

I said that my God, he was going anyhow, pronto. "My God," I said, "you don't mean you'd let that swine stay in this house another hour."

"Of course not, Jim. And I did send for the ambulance. But just at the moment he was so collapsed. He could hardly whisper."

"So you've been talking to him."

"Only about six words. He's too ill to talk—he only saw me about the Pressmen to apologize because he couldn't see them to-day."

I saw at once if Nimmo didn't die, he'd be putting out some lying statement to put me in the wrong or hide the truth. And I'd seen often enough how such men can get their lies received all over the world, so that the truth has no chance against them. Due to their hook-up with all the other brass wanglers in every

23

department who are out to help each other in return for favours expected of the same kind.

I therefore asked my wife if the police were on guard outside the window or in the corridor and if the dressing-room was locked. My dressing-room opened into the bedroom and also the corridor.

My wife seemed startled by this question. She said, "But you couldn't escape now. Would it be any good to try?" Then at once she remembered her society manners. She never refuses anyone anything, flat out. She always says yes, what a wonderful idea, and then somehow if she doesn't like it, it doesn't come off. "But why not," she said, recollecting herself, "that would be marvellous. Wait, I'll just go and see how the land lies."

And she came back in a few minutes by way of the dressing-room, locking the door behind her but giving me the key. She was excited and flushed, and said she thought I had a good chance and she would help. There were only three police on duty outside the house, and they were looking after the traffic too. And Grant in the bedroom corridor. But she would try to distract his attention so I could slip out by the dressing-room and so down the back stairs. She would give me the signal for making the getaway by coughing and blowing her nose.

I was surprised by this, because she seemed to mean it and I warned her she would be incriminating herself and perhaps upsetting Nimmo. For if I did get away, I said, it was only fair to tell her I should probably be making a statement—in fact, that was the idea.

24

But her answer was her duty to me came first and how could I doubt her love.

This gave me very great happiness and I said so. We were both very much moved at this moment, feeling we might not meet again for a long time, or only in gaol. We said good-bye with much love. My wife then made up her eyes and nose at the glass and went out by the bedroom door and engaged Grant in conversation. I at once took a reconnaissance from the window and saw that though it was dark the whole place was illuminated with headlights, a policeman at the yard gate and a crowd of cars and persons outside on the drive. But I considered if I were stopped, I should be no worse off and the crowd might even be an advantage if I slipped among the cars.

Therefore when my wife duly coughed and blew, I unlocked the dressing-room door and looked out. Grant had his back towards me and my wife was smiling up at him—she was an old friend, as they were often out together on Nimmo's speechifyings.

I slipped across the passage in a moment and down the back stairs to the kitchen corridor. From here, however, I could see there was another policeman standing at the back door holding back five or six men, including two cameramen. I therefore stood back against the wall, when I felt a touch on my arm. I turned round and saw a woman beckoning round the larder door. I knew larder had a barred window and therefore shook my head. But she caught my sleeve and pulled me into larder and turned up light.

I then recognized this woman as a person with a grievance against Nimmo—she'd threatened him before, and also been found in the house several times under mysterious circumstances. But Nimmo had taken no action. He considered it bad for votes to use the law against any person.

It is also part of the wangling game not to let people know you are not universally beloved. In fact Nimmo had many enemies in all classes, especially from the time of his being one of the War Cabinet, which was the reason for his bodyguard. This woman was not the worst but more persistent, being in the neighbourhood. She was called Brome and her grievance was Nimmo had caused the death of her son by victimization, that is, not exempting him from war service when she said he was unfit. She had already accosted me before with her grievances, and now took my hand and began to cry and bless me for doing God's work. She said she would hide me so police would never find me except over her dead body. She would die for me. I told her not to talk nonsense.

For I considered this woman a lunatic and pest and I wish to make it plain I had no desire at any time to take advantage of this woman's lunatic grievance against Nimmo, not myself acting from any grievance or petty jealousy but in the public interest and decency. Not wishing to be associated with her in any form nor escape the law by her assistance. I asked her at once what she wanted and how she had broken into my house.

She then pointed to larder window and I saw a young fellow looking in and holding a bar on one side. I recognized him as a man called Drew, a reporter on the *Tarbiton Gazette* who had interviewed me as commodore of the Yacht Club, and I had taken him for a sail to show him the right words. I liked the young chap. He had married a little girl out of a draper's in High Street and he was trying to give her all she wanted in armchairs and curtains.

When I saw him, he made faces and waved his hand at the bar. So I did not hesitate, only ordered the woman Brome to go out first as she had no right in my house and I feared she might make some attempt which would be due to personal feeling and spite.

She duly obeyed and I followed. But it was necessary for Drew and her to help me from window on account of my head. Now I was on my feet and coming in the open air I found myself giddy due to severe knock-out and doctor's injection.

This delayed our progress through kitchen-garden where Drew had left his car in lane just below a gap in hedge. This lane is down a steep bank and when we reached hedge and looked over, we saw it was crowded with cars and a crowd of sightseers. Drew said there were many more, even in ten minutes he had been with the woman Brome who had showed him how to push back the bar. He was very excited and anxious and told me to wait till he had got down and opened car door, then he would signal and I was to run across with my face down in my collar. Which I duly carried out.

Unluckily, owing to the bad state of my head, I slipped on the bank and though the Brome woman assisted me down, we were seen and before I could reach the car, we were surrounded by crowd. One man shone a torch on my face and shouted, "My God, it's the captain." The woman Brome knocked down his hand and Drew pushed me into car, and Brome followed, but the crowd was now very excited and making a good deal of noise. One man at the back was calling "Police," and somebody else was saying to give the poor bugger a chance.

A police constable then came to the hedge and called down to know what the trouble was. This made everyone quiet and Drew answered him in an angry voice his car was blocked in and why didn't police control the traffic. The constable said nothing to this but stood looking on while Drew worked car out and drove off. "That was a near one," he said. "This is my lucky day. But we'll have to be quick. What I propose is we make for some quiet spot on the moor, say Battwell. I can phone from Battwell."

I said no, as I wished to consult my solicitor in Lilmouth. Drew said, my God, this was no good to him. If scoop was going to do him any good it would have to be in London within next hour. And very important for him. Because, as I knew, it was a terrible time for country papers, and *Tarbiton Gazette* very shaky. A strike might wreck it, and thousands of reporters out of work already. A scoop for a London daily might save his life.

I said in that case, knowing him to be a family man with children, I would give him short hand-out as soon as we reached quiet spot. I suggested a certain pub in East Tarbiton, the Water Boy, where there was a back door on the river and a boat. So we could cross if found.

We were now climbing towards the moor and noticed at once several cars had turned off on the same route. "They're after us," Drew said. "It was that fool shining the torch, and this old car is no good on the level."

I said I had no hope of an escape and did not mean to attempt one. I would give myself up as soon as I had given my hand-out. I had done my duty and so long as it had stopped the Nimmo rot I didn't care what happened to me.

Drew said all the same we needed time to get the hand-out and he would take a short cut through the Shagbrook by-road. This he did and threw the cars off the scent. But to our surprise, as we came into East Tarbiton, we found them waiting for us at the crossroads. We therefore made for the Water Boy at full speed through the back streets of the town, but were delayed by unusual number of people in these streets. Also we found the Water Boy, usually very quiet, with crowded bars and even the back garden. I was about to turn away, preferring to go on further, when the landlord, an old friend of mine, came out and said he hoped I would stay and come to his parlour. Crowd was because of a union meeting about Emergency Committee's letter in papers.

This was a set of orders by the Emergency Committee, that is, practically Nimmo, warning against violence in case of general strike and advising against interference with pickets which should be distinguished by arm-bands. Also saying committee was fully aware of general sympathy with miners' hardships due to depressed state of trade, and also sad condition of unemployed, but pointed out violence would prejudice their case.

I said they'd better wait as there was going to be a new committee. Nimmo was out. And I would prefer a bedroom to the parlour as we wanted to be quiet. The man asked me then if it was true something had happened to his lordship and I said, yes, he had got what was coming to him, but there was no time to discuss the matter. Please to see no one came upstairs after us.

We were now in the bedroom and Drew at once pulled out his notebook and asked me to be quick, we only had five minutes.

I said we had plenty of time as landlord would hold stairs. Also I was not like him used to quick composition, and needed time to pick my words. But Drew said he had to get his call through before midnight to get in first.

I saw his point and could enter into his feelings as husband and father. This was why, against better judgment, I agreed to his proposition. I then worked out following hand-out on the washstand.

"The reason of my action against Lord Nimmo was because I caught him interfering with my wife. Repugnant as it is to any decent man to make such facts public in the Press, I hereby give them as a public duty. For many years I have considered Nimmo and his gang of a character without the first idea of honourable conduct, public or private, and this proves it. They have been the ruin of our beloved country—

**30**

have always supported our enemies everywhere and once more in the present terrible danger are only seeking their own advantage to worm their way back into power.

"I do not therefore regret anything in my action and would do it again if it called attention to the increasing corruption of everything in the country, the destruction of family life, and the policy of shameless jobbery and double-dealing in high places, only for personal ambition.

"It is the same everywhere, decent honest people having no chance against the government. They are just pushed up against the wall. No one will listen to them because the only idea is to get all you can by any dirty trick which pays. And family life which is the life-blood of an honourable sound-hearted nation mocked at as too much trouble and going down every day."

I wish here to draw attention to the fact this hand-out was so short, leaving out material facts, as since referred to, because it was done against time. For the same reason, it was not put into good style for publication. I wish to insert here too, on reading over typescript as ready for court, the same refers to whole statement dictated at high speed for short-hand.

My only wish in this statement, as my last say on earth, is to have the truth the whole truth and nothing but the truth, so help me God. Including my poor wife whom I love still with all my heart and Nimmo on his side however clever and misleading.

I have leaned over backwards to give the truth of Nimmo

and all concerned. So that no one shall say I was afraid of it or didn't understand any point.

If I have wilfully falsified any word in this statement, if I have made anything look different from the truth even if against me, I deserve to be considered a contemptible cur. More than Nimmo himself because he has never set up the truth and doesn't know what truth is.

My whole case is this, that if a man or country gives up the truth, the absolute truth, they are throwing away the anchor and drifting slowly but surely to destruction. I say nothing can save but truth and the guts to take it. For truth will always prevail.

I wish therefore to put on record any errors or omissions are not by my will but due solely to pressure of time. Nor any fault of policewoman Martin taking dictation practically all night.

She has given every consideration to me and I desire herewith to express my very high appreciation and gratitude for her great patience and courtesy.

# 5

ACTUALLY while I was working out my hand-out for Drew, Document 1 as put in, some cars had reached Water Boy and Drew, having looked from windows, informed me half the Press was there and if I did not finish at once, it would be no good to him.

Then when I gave it to him he said that he must cut out first sentence because it was libel. I answered that I could not allow it to be printed without first sentence because otherwise it would look as if I had acted from jealousy. And the first sentence was nothing but the truth. Drew said this made no difference. "Truth can be the worst kind of libel because doing more damage."

The following conversation then took place in these words:

"If you cut out Nimmo's act against my wife, people will

think I acted from jealousy and had no good reason. It's just that act shows him up for a hypocrite."

"No paper can print libel."

"I thought you wanted the truth and now you cut out the only important part of it. You talk about the freedom of the Press and then you say you can't give the truth."

"I don't tell lies."

"You make this a lie if you leave out the important fact. You make me act like a lunatic."

"It's not me—it's the law and the boss."

I said if Drew was an honest man and had any feeling for the truth, he ought to take a risk. He said it wouldn't be any good, he would only be sacked.

This situation speaks for itself. I said to Drew, "No wonder the country is in this rotten state if no one can tell the truth." He said, "You'll get your chance in court."

I said, "Yes, and I'll say how the Press acted—it seems to me the Press is simply there to hide the truth."

People were already knocking at door and one of them was shouting to Drew. Also a ladder appeared at window and a man put his head in and said, "If you've finished, Drew—" Drew said, all right, and made for door. But before he got there the man on ladder got in, and when Drew opened door, about six more pushed in from outside.

I turned to these people and said that if they were looking for me, I was Captain Latter, and I would be only too glad to give them the facts if they had the guts to print them. The red-faced man who had come in at the window said he was sorry if I was annoyed but I must understand he was only doing his job. The following conversation then took place:

CAPTAIN LATTER: "It depends what you call your job. To give the truth, or keep in with the wanglers who are rotting the soul of this poor old country."

RED-FACE: "Depends what you mean by wanglers."

CAPTAIN LATTER: "The old gang—the Nimmo gang. All the lot of thieves and liars who are wangling the people along to the ruin of England. But I see it only makes you laugh—you think I'm just another fool of an old soldier."

RED-FACE (getting angry): "You've no right to say that. I wasn't laughing at what you said. What made me laugh was the idea you're going to change it."

A little old man on the bed, with a cock-nose, "That's it, Captain. I've been in the thick of it for forty years."

CAPTAIN LATTER: "And went along with it."

A tall man leaning against the wall, with a green face like a cheese-scoop, "Are you a Fascist?"

CAPTAIN LATTER: "What's that?"

CHEESE-SCOOP: "Mussolini's racket."

CAPTAIN LATTER: "That is a foul lie. You know very well I belong to one of the oldest Liberal families in the West and have always been for the people, against all oppression. My action against Nimmo has nothing to do with politics. It was simply the man is playing a dirty game and leading the country to ruin, including the people. It's too late for politics."

RED-FACE: "Wait a moment, please, is this for the record?"

CAPTAIN LATTER: "Yes, put it down. How long do you think this poor old country is going to stagger on under such a load of vermin. What's going to happen if they bring off this general strike? It will finish old England and finish the lot of you too."

A young man at the back said, "Hear, hear." Red-Face said that the miners weren't too well off.

CHEESE-SCOOP: "Two pound ten a week and risk their lives."

I said this was a scandal and as a Liberal I had always been against starvation wages anywhere. And as an old soldier, against the people who got rich on paying them too. In the services nobody made fortunes as they well knew.

Cheese-Scoop called out that Lord Frant was a Liberal and made thirty thousand a year.

I answered that this was true. Lord Frant was in with Nimmo. And when he was going to pull off a steal, he gave Nimmo a tip. I knew because he wanted me to go in with him. He gave me the tip.

SCOOP: "And did you take it?"

CAPTAIN LATTER: "No, I didn't take it. If you take anything from Nimmo, he'll want something back. That's the game."

SCOOP: "And what did he want?"

All this time there was a lot of noise, not only from the bars and street and also the garden where the men were arguing, but because some of the journalists were pushing

36

out, having got what they wanted, and some others coming up the stairs. So I didn't hear the fellow properly and asked him what he'd said. Then he bawled out, "I said what did he want from you?"

When I understood this, I admit I lost my temper. I made a dash at the swine. But the young man caught hold of me, saying Scoop was a Communist, and only wanted trouble, and half a dozen more got round and pushed me against the wall.

I told them to get out. That I was not going to quarrel with such poor bloody devils. "I know you're not free to say what you think and you know you're in a rotten job simply to sell rottenness, and you can't do anything about it."

"Look, Cap.," said Cock-Nose, "perhaps you don't know it, but we like you. You're a popular man in these parts and you've had a raw deal all round."

"Hear, hear," said the young man who had now come up beside me. And then some of them said, "Hear, hear," and one fellow started clapping and they all clapped and cheered. This took me by surprise. Here were about twenty fellows that had been through all the dirt in the world for years and, by God, they still had hearts to feel. And what were they getting out of it? Damn all. What had I done for any of them except spit in their faces. I got a big surprise and I was ashamed of myself. "By God," I said to them, as soon as I could speak. "That's the best thing that's happened to me for forty years. I don't mind telling you. It's a lesson to me. I don't mind telling you I don't have much opinion of the

37

Press or writing chaps generally. The writy chaps are only a tick better than the talky chaps, if ticks can win on bugs— both of them are out to suck the country's blood. But damn it all, I know how it comes to you. A chap gets married and has kids and he wants the money, and he says to himself, 'It may be dirty work but how am I going to stop it. Who am I to stand out?' And then he says, 'Perhaps I need not eat so much dirt as some of them, perhaps I'll be able to write honest clean stuff and nobody'll notice it.' And then he goes into the job, has another kid, and by the time he wakes up and knows that he's a bug like all the other bugs, he's so jammed up with bills and worry that he don't know how to get out.'

" 'There's a lot in that,' as the chambermaid said," said Cock-Nose, and I could see some of them were laughing at me. "All right," L said, "that's all right. I'm a damn-fool old soldier who's talking out of turn. And you think me a comic cut, and I think you're a lot of poor bastards who daren't take a look at yourselves in the glass in case your guts fall out on the floor and your wives have to go on the dole. But I say it's a damn bloody shame ever you came in such a jam. Because it wasn't your fault. You didn't mean to be on this filthy ramp. Your hearts were in the right place and outside your job you're still some of the best fellows I've ever run into. I'm sorry for you, but by Christ, I'm grateful to you. You've done me the best turn one man can do another. You've made me see what decent chaps there are still in the country, and how wrong I was to judge by appearances. You're just caught up in this slimy web that's wound itself round everything. What you've just said gives me hope—I know now even if I've smashed myself and dragged my poor wife into all the dirt of the courts, I've not been wasting my time. It gives me hope, if we could only blast some way out of this mess, we'd find it only a nightmare and wake up in God's clean daylight again."

"We'll have a drink on that," Cock-Nose said. But before we could get down to the bar, a man came up on a motor bicycle and shouted from the street old man Nimmo was doing well and did not propose to make any charge.

The whole crowd rushed out to question this fellow, and a great many from the street and the bar came round too. Some of them had not heard anything about the case and were calling for information. And after a moment I followed to find out the particulars. For I was taken by surprise, by this action of Nimmo's, as I had seen the police at the Cottage. I found all the Pressmen talking at once and several of them writing, and for a moment no one would attend to me. Finally I asked the young man on the bicycle what he meant. He looked at me and said, "The old chap is taking nourishment." "But about the charge—the police were called." "That was before he came round. But as soon as he heard of it, he said there was no case for them. The thing was an accident and there would be no charge." Then he laughed in my face and said, "What do you think? He's not so green. To let a thing like this get into court."

"Everybody knows the truth," I said.

"It's only your word against his."

"And your word won't make the front page," Scoop said. And I could see in spite of them all being so busy they were amused. I asked then what was funny in a crook getting away with all his dirty work which was a danger to them too and the whole country.

"I don't know," Cock-Nose said. "But you have to take off your hat to the old bastard. Good night, Captain, and good luck with it," and he went off to his car. All of them were hurrying away and in a few minutes there were only the fellows from the bar who had come out to hear the news.

# 6

THIS trick of Nimmo's gave me a surprise. But then I saw
I'd had the right idea—the only mistake I'd made was not
shooting quick enough before my wife jumped in. I said,
there's only one way out with that kind of crook, to shoot
him. He may be as clever and as tricky as you like but cleverness won't stop bullets. And what else can stop him, but a
bullet? They'll call it murder, but what I'm out for is truth
and justice. I've been a magistrate and I've studied law and
I know how important it is to make the law respected, but
if the law goes against truth, then it is worse than useless.
It is an evil thing because it brings fair dealing and decent
conduct into disgust. It brings in the worst corruption because
the people give up all idea of fair dealing and think only of

every man looking out for himself. It turns everything into trickery and bluff.

I said this to the people there. I said, "You see how this crook Nimmo has dodged out of his crime. And I hope you'll tell everyone the truth—that this old hypocrite and faker assaulted my wife. I don't want to bring personal family matters into public, much less my wife's, who is very dear to me, but I do it from the duty to show up this man Nimmo and stop the fearful evil he's doing."

They all looked at me very attentively, and more kept crowding round from the street and the bars, but as I soon saw, they weren't interested in my statement. Some of the boys at the back were laughing and one called out that Nimmo was one up on the day. An old man in front asked me if it was true Lord Nimmo was not badly hurt. I said I didn't know, but I believed he was out of politics which was the one good thing I'd done yet. They did not say anything to this, and then the same old man asked if I thought there was going to be a revolution.

This started them all off, some of them said it was all nonsense. If a general strike were called it would be only in support of the miners and not political. I said if it didn't start political it would end political. Someone at the back called out then he hoped there would be a revolution, it was quite time. I answered the Communists wanted one and Nimmo was playing with both sides, so if there was a revolution he would come out with the winner and a good job. "Look at his emergency orders," I said, "he is practically saying, 'Go on and have your general strike—bring everyone out and we will not allow you to be interfered with.' " A young man said this was a lie and some other young men called out I was a Fascist. I answered he was the liar, and there was a scene. A lot of young people came pushing through to the front and took up a threatening attitude. Also a lot more of them were laughing. Not caring about the truth or country but only making game of everything. I said I wasn't accusing them of being Communists but they were being misled by Communists. Some of them now began to jostle up, someone started a shout, "The army against the people" and "Put him in the river." I shouted I had left the army twenty-five years but they shouted me down. However, just then a young man I knew, and a girl also known to me, took me by the arms and pushed me towards the side of the street.

I wish to record this act of great courage on the part of those I am proud to call my friends, Arthur Cook of East Tarbiton and Miss Annie Bilson of the same place. I had known Arthur Cook for years as he had worked in Potter's boat-yard and also his father. The girl, Bilson, his fiancée, I had seen only once before and recognized only by her red hair.

The girl was small and not strong, but she turned on the gang who were setting on me and told them they were a lot of dirty cowards, and when one tried to get in our way, she fairly went for him with her nails. He had to duck his face down and cringe out of the way. She took them so by surprise with her threats and by this attack they let us through.

These brave young people then conducted me to the Bilsons' home which was a three-room cottage at the dockside. When being taken with giddiness, no doubt due to the same knock-out, I was advised to lie down on a bed, where I at once fell asleep which continued till after ten o'clock on the next morning.

I was then awakened only by knocking on the window and Annie Bilson telling the person responsible to go off. She told me this had been going on for more than two hours, boys and workers trying to look in from the pavement and three cars waiting for an interview. But she had refused to allow anyone to enter though offered sums of money up to a pound, a great inducement for the poor girl.

I may say that on awaking I found myself actually in the bed which belonged to Miss Annie. The young people had put me to bed, of which I remembered nothing. She having slept on the floor in case I required attention. They also wished me to have a doctor being alarmed by my exhaustion. But I told them it was due to the knock-out. I had been knocked out before boxing as a young man and the effects are often delayed. They then cause headache and giddiness and apparent exhaustion.

I cannot speak again too highly of the devotion of this poor girl. The Bilsons were very poor as the father is dead and the mother is only employed at Potter's as char because her husband was a shipwright in the yards. This poor woman was now much afraid of losing her employment and home because of the very bad trade at Potter's.

44

They knew me as a friend of Thomas Potter as I had been about the yards from a child. My own boats had been built at Potter's, and there was very strong family feeling in this good old firm. This, I was told, was the cause of much of the dispute on the night before. Pressure was being put on Potter's men to come out and, of course, threats of picketeers due to Nimmo's broad hint.

I may say it was not only employers in such small firms as Potter's were indignant at Nimmo's statement in support of picketing, but also their work people who knew too well what it meant, intimidation or ruin and the break-up of their homes.

# 7

SEVERAL letters had been dropped in the box and a newspaper pushed under the door. This was the *Tarbiton Gazette* with Nimmo's statement, as follows, marked in blue pencil:

"The report of an attempt upon my life is completely false. It arose apparently from the hasty misconstruction of one of my staff based upon the accidental discharge of a small rifle, little more than a toy, causing a slight flesh wound.

"Further misconceptions seem to have arisen from the presence of police in the grounds. These were summoned to regulate the very considerable traffic, attracted to the place by the rumour of an assassination, which spread with extraordinary rapidity. May I beg the public generally to receive this intimation as final and conclusive, and especially the numerous friends who have been making enquiries by telephone, letter and messenger.

"These are grave and anxious times for our beloved country and such a trivial incident should not be allowed to occupy the minds and waste the time of the post office staff and the police, not to speak of the Press, at a crisis when the national future hangs in the balance, and your Emergency Committee may be faced at any moment with the most momentous responsibilities. (Signed) Nimmo."

A note pinned to this paper read, "My dear Latter, I think you should see this. Of course I don't believe a word of it. But it raises a problem which perhaps you have not sufficiently estimated—the great political advantage arising to Nimmo from this attack—an advantage which he, of all men, knows how to make full use of. Already, as you see, he has taken an attitude which will win him the greatest respect on top of much popular sympathy.

"I do not blame you for your action. We all know how much provocation you have had for two years past. But I beg you most earnestly to pause and consider very carefully your next step, which ought perhaps to be a civil action. Any ill-considered move might well play further into Nimmo's hands with extremely dangerous consequences not only to your private interests but the public welfare.

"I write in my car, which you can see across the street. I shall wait in the car which is at your disposal, as also
Yours very sincerely,
A. M. Brightman, Major (retired)."

I'd met this man Brightman at a gymkhana committee and I'd read a bit of his book called *True Democracy* which proposed to settle the unemployed by national work, and the housing problem by taking over the millionaires. Also he had led some unemployed marches and had a row with Nimmo.

The book was all right but I didn't much take to the fellow who smelt of brass. Also push. In fact, when I came out of the house there he was with two other chaps, waiting for me. But I brushed them off and told them pretty shortly I didn't need their assistance.

I then made my way direct to the dockside and so to the armoury of the Tarbiton Territorial Regiment. I was admitted here, as I was known as a friend of Sergeant Varney, assistant armourer. Also having lectured to them on Bush Warfare and the Luga tribe.

It was here I obtained revolver and ammunition mentioned in the charge sheet. I wish to say most strongly this was by no fault of Sergeant Varney, one of my oldest friends and whom I respect beyond any man living. It would have been the meanest kind of action to incriminate Sergeant Varney even for my just purpose. The reason he did not report my taking the arms was he was otherwise engaged, and did not know it.

I then hired a car from the Green Man Hotel garage and proceeded direct to my home at Palm Cottage, arriving just before twelve o'clock.

# 8

I FOUND about as many cars and people in Longwater Lane below the Cottage as on the evening before. There was a policeman at the main gate. I therefore left my car in the upper road and proceeded through the wood and kitchen garden to the yard and the kitchen door.

Here I was stopped by Wilkins who told me his orders were to let no one in. But I said he couldn't keep me out of my own house and made him send for my wife.

Nina came at once and welcomed me with a warm kiss and said she had been very anxious, not knowing where I had gone. But now, thank God, all that trouble was over and things could be as before.

I could see she was greatly alarmed. She was very white and her lips were shaking. I asked her if Nimmo was still in the house and she said, "Yes, but he's just going. It was only because he was too ill to be moved."

I asked where he was, and she said she didn't know, but no one was allowed to see him. As she spoke, she turned red, and I suspected she was putting me off. I therefore walked past into the house and made my way to the drawing-room in the front half.

This is a double room divided by folding doors and with separate doors on to the passage. There is also a door from the back part into a rose garden. Since Nimmo's visit, this back part had been made up as a bed-sitting-room for Nimmo. He was not allowed to climb stairs owing to his supposed weak heart.

I went straight to the passage door leading into Nimmo's room but found it locked. I therefore made for the other door into the front part which I found crowded with people, so for the first moment I was not noticed.

I had come to the conclusion Nimmo was in the back part of the room behind the folding doors, but I knew also locks had been fitted to these doors since the lunatic Brome's first entry when she had attacked Nimmo with a kitchen knife. I therefore kept by the wall to watch an opportunity of approaching these doors, in order to try if this way was open.

I was, however, immediately recognized and greeted by Sir Henry Bootham, Nimmo's late secretary and son-in-law. He came quickly and took my hand, and I could see he was much startled by my arrival and wished to be very sweet.

Sally also, who is my god-daughter as well as niece, kissed me affectionately and pressed my hand hard.

Sally is a fine girl with plenty of guts and a mind of her own, as honest as they make 'em. The Boothams were old friends. I'd always said Henry Bootham was a sound man who did his best by Nimmo. He'd left only after a quarrel between Sally and her mother. Now he'd rallied round his great man. In fact, he had some London papers in his hand and showed me the headlines—"Lord Nimmo and Tarbiton Riot," "Nimmo's Proposals for Settlement" and "Shagbrook and After," "Lord Nimmo on National Crisis." Bootham is a calm fellow but he was plainly excited. He kept pushing the papers under my nose. "I think you'll agree, Latter, the Shagbrook speeches have struck a new note, and a better one. He's taken the thing out of party politics." Sally looked at me as if to say, "I wonder." As I say, she's an honest girl, and growing up fast.

"He's certainly got hold of something," I said, "for himself. Grabbed it, you might say." Bootham pulled a secretariat face at me and asked if I had seen the Trade Union statement that morning. In his view, a strike was now inevitable and might have the gravest consequences. Playing the regular private secretary. Knowing his Nimmo all through but never letting him down. And I thought him then a decent loyal chap and a good deal of a gentleman—I respected him for returning to duty, even to help Nimmo.

"You can bet it will," I said. "The very worst—if a certain person we both know of has anything more to do with it."

A nice doll-faced countess, Lady Lilmouth, kept fluttering round us all the time, fixing me with her eyes and cooing she was so delighted to see me again at this exciting time. Then a fellow, about eight feet high with a black moustache and another countess, a brown one, hanging on his words, chimed in and said the nation had had a rude awakening but understood at last in no doubtful fashion a strong and united Liberal party was essential to the welfare of the country. He had a paper in hand too. It was just about the time when the London papers usually arrived and they'd all had a nice surprise.

Bootham introduced this fellow as late minister for something, and then he introduced Lord Somebody, a thin little red-faced man, with a blue nose, as late minister for something else. There seemed to be half the old War Cabinet in the room and the rest were wives or secretaries; and two or three reporters. Also, I thought, some detectives. Two huskies who now began to close in on me. I saw Nimmo had made preparations in case I returned home. Lord Somebody began to charm me with his teeth and said this terrible crisis had proved one thing, the Conservatives only knew how to play party politics, and Labour was run by its own demagogues. Neither was fit to lead a great nation. I said, "Oh yes."

Cars were arriving all the time, and just now another old man came in with a stick on one side and his wife's arm on the other. And even in the door he began to gabble. "How is he? What a dastardly thing."

All the others looked shocked to see him and Lady Doll-Face sent her eyebrows into her hair. They were calculating if all these old men turned up, there wouldn't be enough jobs to go round. But the old man went on gobbling and gabbling about the failure of the Conservatives and the need of a national government, so successful in the last war.

All these people, as they gradually realized who I was, were quite as frightened as my wife. They stood round in rings, staring at me like a wild beast. They hadn't expected the audacious villain to return to his own house while red with the great man's blood. The low blackguard who dared to defend his home against the hero who was going to give them jobs. Some of the secretaries and young ladies at the back were standing on their toes to watch—they couldn't take their eyes off me. And the big pots in front were letting off their speeches to pretend all was well. They were bursting with speeches anyhow. Speeches for the come-back. And now they jumped out of 'em like cold sweat in a panic.

I had my eye on the folding doors but the huskies had put themselves between me and it. This made me pretty sure Nimmo was in there as usual. But they couldn't turn me out of my own house and so I kept quiet and waited my chance. My idea was to wear them down and take a dash at the door. I didn't need more than a minute to do my part by Nimmo, and if anyone got in the way, I should deal with him too.

Meanwhile they were all sticking close to me. Bootham was holding my arm on one side and Sally made eyes at me from the other. The little brown countess kept fluttering round me like a hen partridge trying to distract attention from her eggs. The huskies stood looking sideways all ready

53

to pounce. I felt there would be trouble and I said to Bootham, "I agree about a national emergency but it's been going on for fifty years. It's a lot deeper than politics. And I wish you'd get all these politicos out of my house." He said, "Yes, I'm afraid there is a crowd, but you understand a circular letter went out before—" and he caught himself by the head and finished "yesterday morning." "You mean before I took that crack at Nimmo, but you know my wife don't run a political register office, and neither will I."

# 9

TALL fellow with the moustache now asked me my opinion of local feeling. Diplomatic move to make me feel important and draw me into the racket. Everyone silent and pulling respectful faces. Lady Doll-Face cooed, "Oh, Captain Latter, I've been so longing to ask you—" The little partridge almost patted my arm. "I've heard so much about you, Captain Latter."

Of course she had. They'd all been talking about me. Since yesterday afternoon, at least. I said to Moustache local feeling was just like feeling everywhere else. Just feeling about in the fog. "All they know for certain is that the talky boys will let them down." "Who do you mean by the talky boys?" said Moustache. "The politicos," I said. "The jabberwocks. Who think they can talk themselves out of all responsibility while they play the tickle and grab game."

Moustache said, "Indeed," and grinned round as if to say, "The usual ignorant looby who criticizes us great politicos." And some of the others smiled too, but not very much. The ones in front were too near. And besides they knew I meant what I said. That always gives these talky boys a shock. They smile but they step back.

The old fellow said to me he'd always understood I was a Liberal myself. I said not a question of parties but the national crisis. All the parties were responsible, and it was time they were stopped.

"My dear Captain," said Moustache, grinning away, and I told him I was not his dear captain nor even his valuable friend—with something to give away. I said to him, "You think I'm talking a lot of nonsense but I know you're living a lot of worse nonsense—my God," I said, "look at the state of the country—and the kind of people who run it. Crooks like you who would sell your mother's skin for the ministry of piss-pots. And what I'd really like to know is what you're doing in my house. I should advise you, in a friendly and impartial manner, to get out quick."

Then one of the huskies caught hold of me. Perhaps he thought I was going to hit Moustache, and certainly I felt ready to do so. But instead, losing my temper I hit Husky and the next moment there was a bit of a turn-up going on, and a lot of noise. Somebody gave me a push at the back of the knees and I went down. But just when I thought I was finished there was a silence and I heard a voice I knew, though I couldn't believe it.

56

Then the husky let go and I sat up on the floor and there was Nimmo in the half-door to the back room. He was with Grant, the bodyguard. Grant was carrying him in his arms like a baby, wrapped in his red dressing-gown, and wearing a red stocking cap on his head.

Nimmo was always a small man, and at seventy he was much shrunk up. He looked like a sick monkey in the stocking cap which he always wore to keep his head warm at night.

He seemed very irritated and squawked out in his cat's voice, "What's all this? What are you doing? Good heavens, is that you, Jim? What has happened? Are you hurt? Help him up, at once. This is disgraceful."

One of the huskies, who had a black eye, now began to explain in a loud voice I had assaulted him.

"Never mind—let him go at once," said his lordship, and though he looked so comic, he carried it off. He had been giving orders and having his own way for about forty years. He waved his claw at the husky and said in a severe tone, "Captain Latter is a friend of mine and I shall certainly enquire into this treatment. Come, Jim," he said to me, holding out his hand. "Come in. I was just phoning to find out where you were when Nina told me you were actually here. Come in, do. What a delightful thing."

I did not wish to shake hands with Nimmo. But he went on holding his hand out, and smiling. And I saw all at once what it meant. If I didn't shake hands with him, the whole crowd there would say I was prejudiced—full of grievance.

So I shook hands and he kept tight hold of my hand and put his other hand over it and said before them all, "Damn it, old man, we've been friends for forty years. And friends are not so easy to find at our age. I don't lose them if I can help it. Come in. Grant, put me in my chair, and place a chair for Captain Jim. Throw those papers off. Put them on the bed." For the newspapers had got here too. All the chairs and half the bed were covered with them and there were more on the floor. One right in front of me with letters about two feet high—NIMMO TO THE RESCUE.

So there we were in the back room all among the come-back. Nimmo in a wheel-chair with his leg up on a pouf, and the small chair set for me. "Come, old fellow," he said, "sit down. You'll have a drink, I'm sure."

But I couldn't sit down. For I felt this was his room and I could not accept his hospitality as I intended to kill him.

He then told Grant to shut the door and to fetch some whisky, and he slapped the chair as if it was my knee. "This is fine, this is grand. For us to have a good talk and clear up this silly business."

Grant was still hovering over us. He was afraid to leave me alone with his lordship. But now Nimmo turned on him and said, "What are you doing there. Didn't I tell you to go for the whisky? Kindly do as you are told." He said this in a tone that made the man jump. As sharp and nasty as a Glasgow razor. The fellow Grant turned scarlet. "I beg your pardon, m'lord—but I was wondering in the circumstances—"

58

"Get out," Nimmo screamed at him, in such a fury the man fairly jumped to it—he was out of the room in ten seconds. And closed the door after him so carefully you couldn't hear the click.

# 10

THE moment the door shut, Nimmo flew out at me, "I didn't
know you were a coward, Jim—the very last man in this
world."

I saw his game, to rattle me, and said it was he who had
to be afraid, if any.

"Oh, shooting," he said, "I'm not talking about that, that's
an easy way out for a man who wants to dodge the facts—
suicide—murder—all of 'em a coward's way out."

This was just a piece of damned impudence so I said I wasn't
the dodger. It was up to him to face facts. I knew all I needed
to know. I could trust my eyes.

But he snapped back at me, "Yes, you trust what you think
you saw but you're afraid to face any explanation—in case
it made you look foolish. You're afraid to face the basic

60

fundamental fact of what Nina herself is—her character. She is the sincerest, the honestest of women, the most true, the most loyal. But Nina has no complaint against me. Can you believe that she would endure the least real injury to a husband she adores. Are you surprised that I charge you with making a mountain out of a molehill—that I suspect you of grasping at an excuse to vent a bitterness as unexpected and mysterious as it is unjustified?"

I said if he had anything new to tell me, he'd better tell it at once. As our time was short. As I expected, he had nothing to say to this and pretended he couldn't hear. He shouted, "What's all this noise? I can't hear myself speak."

In fact there was a lot of noise in the next room due to all the politicos cackling and moving among themselves. They were arguing what to do with the audacious Latter, and how to stop him murdering the man who was going to give them jobs. Nimmo jerked himself round in his chair and prodded the door with his stick. Bootham at once opened the door about a foot, and Nimmo bawled at him, "What's all the noise, Harry? We can't hear ourselves speak in here. Tell 'em to go away. I shan't see anyone this morning."

Bootham tried to argue the point. People had come a long way. But Nimmo bawled at him again to say he was busy, and to send Grant with the whisky. Had the whole place gone mad? The noise had already stopped short. We heard only a kind of hissing like a lot of snakes tangled together and working up to bite. But Nimmo wasn't satisfied. "Send 'em away," he bawled.

Just then Grant came running with the whisky and both he and Bootham stooped down to whisper in his ear, one on each side. But Nimmo threw up his arms. "What's all this—I can't hear. Speak up if you've anything to say. Go along. Go away," and he waved his stick as if he really meant to hit them. "Get out and leave us in peace." Bootham and Grant got out together very quickly, and Nimmo, still panting with indignation or imitation, turned to me and said, "Sorry, Jim, but you know how things are in a job like mine. You've been in one yourself. Too many people anxious to arrange your life for you. But I think we'll have peace now." He poured out two stiff whiskies. "Here you are, Jim. I'm sure we both need it. Sit down and make yourself comfortable."

I said I would neither sit down with him nor drink with him. "What I need," I said, "is some of the facts you mention, but it's pretty obvious I won't get 'em from you. I don't believe a word you say or a thing you do. But you hinted just now something about my wife. And I give you a minute to speak just to see if you dare to say anything against her."

He looked at me and saw I meant business. This gave him a shock—he began to struggle in his chair and reached out for a bell on the table. But I warned him to sit still and not touch the bell or I would kill him on the spot.

However, when I put my hand in my pocket for the gun, I found it gone. I realized at once it had been taken by the huskies when they had me on the floor, but decided to bluff and kept my hand in my pocket. If I had not, I knew I should

62

be arrested at once and not get another chance to carry out sentence on Nimmo.

Nimmo was watching me all the time. Now he leant forward and spoke in quite a different tone. "I think you know, Jim, how much I have always respected you as a friend and man—and a public servant. Wait a minute. Don't think I'm trying to flatter you—to get round you, as they say. What's the good? You mean to kill me and I suppose you won't miss me this time—this is what they call the moment of truth. What has happened? You saw what you supposed to be something improper—you acted hastily, on the spur of the moment, and produced a certain situation—the situation we now have to deal with. And it is difficult for you, we'll agree, to admit yourself mistaken, that you have wildly exaggerated a very small matter."

I was going to speak but he waved his hand at me as if I were a meeting. "My dear fellow, I am not trying to dodge any issue—I am not bluffing. You have been my very understanding friend, when you allowed me to stay in your house, and Nina to act as my secretary. You are, in the highest sense of that much abused word, a gentleman. You value true justice —you are not the sport of small considerations, mean gossip and petty jealousies. You despise them, and so does Nina. It is not the least of her virtues, her strong grasp of what really matters in life. Her generous sympathy with old friends —her tolerance, her sense of proportion. You have seen how she has worked for me in the last week of crisis which offers so terrible a threat to all our standards, to all we hold

63

dear. I will confess to you that her sympathy, her belief in me at this time when the nation has so unexpectedly—but so decisively and I may say, loudly, called upon me—has been an immense, a most important encouragement to me at a time when I needed every kind of encouragement."

I said I'd heard all this before. "You mean that I ought to let you get away with a vile act against a friend's wife so that you can make your come-back and go on swindling the people and selling the country. But what the people want is a little bit of truth and I think they can take it."

"And in order to give them what you call a little bit of truth, you're prepared to sacrifice Nina—to throw her to the wolves. Yes, I understand. You wish to ruin me, to destroy me and, in doing so, you don't care if you destroy her."

This charge enraged me as no doubt it was intended. I turned on him and for a moment, God forgive me, I might have hit him, old and crippled as he was, in his chair. "That's just like you to believe such a thing," I said, "You're always talking about morals and all the time you have the lowest idea of how decent ordinary people act. You are always talking about the noble quality of the people and all the time you despise them and wangle them with lies because you think they can't take the truth. You are a man so rotted and soaked in cunning and lies you think everyone is the same. You simply don't know honesty when you see it. You are like a cancer spreading poison everywhere through clean flesh—that's why I say you must be cut out, like a cancer. It's the only way to stop infection spreading."

64

"Stop, stop," he began squeaking again, "Stop, stop," he said, "why talk so much? If you do not care for Nina, you need not care for me." I was surprised to see how angry he was— he was in earnest at last. He pointed at the bed. "And if you want a weapon, look under my pillow. I should be very glad to get rid of the nasty thing. Next to men of violence, I detest their paraphernalia."

This move of Nimmo's did not take me so much aback as no doubt the cunning bastard had intended. I saw at once what Grant had been whispering about and why Nimmo had been so cool—he had known all the time that the huskies had my gun. I went to his bed without a word, it was my own African camp-bed which my wife had brought down for him, and turned up the pillow. I found the pistol underneath, not the pistol I had taken that morning but one given me by Nina many years before when I first went into the African Service. I picked it up and turned to the man. "When did you steal this?"

"I didn't steal it. Nina gave it to me this morning for my protection," and he looked at me as if to say, "Put that in your pipe and smoke it."

"I'd rather," he said, "on the whole, be shot than battered to death by a maniac. Do you think that too strong? I say that this noble vindication of yours is completely senseless and wicked. A merely spiteful murder, for which, no doubt, you expect an acquittal. Yes, you will have all the satisfaction, the self-satisfaction, if you'll forgive me, of the husband who avenges what he is pleased to call his honour the honour of a savage—at the expense of a wife and a friend who never

65

wished him harm. In fact, Jim, you are on, as you like to say, a good thing."

"Do you think," I asked him, "that I counted on that—that I will wish to live after this?"

"No, no, no," and he was shouting again, "give me a moment. I was saying, you will escape scot free provided that Nina, the wife who has loved you so devotedly, finds herself able to testify that you had some reason for so violent an act—that is, blackens her own character in public."

"I hope she will tell the truth," I said, "we've had too many lies. And as for the pistol, I'd like to ask her for the facts. For I know your game which is to turn me against her so that I shan't think you worth powder and shot."

"My God," he said, "you think me capable of such an act. Against a woman who—I say it deliberately—has been the noblest, the deepest influence in my life. Who gave her life for me and who would give it for you too. I said you didn't understand Nina and now I know it. You need not ask her about the pistol. It would only wound her—it would only make her wonder at your incomprehension of her—your suspicious jealousy. I'll tell you the facts—they're very simple. That woman Brome was found in the house again last night, and as I refused to have Grant snoring outside the door, Nina insisted that I should have some weapon of defence. She put that pistol under my pillow because it was the only one in the house." He paused a moment to let this sink in. Then he went on, "I see you think this is another sign of my hypocrisy that I should go against my principles in taking up arms against those who threaten my

66

life. I quite agree. I felt that strongly myself. I did not see myself for the first time in my life handling a firearm, and using
it to shoot a wretched tortured creature caught in the net of
cruel circumstance."

This, of course was meant to reflect on me, as well as the
lunatic Brome. But he went on at once, "But you yourself
know, my dear fellow, how hard it is to refuse the woman who,
I venture to say, has been the joy of both our lives—especially
in one of these so impulsive motions that warm an anxious
heart."

He was looking at me all the time, and though he wasn't
exactly grinning, he was full of grin. He knew I was puzzled.
Then he went on, "Of course you may think that Nina has no
right to care whether I get my throat cut by any wandering
lunatic. You may think it extremely imprudent of her to show
any feeling—especially for the man who was her husband for
nearly thirty years."

"She hated you," I said.

"She is incapable of hatred," he said. "That is perhaps her
misfortune—but it is something I find it possible to forgive.
And as for the imprudence—I rather call it courage, a true
courage, indifference to all but the essential thing—you especially should thank God for it. It was just that high soul, that
independence of mind, which brought her back to you. She
faced the scandal, the agony of that divorce, to be your wife.
She followed the truth of her soul, without fear, without hesitation."

I saw of course Nimmo had played the pistol trick to catch

me out. And now he was making the best of it. No doubt of that. But I did not doubt either he was speaking truth about my dear wife. For I believed in her. I did not doubt for one moment she was faithful and true. And so I was taken aback by this matter of the pistol.

"You don't believe me," Nimmo said. "Very well, send for Nina." He picked up his stick, made a dive forward and prodded the bell. "We'll ask her." But this was too smart. I said, "This pistol game is a good trick. But I'll see Nina alone. I'm not going to discuss our private affairs in public."

"Very well," he said. "Take her into the rose garden," pointing to the glass door that led into the garden. "Open that door and you can confer with Nina in perfect seclusion without for a moment taking your eyes off your prisoner. I daresay," he said, and he laughed as if at a good joke, "you can shoot me as well from ten yards away, as ten feet."

I said there was an easier way to make sure. I locked the folding door and bolted the side door into the passage, and also took away the key.

# 11

I own that pistol business had got under my skin. I was greatly
attached to that pistol. It had always meant a lot to me. For
Nina had given it to me at about the worst moment in my life
when Nimmo and even my own family had got up a scheme to
drive me out of England for good. They'd got me into the
African Service with the hope I'd die there. And even if I
didn't die, I couldn't take my leaves in England because of my
debts.

It made no difference then that I came to think my African
Service the high spot of my life, I knew I was through in Eng-
land. I was finished and pretty much by my own fault. When
I came to the ship which was taking me away from home, as
I thought, for good, I was ready to jump overboard. And then
when I came to my cabin, I found a farewell parcel on my bed,

69

from Nina. The pistol, to keep me safe in Africa, and a note asking me to forgive her. Saying she did not know how we had got into all this misery but I must believe that she didn't blame me for anything. I had given her all the happiest days of her life.

Nimmo had stolen the only love of my life and now he was driving me out of the country so as to drive me out of her heart. But I said to myself the heart was still mine—and it was the truest, the sweetest heart on earth.

It was true, I thought, she was loyal, and what Nimmo said now about her taking a chance for a friend was true too. When Nimmo said it was because Nina followed her heart that she'd come back to me, he was very much on the point and I'm not pretending it didn't have a big effect. More than anything else he'd thrown at me.

At that moment I was so sure of my wife's loyalty, I could have jumped in the fire for it. But now something happened that gave things quite another look. As I opened the garden door, I heard my name and saw Brightman standing at the gate which was to one side. This made me angry and I shouted to know what he was following me about for. He asked me if I'd seen the papers, and I said yes, what about them, and the following conversation took place:

BRIGHTMAN: "It's just as I feared, and worse. Nimmo's right back on the map."

LATTER: "In the paper."

70

BRIGHTMAN: "Any violent attempt against Nimmo now would be enormously to the advantage of his party."

LATTER: "He might get a bigger tomb."

BRIGHTMAN: "But his party would come in—have you reflected on Nimmo's real strength?"

LATTER: "Yes, he's as clever as a monkey."

BRIGHTMAN: "The chapels. That is his strong suit. The religious line. Hence these addresses at Shagbrook. Yes, but the chapel side's his weak side too." And he pointed out that a scandal, a real scandal where Nimmo came out in a bad light, as a guilty party, would ruin him. For instance, if I sued for divorce.

I answered, of course, my wife was innocent. Nimmo had attacked her.

He answered he had no doubt of it but I ought to know of a very dangerous statement made by a late member of my household. I said, "Who and what?" and he said these things weren't to be shouted over a hedge.

I therefore admitted him to the garden by the gate, and he at once handed me a typewritten note. "I don't know, of course, what it's worth," he said, "but the matter came under my notice only last week."

This note read:

"Amelia Jones. Nurse at Palm Cottage to Captain and Mrs. Latter, discharged November 1925, ostensibly for incompetence. She says she was turned out at a moment's notice because she caught Mrs. Latter in an incriminating situation with Lord Nimmo. She says this relation was the common talk of the servants and had been continuing for a very long time."

This letter gave me a shock because I remembered the girl, Amelia, had seemed a good sort of person and while I was away at the Lilmouth Regatta she had been turned away at an hour's notice.

# 12

JUST then I was surprised to hear Nimmo's voice. He was actually in the garden, hobbling on both legs and his stick and holding one hand to his backside. He had forgotten for the moment he was a helpless cripple. He was in such a state of spitting excitement he could hardly speak. "It's you, Brightman," he said. "Since you won't deign to come to me, I've been forced to come to you. I don't know what you have to do with Captain Latter's private affairs but I can guess, and I should like to say that I look upon you as an unprincipled scoundrel and that if you do not leave this garden at once I shall have you thrown out."

"You can't do that, Nimmo," I said, "this happens to be my garden."

But the man paid no attention to me. He was crazy with rage.

He went on at Brightman he was a mean sneaking scoundrel who ought to be horse-whipped. And turning to me, he asked, "What do you think of a man, Jim, who gets hold of your servants and pays them to make up lies about you—who gives it out that any blackmailing, spiteful creature who is low enough can earn a pound or two by bringing tales to him—any wild accusation that a low imagination can invent."

"Nothing of the sort," Brightman said. And he kept perfectly calm. "I know nothing but what was volunteered—and as for wild accusations, they have come from your side—and printed in the daily papers for thousands to read."

"I called you a Fascist," Nimmo shrieked, "and so you are—your politics are on a par with your character. You are out for yourself by any dirty trick, any mean deceit by which you can take advantage of the misery of the poor for your own benefit and glory."

Brightman kept his temper and his dignity and answered all these charges could be made equally against Nimmo. As for being a Fascist, that was a term of abuse thrown at everybody who was not a Communist or a left-wing sympathizer.

Nimmo let out another yell of wrath, then suddenly put his hand to his chest and bowed down in a very queer way. It was as if he was bowing to Brightman. But then he began to topple over and would have fallen on his head if Brightman and I had not caught him by the arms and carried him back to the bed. I rang the bell and unlocked the door into the corridor. A husky was standing outside on guard, waiting to get me when I came out. When I told him to fetch my wife, he put out his hand as if to grab me. But Nina called to him and he hesitated; and meanwhile she came past him into the room and I shut the door in his face. Nina realized at once what had happened and ran to take a bottle of medicine from the cupboard over the bed.

Brightman seemed almost equally worried with Nina. He was standing by the bed with a very red face and kept saying what he wanted was a doctor. But Nina would not speak to him or look at him, and I could see his presence upset her. I too objected to the fellow pushing himself into the house. I was fully aware of his game—he was in politics up to his neck. He was just as keen to drag me into the racket as Nimmo himself and I knew once I let myself be dragged down into that slime I should never get out. All the same I had to see Nina hated the man and Nimmo was frightened of him and his information. It was this first made me ask myself if I was being fooled. If, after all, I was as big a fool as people thought. It was true all right, as Nimmo said, my wife could not hate. She liked to be comfortable and she liked everything round her to be comfortable. She liked to enjoy life. I never knew a living soul who could enjoy herself so much at a party or just walking down the street looking at shops and other people's clothes.

Of course she was mad on shopping too. She couldn't resist the shops, and her drawers and wardrobes were stuffed with things she'd never put on. One of the ways Nimmo had held her so long in their marriage was paying her bills and dressing her up like a London society tart.

Her back was to me as she stood over the bed, but I kept looking at her. And I could see her face in the picture that hung over the bed, a big dark Italian picture of Tivoli. It had come from my father's collection.

I say I could see her face in the picture as she stooped over Nimmo, so anxious for her great man. And now I saw something else as well. Half the window was in the picture too and when I moved a little to come in front of the window, my own face came into it.

I saw in a flash that anyone sitting where Nina had sat yesterday with her back to the window could see anyone who looked in. I said to myself, "Nina pushed Nimmo away and did it very violently—but was it because she saw me looking in at the window?"

And was she the sort of woman to make a fuss even if Nimmo, as the nurse suggested, had been at her before? I couldn't help remembering the time when she was seventeen and we were quarrelling at Lilmouth, she turned to me and said, "If you must have me, take me now before you spoil the concert for me with your bad temper."

I had to see a woman, a young girl, who could do a thing like that was not an ordinary girl—she didn't think much of her moral virtue. I had to ask myself if she had been so faithful to me as I liked to think. She had now got Nimmo's hand on her arm. She was pale with anxiety and pity—I thought I'd never seen anyone look so beautiful or so good. And I thought of what Nimmo himself had said, I didn't know a great deal about that woman. She was as tricky as a set of Japanese boxes.

# 13

NIMMO kept panting and gasping for a good while after he was over his attack. We all saw that by the colour coming back in his cheeks. Also by the energy with which he clutched himself by the chest. He was putting on an act. Brightman said at last with relief, "He's coming round." Nimmo then opened his eyes and said, "What are you doing here?"

"I beg your pardon, Lord Nimmo, but I helped to carry you into the house. You have been seriously ill and I think you should consult a doctor."

"I thank you," Nimmo answered in a very rude tone, "I thank you for your help—but it is no longer required."

"That, if you'll believe me," said Brightman, "gives me a great deal of satisfaction. I was very much alarmed."

"The best way out is through the garden," Nimmo said. "We don't want the mob in here."

Brightman turned to me and said, "I'm sorry for this intrusion, Latter, but I think you understand that I did seriously believe I could help to clear the air for you."

I said I fully understood the position, meaning I was up to his game, quite as much as Nimmo's, and he went out.

Nimmo at once sat up in bed, and said, "The damned blackguard. I suppose he has been trying to plant his slanders on you, Jim. That letter he was showing you—was it anything to do with the Amelia woman?"

"Yes, she makes certain statements about what has been going on here for the last two years."

"The lying Jezebel. She was turned out for stealing—that's why she's so spiteful. She threatened reprisals if she didn't get a character."

I said, "I never noticed before the Tivoli picture acts like a periscope. You look in it and you can see behind you. For instance, you can see anyone looking in at the window."

Nimmo stared and said, "What—what's this?"

But I looked straight at Nina and said, "Nina knows what I mean." My wife got as red as fire and turned quickly as if to speak. But I knew already Brightman was right, and Amelia's story had had some truth in it.

I was so knocked out by this turn I didn't know what to say or do. Then all at once I saw my wife's expression change. She looked as calm and cool as a waxwork—and I knew she had gone mule, as I called it.

And this had always driven me mad. She had played it that day at Lilmouth when we went to the Hotel. First she says,

78

"All right, I'm yours, but hurry." Then because I take her at her word, she turns herself into a limp little doll with a china face and lets me tumble her about as if she had no bones and no feelings either.

She has always accused me of spoiling the first great moment of our love by that day's work. But I say she spoilt it by her mulish tricks.

So now I said, "For God's sake, Nina, don't play any games but say something. Is there anything in Amelia's story?"

Nimmo kept babbling, "A pack of lies," but neither of us paid any attention. When Nina had gone mule she did not care for anything or anybody in the world.

I said to her, "When you helped me get away yesterday, did you know there wasn't going to be any charge? Was all that business with Grant just a fake?" She said nothing to this.

I said to her, "You know what you're doing, Nina, you're trying to drive me mad. You've done it often enough before. But this time you may do it once too often."

She kept on staring at me, as calm as a dummy with glass eyes. But you could see she was making her eyes like glass.

I pointed the pistol at her and said, "Tell me, Amelia told the truth?"

She raised her eyebrows and seemed to think for a moment. Then she nodded her head at me, quite slowly and politely as if saying good morning to the grocer's boy.

And I couldn't bear her temper. I pulled the trigger. But the pistol only clicked. I pulled again and it clicked again Nimmo, still gibbering on the bed and scrabbling to get up, fell back and said, "Oh, I forgot—I took them out as soon as Nina gave me the nasty thing. Thank God for that, Jim. Thank God, thank God. What a providence."

Then, God forgive me, in my blind mad rage, I threw the pistol at my wife and hit her on the head, cutting her forehead. She fell down, and she was trying to get up and I ran to help her. But she held me away. I saw she was half stunned and I told her not to move—to lie still while I got a doctor. Seeing her so much hurt, I forgot everything else. But of course, just because I asked her to lie still, she would not but tried all the harder to drag herself up, and at last managed to get into a chair. She did not utter a sound the whole time and she was as green as glass. The blood was running down her forehead from a deep hole, and now when she felt it on her cheek she put up her handkerchief. But still she sat straight with an indifferent air as if nothing had happened; as if she did not care what happened. And this was always the way she won these fights. Even as a child of seven or eight she would play mule and drive me mad, till I hit her, and drive me to be ashamed of myself and apologize.

Though I knew it was the old trick and she was beating me again, that she had done the wrong and now she was getting away with it, still when I saw her there, so white, and with the blood on her face, I could not bear it. What man could who ever loved a woman truly and had had so much happiness with her. For I want to make it plain I owed all the joy of my life to this woman. I knew it all the time. I never forgot what I owed to her.

So now, seeing her sick and fainting and only holding herself up by her mulishness, I couldn't stand it and said we must have a doctor at once. But she shook her head and said the cut was nothing, and we didn't want any more talk in the papers.

"No—no—no," Nimmo said, "she's right, Jim."

"I'm not worrying about your political racket," I said, "but about Nina." And I took the telephone and called my own doctor, Kilbie. I said that Nina was hurt.

Luckily he was in and he promised to come at once. Nina said suddenly, "Tell him to come in the back way—by the garden."

I saw the force of this and told the man, "Give me a whistle and I'll let you in by the garden door. The house is full of statesmen and Nina doesn't want a fuss."

"No, no," Nimmo said, "there's been too much already."

"Much too much," Nina said. "And I don't need a doctor."

"Damn it," I said, "if you don't get that cut dealt with now, you'll be scarred."

"Why should you mind?" she said. "You wanted to kill me."

I said that she was still my wife, though she seemed to forget it.

"She never forgets," old Nimmo said. "She never forgets it." He was gibbering like a monkey still, and panting like a dog.

"Then what's been going on in this house?" I said.

"You wouldn't understand," she said.

Nimmo said, "My dear Jim, let us admit that you and I have been at fault to Nina—I—if you like, I will say it—terribly at fault. I do not urge any extenuating circumstances except perhaps that of my old and devoted attachment to the woman who was my wife for nearly thirty years and who, in a fit of madness, I divorced. Yet I must urge you to remember that I divorced her, as I thought then, as I think still, for her own happiness. So that at last she could be with the man she had always loved. The one man on earth who could make her completely happy. For I know, Jim—I have known all my life that she did not, could not love me. I was too different in all ways—in mind, in preoccupation, in my very class. Yes, and that goes deep, to the very roots of our grief. I am a cruder, a rougher clay. I made her suffer by my very devotion—I needed her too much. When I came here two years ago to write my book, I was a broken, a finished man. It is to you as much as to her, to your large generosity of mind, that I owe my rehabilitation. And if at this crisis, I can, after all, be of decisive service to the country we both love," and he went on babbling about men of goodwill and experience getting together, till he ran out of breath.

Even Nina, half fainting as she was and leaning sideways against the chair, looked with wonder at the old man while he sat up on the bed, gasping out this rigmarole and waving his arms about.

"What's all this?" I said. "You admit you're a damned old swine, and you say I'm a brute. I know very well what I did for Nina. I was a brute and a young fool too, and I was a brute just now when, God forgive me, I lost my temper. But how does that excuse the foulest treachery one man can show another?"

He fell back as if he thought I was going to hit him, but I

could not have done so if I'd wanted to. Nina had caught my sleeve. She said, "I must go out, please take me out." She struggled to her feet.

I looked at Nimmo. He was flat again on the bed, all among the headlines, and I thought he was safe. And certainly Nina needed all my care. I was afraid she would fall, and when we reached the garden I asked if she would wait while I fetched out a chair. But she only shook her head. She was nearly fainting and I was holding her up with my hand beneath her arm, but the arm hung as limp as an empty sleeve. She was still the mule, too proud to take help even from my hand.

I asked her again to forgive me for that cowardly blow. But she made no answer.

"It's all these lies," I said. "I don't know where I am."

"You couldn't understand, it's no good."

"You don't explain very much."

She looked at me with the same hard face, and I didn't want to talk to her any more. I didn't want to look at her in case I should see how corrupt she was. Even now I didn't want to believe she was hopelessly rotted, all through. But it was hard not to believe. For just as the doctor was coming and I moved to take her to the garden gate, there was a noise from the room behind as if someone was trying to break in at the door. I turned at once to run back, but at the same moment Nina's limp arm stiffened and held me. Luckily the doctor was quick. I did not lose a minute in getting back to the house.

# 14

AND I was only just in time—Nimmo had once more miraculously recovered his strength, hopped off the bed and was working at the lock of the side door. As I came in, he hopped away and faced round. But he couldn't quite carry it off, he was shaking and staring.

"Now," I said, "we're beginning to get at something."

"A message from Whitehall," he said, trying to throw out his chest and carry it off, "but I told 'em to wait. Far more important things. Jim, that poor girl, hasn't she suffered enough?"

He made a dive at me and caught my arm. "Why do we go on torturing ourselves? I love your wife and you know it. I've always loved her—from a child. I took her from you—I am guilty before you—I've been guilty all my life. But my excuse, my only possible excuse is something that you of all men ought

84

to understand. You know what it is to be in love, and I'm not talking of that feeble emotion which passes for love in the ladies' magazines. You are a man of deep feeling, of passionate attachments, let me say it, of ideals. You can enter into the situation of one who has similar springs of action. Jim, we both saw that poor girl just now, in her suffering, her despair. You say you were a brute to her, and God knows, I have been no better."

He was staring at me all the time as if he wanted to see how my wheels went round. "But what is the truth—the real truth?" he whispered, and he took a harder grip with his claw—it felt like a claw, harder and sharper than I could have believed from the man. He was whispering now and fairly trembling with excitement, and I thought, "Is he really going to admit anything?"

"The truth—the whole truth," he said, "let us face it, as guilty men. Let us have the courage to face it. You were a brute, you say, to that young girl, and I have loved her, let us say, too much. But aren't we forgetting something—something without which we are merely piling up one falsity on another—throwing words about and getting nowhere. The actual situation *at the time.*" He shook my arm. "At the time, Jim, that is the vital factor so easy to forget. We were young, young—that is the big truth. We were young—that's to say, we wanted everything we could get so long as we didn't despise ourselves. And we weren't sure how bad we could safely be—how selfish—how greedy. No, no, Jim, you are too hard on yourself—you were not so evil as you say. You were only young and lost—groping your way. And I think you forget that Nina was young too—

85

she was in love, and she was of a nature—how shall I put it—there was that in Nina which—God knows I am the last man to say or think evil of Nina, your Nina, my Nina, but she too knows what love is—in every aspect. Jim, if Nina was a feeble thin-blooded creature, should we have loved her—should we have been guilty?"

"So you're putting it on her."

"No, no, no," he screamed, and then I thought he would fly at me. But he caught his breath and said calmly enough, "I'm risking the truth with you, Jim—the whole truth. And you're going to have it even if you kill me."

"You talk of truth and then you play act. How can I shoot you with an empty pistol? You haven't forgotten again you took the cartridges out."

This was telling him pretty plainly I hadn't swallowed his yarn about forgetting he had unloaded the pistol. And I thought it would sting him. But Nimmo never gave anything away, too old at the game. He looked at me a moment, then pulled out the drawer of his bedside table and offered it to me with a polite bow. "There you are," he said.

Inside there was a lot of stuff, a gold watch, a dirty handkerchief, a brandy flask, two or three pill-boxes, and some rounds of ammunition. I said, "It's a good idea but why should I lie down to it? Why should I do the noble act because you know how to play at it?" And I picked up the pistol and charged it. But he put back the drawer as cool as you please. He didn't really believe I'd shoot him.

86

"Even if Nina is guilty," I said, "why should that let you out? And don't look murder at me. Who was it murdered Nina's soul? Which is the real murder, to poison a soul year after year till it goes blind and deaf, or to shoot the poisoner?"

Nimmo waved his hand, and bent his head sideways, a platform pose meaning, "What a lot of nonsense," and said slowly, "I think you deceive yourself, Jim—but you also do yourself an injury. As you did just now. I mean with Nina. She never could stand claptrap."

I said, "Christ, are you calling me a hypocrite?"

"Yes," he said, "and you know it. All this exalted sentiment is simply a piece of hypocrisy—no doubt you are trying to deceive yourself as well as me. But it doesn't work and Nina could not bear it. She says you can't understand. But I am not so charitable. I say you can if you try—if you dare."

"My wife seems to have her own ideas of the truth."

"Nina is one of the truthfulest women I have ever known— the most fearless of truth, the living truth."

"She was a truthful girl before she met you."

The very thought of Nina at seventeen gave me a choke in my throat. The straightest, sincerest creature I ever knew. And no doubt Nimmo saw or felt something in me. For he jumped at me again. "Ah, who could forget her then," he said. "And how can we forget her now, Jim, I beg of you. As men in the very presence of death. Let us face it, we are poor things, poor rags beside her. Do you really know Nina, Jim—do you realize how complete, how absolute is her forgiveness? Because she

knows that the boy who was so cruel to her is no longer you—
he has passed away more completely than the dead. She knows
that the wrongs of yesterday are but the tale of those selves
that are dead. My dear fellow, you know this noble creature—
you know her genius in love, in tenderness, the faithfulest of
friends. You know her horror of ingratitude. What is her message to us both, forgive and forget. From Nina who is our
victim, who has suffered most. She says let us start again here,
with hearts renewed in sympathy, in our old tried friendship.
Let us start again in truth—the truth of mutual sympathy, the
reality of affection, the fact of to-day and its lesson. Let us not
throw away this great precious substance for the shadow of old
prepossessions. Above all, let us avoid any step that would give
a handle to malicious gossip and bring fresh misery to Nina."

"What's all this?"

"You understand, of course," he said, "that the circumstances
of the household are now going to be quite different. For one
thing, Sally is here, and I'm perfectly willing that she should
always be present when I work with Nina."

I could scarcely believe my ears. "My God," I thought, "he
really means it. He thinks he is going to stay on in this house.
He's so used to wangling that he can't believe there's anything
on earth that can't be wangled."

"My God," I said, "do you still think you're going to stay
in my house after yesterday? And what's the point—everyone
knows what's happened."

"Exactly," he said, "and that's why we must not do anything

rash. I have had some experience of gossip, Jim. The great secret is to act as if it were false. They daren't print it, you know, whatever they believe. And if they see that we're going on as before, they'll begin to doubt the whole tale or some of it. My dear fellow, I speak from what I know."

"Look," I said, "unless you are out of my house in twenty minutes, I'll put another hole in you, a finisher this time."

"Do you threaten me?" All at once he pretended to blow up. But he also sat down in his chair, thinking, I daresay, I wouldn't kill a sick man sitting down. In fact, I was just about to pull on him as he got into the chair. But he went on bawling at me from there, as bold as the brass he was, "You take advantage, in short, of my position as a public man, to blackmail me. No, no," he waved his hands at me, "don't talk about your honour. What is it worth? The country is tottering on the edge of revolution and you seize this moment to gratify a private spite. At last you see your chance to ruin the man who has never done you anything but kindness—a man over seventy, in any case condemned to die. But you can't wait to dance on my grave and vilify my memory, like all the other jackals who have preyed upon me in life—you are resolved to drag me in the dirt during my last months. And this at the cost of your country. My dear Jim, at least allow yourself to believe that I am not speaking a vain thing. You saw the Press this morning—if not, the papers lie there on the bed. I have some influence still. Say if you like that I have done nothing to deserve this position, but you can't deny or ignore it. Since this last week the whole picture has changed, at this moment my intervention could be decisive. Forgive me if I say that you don't realize the situation."

"God damn it," I said, "I think of nothing else. Fifty years of it. Since you and your gang set out to pimp for every gimme in the game. And bought your first ponce's pants with Nina's money—and Nina's soul. The situation. A whoreshop for syphilites—everything goes because you'll all get in. And how smart we are at the dirt. You've poisoned everything you touched and it's still working. A living shanker. And you think no one'll notice if you talk big enough. You think you can talk it away. Like a bill in your talky house. Good or bad—talk it out—talk out the loyalty and the truth. Talk out the man who dares to have some faith—some principles."

He grabbed at me and fairly screamed, "I'm not blaming you, Jim—"

"No," I said, "you don't blame anybody for anything. That's the password for politicos—that's the pill for punks—that's the joy call to the love feast. Come on, boys and girls, we understand each other. We're a putrid lot. Let's get together and sing unto our putrefying lord the hymn of the putrid. Don't blame anyone for anything. You don't blame me," I said, "because you want me to let you off. But I know bloody well what I was and what I am. I was a bloody young brute who took advantage of a girl because I knew she was good and true—because I knew she wouldn't give me away. And I know what you are—a poor old fester on a dying ramp. A shit-merchant who's so buried in filth he can't smell himself. But I can and I can't take any more.

Thank God I didn't kill you. It would have been a crime. You aren't responsible for your own dirt. But get out now—get out quick." And I took out the pistol and fired a couple of shots into the floor, one on each side of him and pretty close too—close enough to make his trousers shake in the breeze. And there was a noise next door like a farmyard when the cowman chops a chicken. None of that crowd had gone away. They simply couldn't tear themselves away from the man with jobs. They charged the doors like one gimme, burst the bolts out of the wood and came bursting in. About forty of 'em. They hung back a bit when they saw me with the gun in my hand. And Nimmo jumps out in front of me, stretching out his arms and squawking, "It's nothing, calm yourselves. A demonstration merely." Then Bootham catches the idea from Nimmo, and calls out in his best front-of-the-house voice, "Don't alarm yourselves, ladies and gentlemen. Nothing has happened. Pray give us room. There is a great deal of urgent business to be decided. Security measures." Nimmo clutches his chest and falls back into his chair. Sally runs for the medicine, the two countesses and about fourteen politicos stand round making anxious noises. At least a million pounds' worth of political sympathy. And then they look at me as if I were the devil. But they don't say anything.

I was standing against the wall with my hand in my coat pocket, and they knew I meant business. They recognized a bit of truth when it had a gun in its hand.

Then Bootham stoops down to get his lordship's orders, and Moustache and he push the chair out of the room and out of the house. They lift him into the Daimler and drive off.

And the whole lot go trooping after; all round they're starting up their cars in a hurry. Daren't let him out of their sight
or he may forget 'em when the good time comes. In five minutes,
not a soul in sight, nothing in the drive but a few drops of oil
and some dirty newspapers blowing over the spring flowers.

# 15

I WENT and poured myself a drink. I don't drink but I needed a drink after that morning's work. And it wasn't till I rang the bell for a syphon I found the house was as empty as the drive. I was alone in the place. No one in the kitchen, no car in the garage. Nurse and son Robert probably gone off in it with Wilkins to drive. Leaving the doors wide open. All the doors wide, yard door, garage door, garden door, both back doors. As if people had exploded out of the place. To get away from that wicked man Jim Latter, who asked for a bit of truth.

I was just getting a line on this position when an old Tarbiton taxi came clanking and wobbling up to the door. Young man like a snake driving. I'd seen him before at the dockside garage. A bad type—Bolshy I should guess, or near. I asked him what he wanted and he said he'd had a call from Chorlock Manor to fetch Master Robert and his nurse. They were to join Mrs. Latter there. Chorlock Manor is a house belonging to Lady Gould, a friend of Nimmo's and a friend of my wife's too, but none of mine. "So she's gone," I thought, "bolted. This is the end of that. This is the end of Palm Cottage, with roses round the porch." And I didn't want to go into the place again. Not even to close the doors or fetch a hat and a toothbrush. I told the snake Master Robert and the nurse had gone already and I said to him. "Tarbiton, quick."

It was the first idea came into my head. I didn't know where I should go. But I thought, "Sergeant Varney—" and the moment I thought the name, I wanted to be with the man. And his people. Honest true people. And I wanted them quick. To get way from all these other people—grab merchants—gas experts. And their flash patter.

"She couldn't stand the claptrap," meaning I was using the big words. Truth and honour. But hadn't I the right, before that pair. "A genius for love—a horror of ingratitude." I saw her standing there, playing mule, white as paper and that handkerchief stuck on her forehead. To hide the blood. Too proud to let me see it in case I said, "She wants me to be sorry." And I remembered the times when we were children and fought. And she would win by her mulish game. And then creep back to me and call herself a beast. For winning. A genius for making a fool of young Jim—a horror of not having her own way. "The faithfulest of flirts," I said. "Dammit, the facts are pretty plain. She's been letting Nimmo do what he liked with her—as far as he could get—for two years in her own house. And now she's

94

off and taken Robert with her—she's off to join his lordship and his lordship's gang of swindle-cookers. That's what the whole country will say, and what anyone would think."

And then I banged on the window and said to the snake, "Do you know where Major Brightman hangs out—somewhere on the Lilmouth road?"

"That's the other way," he said. "I can ask but it's the other way, a long way out." And he looked at me crosseyed.

"I'll pay you well," I said. "I want to get there quick."

He grumbled something about his lunch hour, but he took the next Lilmouth turning.

"The faithfulest," I said. "And why did he invent that one? Because she has no faith. He sticks the lie into me because it is a lie and he knows I've got the truth. A lie was the only answer."

That was always Nimmo's game, to confuse things. Bunko. Whenever you went near Nimmo, you got in a blind spin, a mass of dirty fog full of wreckage like London in a November bomb raid. You could only bash yourself against the walls and break your nose if it wasn't your neck. I wanted something to steer by. I was after it now. A man who spies on his wife is a tout. I felt like a tout now but I was lost and sick of it. I wasn't going to take any more lies.

All right, but here were more words of Nimmo's. "She doesn't know how to hate." "Yes," I thought, "but she's afraid to hate. She's told me so." Just as she was afraid of the dark when we were kids. Old Aunt Latter wouldn't give her a candle at night because she'd been spoilt. She said that Nina's character was half-way to the devil already—she gave way to herself. And Nina agreed with her. She knew she was spoilt. She knew she didn't deserve a candle. Good kids don't need to be frightened of devils in the dark. So she used to come to my bed at night. That began it all. I'd never met anything like Nina—I hadn't a relation in the world that gave a damn for me. My mother was dead—my father was abroad with some woman and my brother, Rob, was with him. I didn't like my father or his women and they didn't like me. I don't blame 'em. I was up against the whole setout. And now Nina came running to creep into my arms. Of course she would flirt with anybody. I knew that. She would climb on anyone's knees and open her big eyes and say, "Love me." But she hated boys because she could not turn them round her finger. She hated me when I first came because I called her pussy and pulled her hair. I didn't know how to do with girls. And she didn't understand boys. When I teased her she would turn white and say, "You are a fool and nobody loves you."

But one night, I say, she came running and threw herself on my bed—she said there was a creature in her room, she heard him breathing in the cupboard. So I lit my candle and took my knife and went in. Of course there was nobody. But she wouldn't believe it. She said he would come back—she begged me to let her into my bed. So she came into my bed and clutched hold of me. She was shaking all over and I stroked her like my pony when it was frightened. I stroked her and she said, "Hold me tight, don't let it take me away."

She thought it was some kind of devil had come for her because she had stolen things. She used to take money from the aunt's purse to buy chocolate, she wasn't allowed many sweets because they were bad for her teeth, but she had to have them. I told her it was low to steal, and she would say yes, she knew it was wicked, but she didn't care—she didn't care if she died and went to Hell. But that was in the daytime. At night, she would get the terrors and come to me. I told her then she deserved to be frightened. If she went on stealing she would have to get the terrors, and she promised not to do it again.

That was the time I had religion. All our prep. school had it from an old boy, a missionary. He'd had an eye shot out with an arrow, he used to come and give us lectures with a magic lantern. Then he would preach about the duty of the Christian to spread the light of love, and brotherhood, justice and truth. He said our Empire was a trust from God to open the eyes of the heathen and enlighten their darkness—to abolish superstition and human sacrifice, to rescue the poor Hindu from his blood-sucking money-lender and the poor Kaffir from the Boers. He was a great man, one of the finest men I ever knew, and he gave his life for Christ. Some slave-raiding Arabs murdered him in Central Africa when he tried to protect his converts. Now he's forgotten. His name is nothing and his work is nothing too. The talky boys have talked him out and sold poor bloody black man to big business. And now poor black brother has got his own talky boys to wangle him with lies and double talk, till his brains are as fuzzy as his hair.

And as I sat in that old taxi, I said to myself the world was mad with cackle. Cackle that nobody means for truth and nobody takes for truth. Copy-cackle. The truth, I said, give us some

97

truth. That's all I want. To give us all some peace. You can sleep on truth if it's a pile of stones, honest stones.

Brightman's place was an olde Englishe farmhouse just outside Queensport, built two years before with half-inch deal timbers nailed on brick and pebble-dash between. Steel casements with bottle-ends for panes. Roses round the door. His drive was full of cars too—just like at the Cottage. Only chiefly sports cars or old tin Lizzies. Young pups on the dash or old soldiers on the dole.

The snake wanted to be paid. Said he wanted his lunch, and had to get home. Two pounds odd on the meter and it turned out I had nothing in my pocket-book but ten bob, cards, a cheque form and a few addresses. So I wrote out the snake a cheque and told him to call at the Queensport bank.

All this time waiting at door. At last young fellow in a white jacket condescended to answer my bell—and asked me to wait some more in the porch. But I didn't see it and walked into ye olde tyme lounge hall, panelled in Elizabethan linen-fold oak made out of chewed paper painted olde shitte colour. Full-length portrait of Brightman at east end, olde shitte, about eight foot high, as olde Englishe good chappe, with shorts, open shirt and pipe. Slap-up bar underneath with olde chromium fittings. Full and humming. Only not same noise as other statesmen. This lot were drinking free and their clack was more like a race row than a tea party. They were bawling out the foe instead of taking his character to pieces. They were not saying, "How d'ye do" to their rivals but yelling, "Hullo, you old bastard. What are you here for? Thirsty again?"

When I came in, they stopped talking one by one as the news spread and turned to look. You could see them nudging each other and saying, "Latter, Latter himself." I hadn't known before I was a celebrated person. Nearly as much as Nimmo.

They looked at me and I looked at them. I didn't like 'em much and said, "Good morning, gentlemen—have you used Pear's Soap?" But nobody answered. They didn't like me either. At least three of 'em had been blackballed from the Yacht Club, men with their own boats. And it's hard to be blackballed from a little yacht club like our show. We'll take most offal if it has a real boat.

White-Jacket came popping in to look for me. Faster than he went to announce. He'd heard who I was. Almost bowed when he asked me to come on—Major waiting. Took me upstairs into a study. Spears and guns on walls. Brightman behind large desk. Four serious gentlemen in conference round. Brightman gets up, shaking hands, and takes me into olde Englishe window hanging over porche. Doesn't say anything but looks enquiring.

I say, "Look, Brightman—I'm not here to join your show. I don't like it. But I want to know about this story of yours this morning—about an old servant of ours."

"Yes, yes. I'm sorry about this new development, Latter. You have all my sympathies. Or perhaps you welcome it."

"What new development?"

"I gather that your wife has left—"

"You have your spies," I said, "and you seem to like the idea. I don't. I don't like this Amelia business either. Servants' tales.

**99**

But I want to get things straight. As straight as I can with all these Napoleons about."

"You saw the particulars. I took them down myself from her report. And I've kept them to myself—strictly confidential."

"I want to see the girl."

"I can assure you that there is plenty of evidence for a divorce."

"I don't want a divorce. This thing is too serious for a divorce. It's got to be settled between me and her and Nimmo without any poodle-faking by lawyers and talky boys—or writy boys either."

"You can't hope to keep the thing out of the Press. Your only choice is between some ill-considered piece of violence which will go far to establishing Nimmo or his party in power—or some rational appeal to public feeling which will ruin him."

"I tell you I won't have a divorce. That means lawyers and talk, more wangling, and a fine chance for Nimmo to tie everything up again in a lot of big words."

"There's another way—give the facts to the public and let him bring an action for libel."

I saw the force of this but I didn't like it. "I don't like it," I said to myself. "It's Brightman's game, and I don't want to go in with any of these career boys' dirty work. Let them hit each other below the belt but leave me out of it." And said so. I said all I wanted was to see the girl Amelia. And at last, he said, very well, he'd send for her at once. Would I take luncheon?

No, I wouldn't lunch. And I wouldn't see the girl there. I'd see her in her own place. But he said he hadn't got the address, and began again about the public statement. Would I call it a libel if it was a statement of the truth?

I said whatever it was, it was a dirty back-door job. And I was tired of tricks.

Just then White-Jacket came up to say my driver wanted to see me. I said, "Send him up." And the man came up more snaky than ever, hissing and spitting. He'd been to the bank and they'd refused my cheque.

This gave me the surprise of my life. I hadn't had a cheque of mine R.D. for thirty years at least. I was staring at the thing and Brightman offered me his phone and I rang up there and then. "Captain Latter here, and what about this cheque you've refused?" "You're overdrawn." "But I've been overdrawn before. I've got securities." "Not sufficient to cover a further advance." "Damn it all, I own a house and grounds." "I understand there's a mortgage. I paid out more than a hundred pounds last week and Mrs. Latter was good enough to make up the sum from her own account." "Why wasn't I told?" "All we know is that we phoned and Mrs. Latter answered and sent a cheque."

This didn't surprise me so much. I'd always left the bills to Nina. What surprised me was the tale I hadn't enough securities to cover a couple of thousand overdraft. I told the bank to send me a full account at once of the whole position. And I considered they had behaved very badly in refusing a small cheque without notice to me.

I hung up then and Brightman said, "I suppose they've heard about your wife's move."

"What difference does that make?"

"It might make a good deal to your credit."

"I don't know what you're talking about."

"I beg your pardon—but I always understood that Nimmo paid his way. That, at least, is the general view. Bed and board."

For a second I didn't get him. Then the blood went to my head so hard and quick I thought I should have a stroke. I couldn't speak. And about three of Brightman's men came between us before I could speak. Then I called out, "You won't escape like that, Mister Major Brightman. I'll make you swallow that lie before you're much older." Brightman answered something to the effect that if I was determined to be a blind fool, he couldn't do anything about it. But he was speaking "by the book."

I thought this was politics. I said it was a lie, and so it was a lie. But what I didn't know it was so near the truth that nobody would take it for a lie.

His three chaps were handling me all the time, but I put my hand in my pocket and said, "Don't ask for it or you'll get it."

Then Brightman called them off and I made for the stairs with the snake right on my heels. And when I got to the car I said, "Look, driver, you know me—it happens I'm short of cash at the bank, but I've plenty elsewhere. You'll be paid all right and paid well too. So drive me on to the Manor at Chorlock."

But the fellow turned more snaky than ever. He'd heard Brightman, no doubt. He said he'd certainly get paid, he'd see to that. But he wasn't going to Chorlock on tick. Twenty miles in the wrong direction. No fear. So let me get someone else to drive me. And he got into his cab and left me flat.

102

I wasn't going to ask any of the Brightman politikites for a lift, so I set out walking the five miles to Tarbiton. And this was a lucky thing. It gave me time to cool off and to think. It stopped me from going to the Manor where I'd only have got more lies. It brought me back among true decent people, my true friends. When I had gone a mile, a trap came along with the Battwell butcher and he asked me if I wanted a lift as far as Tarbiton. I said East Tarbiton was far enough. "Put me down in Water Street for the Water Boy. Sergeant Varney ought to be coming in about now for his morning half one."

"A good old sort of a cock," he said.

"Yes," I said. "One of the best, one of the finest truest chaps in the world. And he's my sergeant."

"Your sergeant, Captain?"

"Why yes. In the Specials."

"Well, sir. What do you think about the strike?"

"I don't know if there'll be a general strike. But I do know that if we get one it will be because of the way the government and the unions and the Emergency Committee and the whole gang have run away from their job which is to give a lead to the country. Because of funk and wangle."

"I couldn't agree with you more," he said.

# 16

It has been said against me, "Here's a man who talks about honour. But during the strike and the national danger he does about the most dishonourable thing possible. He disobeys orders and breaks his oath out of personal spite against his commanding officer, with the object of bringing Lord Nimmo into trouble with an important group of his supporters."

This is a lie, and a deliberate lie. But it doesn't surprise me. I saw it coming. Look at the facts. On May 1st I caught this man with my wife. I had a right to kill him but failed. On May 4th, when the strike was on, I found myself, as a Special Constable, under his orders to keep the peace. I was immediately approached by him, that is, by his committee, to take charge of all the specials in the area. I refused that offer on the grounds I did not approve the emergency orders, but being asked if I wanted to resign, I said no, I would serve as a ranker. That is, I did my plain duty which was to take orders from my superior officers, but I would rather not give orders carrying out the Nimmo policy.

The general strike was called from midnight, May 3rd. That evening, just before dark, I took a walk with Sergeant Varney along Tarbiton water-side, both being off duty, that is, as private citizens. We'd been sworn in four months. Instructions to make ourselves acquainted with the Tarbiton area, all lanes, back alleys, cellars, etc., especially along the dockside. Also any likely trouble spots. Trouble spots either way for attack or defence like town halls, armouries, political clubs, committee rooms, including all parties. And we had Pincomb's place, the Communist place, high on our list for both reasons. It might make trouble and it might bring trouble. Because there was a lot of feeling in the place against the Bolshies on account of boring into the old unions. Also with some of the small firms that didn't have many union men and didn't want to come out.

We all knew the dangerous time was first night. Trouble-makers, lunatics, commies, would say to 'emselves, "Now's our chance before the police are ready." First definite news of strike when Varney comes to me in Water Boy just about closing-time and says, "It's broke. Zero hour at midnight. And I've got my first orders. Take a look along the docks round midnight and after." I say, "Any order for me?" He says, no. I say, "Some nasty spots along the dockside. Spots and chaps. I'll come along," and I took out my arm-band. But he shakes his head and says, "No brassards. Nor truncheons. It's not a uni-

105

form job. We're to go on our own like." I say, "Whose orders?" He says, "Police—verbal instructions." I say, "My God, you're not going to fall for that one." He says, "It's all right, Cap. They told me why. And reasonable enough, too. Essential not give unions any chance to say government mobilized first and gave provocation in order to provoke violence and crush workers. It's like, who's going to throw the first stone."

Sergeant Fred Varney is one of my oldest friends. It is wondered why I chose to serve under him. It's because I had so much respect for him. And I know him through and through, the finest man I ever knew, bar none. The truest, the straightest, the bravest, the loyalest. And a real Christian. He was a Tarbiton man but the first time I met him was when he turned up one day in Africa in my division on his way to the front. Sergeant with a Southern Company. I thought he looked damned ill and I didn't take to the C.O. or his pip-squeak subaltern. A couple of Aldershot Cuthberts falling over backwards with their own importance. About half Varney's age and a tenth of his manners. I gave them all dinner but when the young entry were packed up I went in to see Varney in his hut to ask if he was all right. Offered him a dose of my quinine. He was a bit reserved at first. Not sure if I wasn't cutting in behind his officers. A bit suspicious of me too on the civilian side. But as soon as he saw I was on the square, he came out freely. And so did I. We took to each other from the start and we talked pretty well all night. He'd joined up under the Derby scheme for the forty-year-olds. Brought in because the talky boys wouldn't have conscription. The country could take it but the talky boys said to themselves, "The first man who proposes conscription will have it pinned on him by someone on the other side, that is, by some other talky boy on the make, and it will lose him votes. May cost him his chance of being Prime Minister. So after you, sir. And come on all you fellows who have guts enough to fight for your freedom, come and be killed." Varney was just engaged to be married, also a mother dependent on him, but he felt he ought to go. Didn't like the idea he was safe at home eating three good meals a day while others were dying for him. So off he went and got a bullet in the guts. Twice gassed. Not fit for trenches so sent off to Africa. But it struck me not fit for Africa either.

Worried about his girl. Showed me a picture. Round-faced girl with pop eyes. I said nice girl, lucky man. He said, yes, luckiest man in the world. But a bit worried. A nervy girl. On the young side for him too. Came home and found the girl going with another chap. Who hadn't volunteered for anything and not likely. Reserved occupation. Making eighteen pounds a week after two strikes. House of his own and a nice lot in the bank.

Varney's first idea—shoot 'm. But then he thought a bit and said, what's the point. Won't get the girl back. And won't stop her new chap thinking him a damn fool for volunteering. Besides, his health was bad. Lungs still gassy. Sitting up half the night with asthma. Not attractive to young girl. And he hasn't even got a job. Living on his sister Margaret. She's got a husband and three children, but Freddy's her brother and he needs looking after. Also husband doing pretty well in Behrman's machine shop. Motor parts. Fred has applied for a disability pension in the usual course. Also in the usual course, the Ministry takes time to look into the claim, a lot of time. Meanwhile he lives on his savings and his sister's husband.

Then the 1920 slump. Margaret's husband, Teale, out of a job at Behrman's and goes north to look for work. Old Mrs. Varney, Freddy's mother, over eighty and crippled with rheumatism, turned out of her caretaker's job because the owners can't afford a caretaker. So she comes to the Water Lane house too and shares the bedroom with Margaret and the children. Varney's savings sinking fast now. Margaret goes out charring, but not much doing. Too much competition. Half Water Lane half-starving and strong young women going out to work all day for two shillings and their tea.

When the slump hits the poor, it hits them hard. Gets them on the ropes and gives them one, two, three, like lightning. Knocks 'em silly. They don't know where the next real smasher is coming from. The next one came from the Ministry when it refused Fred's pension. Said his chest had always been weak and his disability not due to gas. In fact, they were playing the game governments always play on the soldier as soon as peace and slumps come and the office boys take over. It's what Kipling says:

*A making mock of uniforms that guard you while you sleep*
*Is cheaper than them uniforms, and they're starvation cheap.*

This is how I came across Varney again. He saw my name

108

up on a notice as Commodore of the Longwater Yacht Club, and came to ask my advice. I put my friend Kilmain on the case and made a stink. But the government bilk-experts were in a strong position because of the slump. Thousands were suffering so why do anything for one. Varney was a bore—let him die.

Luckily Kilmain found a job for him, as general superintendent Unemployment Works Centre at East Tarbiton, with quarters. This suited everybody. Poor Varney and his family desperate for a roof, Kilmain and his crowd desperate to save the Centre which was giving lots of trouble.

These centres were a scheme by a local committee to help the unemployed. Idea was to give them recreation rooms, canteens, nurseries, workshops. Half a dozen of them were started in various spots, an ex-cloth mill at Batwell, the Parish Hall at Terryport. In Tarbiton at an old tin chapel in Water Lane, joined on to what had been the minister's house.

Kilmain was first chairman of the county committee, and ran the thing like army welfare, put in a lot of old sergeants as managers. Kilmain was a crank and a Plymouth Brother as well as a sapper, but he was also an honest man. He believed in a jealous god but not jibbercats. Thing went off to a flying start and got a good Press. So then Nimmo volunteered. To general gratification at this mark of confidence, adding so much to prestige and usefulness of humble labours. See Press hand-outs. And Nimmo did bring in a lot of money, from his millionaire friends. Next thing he was chairman and reorganizing whole set-up. Lady Gould got job on General Welfare; Countess of Lilmouth, Entertainments; Mrs. James Latter, Canteens; Mrs. Bill Pincomb, Children's Care. Nimmo's usual game, hang a nosebag on everyone, keep 'em quiet. But trouble from the start. Mrs. Bill, the Communist, wanted to put commies into all the nurseries, Lady Gould had Liberal candidates and Lady Lilmouth a string of Colonels' widows. This started politics in the centres— unions, the commies, the Liberals, all pushing for control. At Tarbiton a chap couldn't mend a chair leg unless he was in the union. Because the instructor was a unionist and wouldn't let anyone else in. And his wife couldn't leave her baby in the day nursery unless she was a Bolshy or nearly. Because Mrs. P. had a good party member in charge. Varney managed to keep the peace by getting the steadier men behind him. And standing no nonsense from the troublemakers. Also he lived on the spot. His quarters were three rooms at the top of No. 11, the old minister's house, with a door into the gallery of the chapel, which was now the hall of the Centre. For dances and whist drives. So he was always able to pop in and out.

Personal influence is what matters in a job like that, men aren't machines. Especially Englishmen. All the worse when they get pushed around by machines: Varney got such a pull at the Centre the only place where politics had the last word was the nursery. That stayed solid commie—for good party babies only. Everywhere else the poor devils of unemployed and half-timers began to forget to fight each other. They shared the same work benches and even played billiards together.

Of course he was helped by one thing. When Potter's went on half-time and their men became eligible for the Centre, as partly unemployed, he got a lot of new members who were steady middle-aged men and chiefly in the small craft unions or none at all. And they weren't interested in the political push-pull run from London by the big mouths and the puffballs.

Varney, I say, proved his worth. He did a grand job and got no pay for it. Only quarters. For himself and family. The whole family, mother, sister Margaret, three children, in the three rooms. And they couldn't be grateful enough. To me. I'd only put old Kilmain on the job. But their view was I'd taken trouble about the pension too, even gone to London about it. Worried my friends. They couldn't forget it. They were that sort of people. The best sort—the only sort that matters. The people who would be ashamed to forget an obligation. Call it pride, if you like, but it's not the pride that swaggers about its dignity. Just the other way. They didn't talk about personal honour. Too big a word. But they had it strong. In their bones. I was their friend for life. Nothing too good for the Captain. From the first time I came round, it was, "You'll have something, Captain?" and I was to stay to tea and one of the children sent out for saffron cakes. I heard it all going on behind the door, and it brought the tears in my eyes. These poor people laying out their pennies for saffron cakes, so full of gratitude for what I'd done for Uncle

111

Fred, which was nothing. So I told them. I told them too I had one in for the government all to myself. I had been practically thrown out of the African Service for trying to protect my poor pagans from exploitation, and so I knew how Uncle Fred felt, I had been glad to make a stink for him.

But they wouldn't believe it. There was Margaret fussing with a table-cloth as if the angel of the Lord had come. And telling me how good Uncle Fred was to them and how ill he had been and how the children loved him. Flushed up to the eyes and ready to cry herself. The free quarters made such a lot of difference, she said. Mother with her bad leg, Potter's on half-time, and no charring anywhere within reach. Three children to feed and little Fran so delicate. You could see she was pretty near worried to death, but not for herself. All for the others. And not pitying herself, and not bitter. Though God knows she had every excuse. I thought to myself, "The salt of the earth and some government clerk in London tries to cheat them out of a few shillings a week."

And why? That's why. Because they're the salt of the earth and trust the nice gentlemen in black coats to do the right thing by them. Because they won't complain when they're cheated. Because they don't shout for their rights but do their duty. Because they are not gimmes but givers. I tell you, just to go up the Varneys' stairs gave me a new feeling about the world. It made me feel there was real goodness and loyalty in it. In those bad times after the war, it came so I went every week. And I would have gone oftener if I hadn't been afraid of being a nuisance to them and costing them too much

112

money. For I couldn't insult them by offering money and yet they would always spend on me. And if I drank with Varney, then he had to pay his turn. So I kept it down to once a week. But it got so that then I was expected. The children would run down the street to meet me. Mary Teale, Varney's little niece, would be at the bottom of the stairs to welcome me at the door, and upstairs there was the old mother, if well enough, and Margaret and Varney himself, to do the honours.

And I said to myself, "This is the best of England," and I was forgetting it. I was forgetting it had any best at all. I was looking at the outside, the thing you see in the papers, all lies and dirt and grab and the gimmes ready to sell their mothers for loot—monkey-hill at scratch time.

# 17

SERGEANT VARNEY is a fine man, but no fool either. So when he talked like that about the verbal instructions to act as a policeman without a policeman's powers, I was considerably surprised. The racket was obvious. If there was any trouble and he tried to stop it, it was on his own responsibility. Suppose he stopped the Bolshies proceeding to the boat-yard with bottles of paraffin and pockets full of matches. There'd been threats to burn the boat-yards, because boat-yards didn't want to strike. All right. Local commissar runs special in, says unwarranted attack on private citizen taking home his weekly lamp oil. And Nimmo says, "Quite so. No authority from my committee. Sergeant Varney is an enemy of the people. Old soldier—brought up to butchery. Throw him into quod. Run him in for damages. Hold him up to public disgust and contempt.

114

Turn on the Press gang—chew him up in best printer's ink all over the world." All right. But suppose he doesn't interfere and these boys go and set fire to the boat-yard. Why, then the committee wants to know why Sergeant Varney didn't do his duty. Duty of every citizen in such an emergency. Much more sworn special, even without instructions. Act of cowardice. Shocking dereliction. Old soldier too. Man with full understanding obligations of loyalty and discipline. Disgrace to the country. Blacken him. Hound him. Charge him full damages. Ruin him. He can't answer back because nobody will listen. And he's only got one vote.

"My God," I said to Varney, "don't you see the racket? Who's going to carry the can?" He laughed and said, "I suppose me." "But look here, old man," I said to him, "this isn't joke. It's the old game they played on us in Africa— the everlasting Nimmo game. The everlasting game they always have played—nothing in writing. Nothing definite— nothing you can pin on them afterwards. The verbal instructions gambit specially invented for mugs like Tommies and coppers. Theirs not to reason why. Theirs to take it in the neck both ways. And save the bunko-boys from the cruel fate of losing votes and even pay. Not what you do but what the papers say. To tickle the mob in the right place. One hand dirties another and both of 'em to push the man in the ranks into the mud. Let him choke, the silly bugger. He's only a bloody fool who doesn't know how to dodge out of keeping his word."

Varney only laughed and said I would have my knock.

**115**

But I had a kind of feeling about that first evening. Every old soldier knows it. First moment of a war is the time to expect the unexpected. Something tricky and something that will make a big effect. Before the other side is on its toes. And I was right.

On that night, the 3rd, Varney and I had been patrolling from about 23 o'clock, about two hours, and found all quiet. At a certain back lane called Butcher Row we separated by agreement, I took the front street and Varney the lane. About twenty minutes later, that is, 23.20 on the 3rd instant, not meeting Varney at the corner, I turned back up lane and found him standing by an entry with a big parcel leaning against the wall. He said he'd removed it from an open yard inside and asked me for my opinion on the contents. What had happened was this. The special called Nolly, afterwards a witness in the case, then a night watchman, saw some suspicious movements round a yard opposite his warehouse. He knew it was the yard belonging to Communist H.Q. That is, it was on the special list for protection. He sees a couple of fellows dodging in and flashing torches. Varney has just passed that way, given him a word. He runs after Varney and reports. Varney goes back to yard and out pops a couple of fellows. One runs off. Varney grabs the other, who says, "Hullo, aren't you Sergeant Varney?" Varney says, "Yes," and the fellow says, "A special." "Yes." "Then I've something to show you," and he takes Varney into the yard. At the end there was a small motor van with an open back and at the back this parcel. The young man flashed his torch on the

116

parcel which was partly open and pulled out a folded paper. "Look here. They're going to stick 'em up to-morrow night."

Varney read the paper which was a small poster, about twelve by eighteen. There was a big heading, "Workers, now or never." And it went on to say the English Government had copied Mussolini and started a plot to provoke violence by means of the specials. The object was to bring out the troops, in order to shoot down the workers, smash the unions for good, drive down wages still further.

And it declared this plot would fail if the workers were firm and struck at the means of communication and transport. They were millions against a few hundred cowardly capitalist stooges and their victory was certain. But they must take decisive action immediately and together.

Varney saw this poster was certainly seditious and dangerous, and he decided at once to carry off the parcel. Also another of the same type in the van.

While he was getting this second parcel out of the van, a young woman came out of the back door of the building and asked him what he was doing on private premises. Varney pointed to the wording of the poster and said it was seditious and he meant to confiscate it.

The young woman said of course the poster was true, Varney was a Fascist tool, and she would make a protest to the Chief of Police and the Home Secretary. He was breaking the law. He told her, very well, he had to do his duty, and dragged the parcel into the street. The young man had made off when the woman appeared.

As the parcels together were too heavy for Varney to carry alone, he had then waited for me. I agreed with him of course the posters were seditious, but said in view of absence of direct instruction we should not destroy them, but merely convey them to some safe place until we could get a decision from the committee about their disposal.

So we carried the parcels round to the armoury. We retained only one poster to go with our report. We weren't surprised next morning to hear there'd been a protest from the commies. But what we hadn't expected was they also called a meeting at the Centre, packed it with commies and voted to get Varney sacked. Also Nimmo's next move was a surprise. On the evening of the 4th when I was sitting in Varney's room, a little girl came over from the Water Boy to say there was a call for me. I went over and the lady secretary, Emergency Committee, says, "Is that Captain Latter?" "Speaking." "Hold line for the chairman." And after another five minutes, I hear Nimmo's voice, his sweetest, his richest— the wedding-cake voice. "Is that you, Jim?" "Speaking." "Jim, you're the only man for this job. Don't think I'm trying to flatter an old friend. I come direct from the first plenary session of the committee, and they were unanimous. I speak simply as their delegate." "What are you talking about?" "They want you to take over the specials." "Can't be done." "My dear fellow, no one else can do it—no one else has the necessary influence with rather—what shall I say—independent material." "Not a hope."

There was a pause here and then I heard another voice.

118

Nimmo had pulled out another stop. This was the one he used for funerals, deep grief combined with hope. A bit of a wobble underneath and a touch of angel's wing in the wind. "I don't know, Jim, if there is any personal reason for your attitude but—believe me—I could well understand it. I can only say how sorry I was on Sunday—and how right you were. And you need not fear that I shall ever enter the Cottage again. I have actually told Nina of that decision. Of course she is in full agreement." I stopped this rigmarole by saying my refusal was nothing to do with what had happened on Sunday. Or any other day. I was serving as a special because it was an obvious duty. And the reason I wouldn't take command of the specials was because as C.O. my duty would be to carry out the orders of the committee and I didn't like their orders.

"What don't you like about the orders, Jim?" A brisk note like a cracked bugle—defaulters. Come and be argued with. But I wasn't going to argue. I said I'd made up my mind and rang off.

But half an hour later, Varney's sister Margaret, Mrs. Teale, came upstairs to us in a great state of mind. "There's a big car at the door and the driver says it's some lord." To this poor woman big cars and lords mean bad news or some kind of demand. And she hadn't much left to give. Even when I explained, she was in a fluster. But she dusted down a couple of chairs and Mary Teale brought the visitors up. Frant, a big man, who looks small, with a round baby face and little silly features, and Winfield. I hadn't seen Winfield before, but I knew the name. Chairman of Winfield's Chemicals. A sharp little man like something you see in a race crowd, picking pockets or selling winners. I introduce Varney, "My friend Sergeant Varney." They shake hands and you can see they think, "One of the Captain's crack-brain whims—introducing us to his friend the Sergeant." Margaret has another dash at the chairs and they sit down, and Freddy makes for the door and I say, "Where away, Freddy?" "I thought the gentlemen might like to see you by yourself." "Not at all. I'm not going to turn you out of your own room."

Frant murmurs something in agreement. But you can see he's put out. "Captain Latter, I daresay you know why we called." "Yes, to get me to take on the specials," and I said why I wouldn't. "What is your objection to the committee arrangements?" "That letter about picketing. It was simply an invitation to the Communists and the left-wingers to stop all the roads and starve the country." "Excuse me, but the object of the committee is simply to avoid interference with pickets which would lead to fighting." "It says nothing about control of pickets—they get a free hand." "We thought it wiser to leave that point to the discretion of the police and specials, on the spot."

Little Winfield starts in here, "You don't like Nimmo." "Let's stick to the point." "It is the point. I don't like Nimmo either. I don't like his politics and I don't like his face. But I'm backing him in this emergency because he's the man for the job." "Whether I like him or not is nothing to do with my refusal." "People will think it has." "You can't help people

120

thinking." "No, but it's damned important what they think just now. They think Nimmo is a wonder in an emergency— due to the war. And that's why we'd better think so too. And why you ought to come in when he asks you."

Frant puts in, "He says he's been your friend for forty years and he has absolute confidence in your loyalty."

This made me laugh. All down the back and up the guts. It was plain enough why Nimmo wanted me to serve. I couldn't go shooting him while I was under his command. And I couldn't put out statements to the Press while I was a police-man.

# 18

THE two wanglers looked at me laughing and didn't move an eyebrow. They knew what I was laughing at but they didn't care. It wasn't business.

Winfield fired off again like a gun. "You were a police officer in Africa." "I was a political officer in West Africa till the government pushed me out. With Lord Nimmo's approval." "You had the police in your charge." "Most of the time." "And put down a rebellion." "No, just a spot of trouble. No one got hurt."

"Exactly," Frant says. "You knew your job, and carried it out in such a manner that the Governor sent you his special thanks. That's just why Lord Nimmo is so keen to get you now. You've got the all-important experience and a cool head. There's no one else in the country measures up to the work as you do."

Winfield cuts in again, "You won't serve because of your row with Nimmo?" "I am serving." "Not in your proper job." And Frant puts in again that I'm the only man for the post. No one else commands the same confidence, and so on.

"If we get trouble," Winfield says, "it will be your responsibility." "Not a bit of it. It will be because the committee won't give proper protection to firms whose men don't want to come out." "You've heard Frant's explanation. If you take the job, you can keep an eye on pickets." "Pickets should not be allowed anywhere unless the majority of men want a strike. That's what I thought we stood for. Democracy."

"That raises a new point," Frant says in his soft voice. "About fifty new points," Winfield cuts in, "and we haven't time. The thing is simple. You've got a personal grievance against Nimmo and so you won't do this job which cries out for you. This stuff about pickets is a smoke-screen and you know it. You can settle about pickets when you take on the specials."

I was still taking a look at this proposition when old Frant turned to Varney and said, "And how's your chest nowadays, Sergeant? Better I hope." "Why, yes, sir," said Freddy, surprised. "It is a bit better." "That's good news. Very sporting of you to volunteer like that. Most patriotic. And now in the specials. How do you find things?" "People are a quiet lot round here, sir. They don't want to make trouble." "And what do you think about having Captain Latter in charge?" "Just the man, sir—I said all along—"

I couldn't stand this bit of nonsense. I said to Frant, "You

123

have a wonderful memory, Lord Frant, or a first-class secretary." But before he could answer this, Winfield jumped in again with both feet. "What about it? We've met your objections. You know damn well where your duty lies."

I liked Winfield. He might be a crook but he wasn't a mean crook. And I saw his point. I said I'd take the job if they gave me a chit confirming my power to regulate pickets.

And when they looked at each other and Winfield said a chit would be unusual, I agreed to take a private note, anything in writing to cover my field of action.

"Certainly," said Frant, "certainly, of course. And may I say how grateful we are for your co-operation. We wanted you from the beginning, it was the obvious choice. All the committee agreed on that," and he went on with his flummery.

Margaret then knocked on the door to know if the gentlemen would like some tea. But no, they wouldn't take anything. Most grateful but no time. That is, Frant was most grateful, Winfield didn't bother to say thank you. He gave Margaret one look as if to say, "Who's this poor fool who offers Lord Frant and James Winfield tea in the middle of the morning?" and then made for the stairs.

Frant spent three minutes shaking hands and saying how charmed he was, how much he hoped these economic troubles would soon be over and prosperity return to Tarbiton, before he smiled himself out of the door. Varney and Margaret both thought him a very nice man. And when I pointed out he had certainly never heard of Varney before that morning, and had simply put on some secretary to find out some facts,

124

Varney said, "Well, he took that trouble." "Yes," said Margaret, "he wanted to be nice, didn't he? Oh, dear, I hope he wasn't offended about the tea. But we haven't any whisky."

I said it was a pity they hadn't had some prussic acid. But they did not answer this. Both of them thought me prejudiced against Frant, and even against Nimmo. They looked upon me as slightly cracked in my view of that great and noble character, whose picture had been in all the papers. Old Teale, in fact, Margaret's uncle by marriage, had a war caricature of Nimmo framed on his sitting-room mantelpiece. The usual caricature showing him with a great bald dome and deep-set flashing eyes. Nimmo's head is quite an ordinary bald head, and his eyes are ordinary eyes. But caricaturists must live. So they blew up his head and deepened his eye-holes, and handed him on to the public as a sage full of brains and holy enthusiasm. And people like old Teale, half the people in Tarbiton, especially over forty, couldn't see any other Nimmo. Not even if they had him in front of their eyes. I've heard Varney himself say, after Nimmo had been speaking at the Town Hall, "All the same, he's got something about him. You see at once he's exceptional." "Exceptional what for?" "Well, brains of course. But there's the religion too—something in his eyes." "My God, Freddy. That rat. Are you falling for the yarns in the radical Press? And after what he's done to me?" "Ah, that's a funny business if you like."

But he still thought Nimmo a wonderful man, a great man full of noble thoughts. Nothing could shake him on that point. He'd drunk in the idea with his mother's milk. Chester Nimmo,

125

the champion of the poor, the voice of a merciful god. And when he said, "That's a funny business," he did not mean it was a wicked business but a mysterious one. How had this great holy Nimmo done such a dirty deed upon a friend's wife?

I don't say Fred Varney thought I must be inventing the whole crime, or exaggerating an innocent gesture. But he thought there must be some explanation which would save Nimmo's halo and excuse me for shooting him, all at the same time. And so did nearly all the older people in the place. One of my difficulties in this whole affair has been this feeling about Nimmo, built up by the Press, as a political racket. Old honest Baldwin with his pipe was nearly as bad. Always draw him with a pipe and the people will feel, "There's an honest simple Englishman—no flimsy cigarette-smoker but a real good chap like you would meet in any pub." Old Baldwin! As cunning a diddler as any in the book. What do they do it for? Why do they build up these grabbers and fakers into noble souls and heroes of the nation? It's all in the game. Poor devil of a Press artist has to get a job, catch the public eye. Tickle 'em somewhere. Poor devils of the mob want to think they've got a genius to look after 'em, hold off the next slump, keep out of the next war. And the politicos make hay between, with their tongues in their cheeks. It's the whole system is wrong. It's the way we've got fixed. By drifting along and not asking where we're getting to.

126

# 19

THE moment I took charge, I ran into trouble with Bill Pincomb. I also discovered he had a pull with Nimmo. The two had a closer hook-up than even I had suspected.

Pincomb'd made a speech, on the first strike day, outside the Town Hall, pointing out that members of the Watch Committee, including Nimmo, had large investments in Frant's and other firms. And trade was bad. Therefore a strike was an advantage—it would enable the firms to save all costs and wages instead of going on half-time. "That's the real reason for the Emergency Committee's orders about pickets. They're not out to protect the workers' right to strike. Not much. Their game is the old capitalist game of heads I win, tails you lose. There's only one hope for the worker, smash the whole racket—

seize the means of production. And this order about pickets is your chance."

I called up Communist H.Q. on the phone to warn Pincomb against incitement to violence. Some young woman answered Comrade Pincomb was out but she would give him my message. But my man, stationed in the house opposite to keep an eye on the Communist H.Q., reported ten minutes later Pincomb had spent the night in the building and was certainly there still. There was no way out except into the yard which opened only by the gate on the lane, alongside the front door.

I concluded Pincomb's secretary was afraid we meant to arrest him and told the man to go back and keep his eyes open. I then went round to my office in the Town Hall. This was just an attic allotted to me during the emergency. I found it crowded already with people wanting to see me.

It had been divided in two by a wall of file boxes, about three feet high, but there was no privacy, and no furniture except a desk and chair for me in the inner part of the room and three chairs in the outer. About fifteen people waiting, but all of them on their feet. They pushed forward as soon as I came in and began to talk. Each of them thought his business top priority. One wanted protection for his van while he moved ice from a store to his shop; another, a shopkeeper, complained an assistant had been threatened; several wanted to move food about or collect it at the station.

Strike Committee was issuing permits for movement of essential food stores, but hadn't made up its mind about what was essential and what wasn't. Tarbiton committee didn't agree with Lilmouth, which had stopped the ice. But the ice was wanted for Tarbiton hospital. Or some of it.

My orders were to avoid, as far as possible, a direct clash with Strike Committee. Therefore sent the fish-shop man back to Tarbiton committee with a note explaining problem. Could they deal with Lilmouth?

I want to emphasize this point. I backed up the Nimmo committee, from the start. I actually refused protection to another merchant, a woman who wanted to shift a load of bicycles from the dock. My ruling was bicycles were not essential stores.

This led to some argument, in which other women joined. And in the middle of it I was startled to hear my name spoken close beside. I'd been aware of two women pushing towards me through the crowd, but both wore the new hideous fashionable hats, pulled down to the eyes, and I'd not taken special notice of them. Now I turned and, after a moment, recognized my wife. After a moment because there was a moment I said to myself, "Who is she?" It wasn't only she looked thin and ill—her whole face was different. The way she looked at me. As if she hated me. I didn't know how to speak to her. I was embarrassed by this visit. I had a letter of hers in my pocket at that moment, but I hadn't answered it because I didn't know what to write. The letter was an affectionate letter such as my wife knew how to write better than anyone. "My dearest, you see I write from the Cottage. I came home last night because I can't be happy anywhere

129

else. And even if I'm never happy again, I can *remember* happiness here (whatever you say, we were happy together as children). But I hoped to find you here and it doesn't feel like home without you, and it never will. You are my home, my dearest, you are my comfort and peace as well as my roof and shelter. I never had any peace till I found you again. I hope you aren't blaming yourself for anything that happened on Sunday because it was *entirely* my fault (this sounds rather comic after I've been so terribly in the wrong) but what I mean is the *special* fault of not speaking which you might blame yourself for. In fact I *know* you do (you'll say this is a typical piece of my 'diplomacy' and 'dodging round the point' but I'm never sure if you would say I 'know' anything unless it was proved). You don't believe in intuition, do you, but really it's not intuition. It's only that I love you and understand how really gentle and long-suffering you are by nature—I deserved very much worse than happened. I'm even glad I was cut a little, though I suppose this is something I oughtn't to confess (I mean I've no right to feel relieved just because I got a little cut on the forehead where it doesn't even show) because now I have your mark on me. Does this sound mad? I'm afraid it sounds silly which is worse, and which you will hate. But after all I ought to have been punished—I oughtn't to have 'got away' with everything. This sounds rather muddled, if what I liked was also a punishment. What I mean is I liked feeling that you had punished me, even though you were so disgusted with yourself that I suppose you feel you only made things worse for yourself. But

130

I don't want you to feel that—I hate to feel that I'm getting the advantage 'all along the line.' It's so unfair, and so hard to forgive. My dearest, however I seem to 'score,' I know perfectly well exactly what I am—a worthless kind of woman. Perhaps you can never forgive me or love me again. But do believe that if you *can* forgive me and let me try again (and you have said I did sometimes make you a little happy) or not even forgive me (I quite see that may be *impossible*) but just allow me to be with you, I will do my 'damnedest' (as you would say) to 'work my passage.' For unless I can 'make it' I shall be truly a lost woman, I shall want to die—"

There were three more pages of the same kind. My wife wrote letters eight pages long even if I was away for a couple of days. Her letters were something I'd valued all my life. They had, I really believe, kept me alive in Africa when the government was trying to break my heart and kill me in a death station.

But when she wrote those marvellous letters to me in Africa full of love and tenderness, she was Nimmo's wife. And I asked myself even as I read this one, if she wrote so to Nimmo now, while she was mine.

What could I say to this woman who had a mind like a conjuror and a different name for everything. Love without truth. What does it mean? Loyalty and lies?

I'd tried to answer her last night but everything I wrote had seemed false or priggish. And I'd noticed this before in dealing with my wife, or Nimmo himself. Because they were tricky, they made you feel tricky. When they struck attitudes, you felt as if everything you did was a pose. I'd torn up three or four beginnings of an answer to that long letter and now when I saw her suddenly in front of me, so pale and ill, I didn't know what to say. But she spoke easily enough to me. No difficulty at all, quite cool and looking me right in the eye. She said she wanted to see me and it was rather urgent. "Is there anywhere?" I said there was nowhere at the moment.

"I've got the car outside."

I said I was on duty twenty-four hours a day and as for a private room I only had my office.

"Very well. What about the passage outside?"

We went out into the passage which was luckily empty at the moment—and she said to me at once, "It's about the Cottage—what are you going to do about the Cottage? I'm going away as soon as I can pack."

I said I had her letter and was going to answer it. But she cut me short with a wave of her hand and said, "Never mind—it's not about anything I wrote. It's about the Cottage. Who will look after it if I go?"

It took me a little while to understand what all this meant. I asked her if she was angry because I had not answered her letter. "No—of course not. I'm not angry at all—it was a stupid letter. I'm not surprised you didn't answer."

"When are you going to leave the Cottage?"

"Does it matter? I haven't thought."

"What about Robert?"

"We'll have to arrange—what do other people do when they break up?"

132

# 20

ASTONISHED as I was by this about-turn, I kept cool and said I'd come to think divorce wrong. Especially with a child. Our first duty was to Robert.

"Very well," she said, "it will have to be a separation. And don't think I'm daring you. We can't go on. If you don't trust me—and you never have trusted me."

She said this as if accusing me. I was so surprised for a moment by such a charge from her after what she had done I couldn't think of an answer. Then I said she knew better than anyone how much I had trusted her.

"No, never. Never in your life. I've always known you were watching me—judging me. I've always been afraid of you. These years since we've been at the Cottage have been an agony."

133

"You said you'd never been so happy before."

"Yes, to keep you happy, to keep you from digging at me all the time to find out what I was really thinking."

This was such nonsense that I lost my temper. I said if she was trying to provoke me by lies she wouldn't succeed again. "I hit you once and I'm sorry—I'm ashamed of that cowardly blow."

"You didn't only hit me—you meant to kill me. You hated me—you've always hated me."

I said nothing to this. She was obviously surprised I did not answer, and after a moment, she said in a careless voice, as if talking about the weather, "I made a visit to Drake Lane this morning and saw Pincomb." I knew from this casual tone she was spilling something big. Probably the whole thing she'd come about. I suspected at once she had gone, as several times before, on business between Nimmo and Pincomb, and I walked carefully. I said, "Well, why not—why shouldn't you? I know he's a friend of yours. Did he say anything, by the way, about the specials breaking into his room and stealing private papers?"

"No—what papers?" And though I was watching closely, I could not get a clue. Trust your London society woman. For as it now appears, the lying complaint against Varney was actually the first excuse for the whole conference.

"What papers?" my wife said, opening her lovely eyes wide. "What papers?" and then she said, "Unless you mean this thing, and that speech he made." She showed me a leaflet, a cyclo-styled paper in green ink, headed NIMMO AT IT AGAIN.

134

There were a lot of these things floating about already. The machine-printers had come out on strike and most of the papers were stopped. But at once there were people handing out leaflets at every street corner, sticking them in letter-boxes or posting them up on walls and lamp-posts.

The government had started a gazette on one double sheet, but the Communists were selling their own sheet, there were dozens of labour circulars, and any number of leaflets put out by religious people, crank societies, and plain lunatics.

This cyclo-styled paper brought me by my wife was one of these leaflets. It simply repeated the charges made in the speech, about Nimmo's investments and the strike suiting him, as it would save him money. It also referred to an old scandal when Nimmo had been accused, as a minister, of using his private information to make money on the Stock Exchange. And the last sentence read, "Nimmo belongs to the class of capitalist stooge who buys and sells everything and everybody. Everything has its price for a Nimmo, workers, women, children. He buys them body and soul and when he has paid, he wonders why anybody should shoot."

I read the thing and I said I supposed it was true.

"No, it isn't true. But I'm not bothering about the old lies. It's the new one—about Frant's. That's nothing to do with Chester—it's the money invested for me and Robert. Aunt Latter's money."

Aunt Latter was the old aunt, of Nina's and mine, who had died the year before and left her fortune all to Nina for

135

life with remainder to my son Robert. And she had appointed "her old and trusted friend Chester Nimmo, Lord Nimmo, as trustee."

"Very well," I said. "And you went to Pincomb to ask him to stop the libel." "Yes, and in case you believed some new lie about me." "What lie?" "About my taking money from Chester. These investments he made for me are my own money." "Very well, what about it?" "Pincomb said it was nothing to do with him. It was more likely Labour or Fascist propaganda." "Very likely," I said. "They're all throwing dirt. By the way, did Nimmo send you along?"

"I knew you would think that," she said angrily, turning pink. "But don't you see it's dragging us into it—it's suggesting that," she made a face as if swallowing a lump, "we've had some financial advantages from Chester?"

I said I didn't know anything about Chester's investments for her, as trustee. They weren't my business.

She answered in a furious tone, "But I want you to know about them. I'm telling you about Pincomb this morning, so you needn't wonder what I'm doing there or have me followed." I said that I'd never had her followed. I wouldn't do such a thing.

"I beg your pardon," she said, "but that's simply not true. You had a man this morning in the lane. He thought I couldn't see him in the doorway opposite but the poor thing was too stupid even to pretend." I said I'd never sent anyone to watch her. The man in Drake Lane was watching the Communists' H.Q. in case of trouble—it might be attacked or it might start

136

trouble of its own. And if she believed I was capable of spying on her then we had certainly come to an end.

"I'm very glad. You've always hated me. I'm not surprised you wanted to kill me." She raised her shoulder and shivered. "It's a miracle I'm not dead." I lost my temper at last. "You know you drove me to it. You've always tried to drive me mad, deliberately."

"That's what I say, we always hated each other. It's silly to go on."

People had been passing up and down all the time and interrupting us. Now a special came up to me with a note, but seeing my wife was talking to me, he hesitated. At once she turned to him and smiled—her whole face and look changed—she became a pretty, charming woman again, she even coloured a little. She said to him, "I'm getting terribly in the way, aren't I? I'm so sorry," and then to me with the same smile, for the fellow's benefit, "Don't mind me, Jim. I can wait. I've no right to be here really."

I took the note and looked at it. It was about Nimmo speaking again at Shagbrook. Nimmo had put out bills for his third address. Place was plastered with 'em as far as Lilmouth. And we'd already had a lot of trouble about it. First the Strike Committee gave a permit for special buses for Tarbiton and Lilmouth. Then they stopped it. Then they had allowed it again if the Communists gave an undertaking not to interfere.

There were also demands from Shagbrook people for protection against the mob. It had knocked down garden walls

137

and trampled over the grass during the last address. The Chief Constable now sent the thing to me, saying it was a job for the specials.

I told the man to go into the office and get my duty roster. Nina was watching me. And again she'd changed. She'd stopped being a London charmer, or a furious bitch—she had a wise sad look like an elder sister talking to a little boy that has dirtied his trousers. "Jim dear, you know we can't go on—you know you're longing to get rid of me. Only you so hate to admit it's all been a mistake. But really we are past the age of pretending—we need some peace."

"What did I ever pretend? God knows I never loved anyone but you. I still love you. And now I don't know what to do. I don't know what to think. Why did you write that letter if you want to leave me? How can I believe a word you say or anything you do either?"

"That's what you always say. But you don't know what love means, not proper love. You've never been really in love with anyone. You're afraid of being let down. No, don't contradict. When just this morning you had that man following me through the streets."

This false charge repeated like this, deliberately, made me rage again. I wanted, God forgive me, to strike her. I saw she even expected it. She flushed and stared at me—her mouth was a bit open as if thirsty. And I'd seen that look before— in such fights. She wanted to be struck, though if I had struck her she'd never have forgiven me. She remembered every time I'd touched her. She was too proud to bear it.

The man had brought my roster and was standing two yards off, waiting to catch my eye. I turned to him now because I didn't know how to keep my temper, took the roster, apologized to my wife and went into the office to pick two men for the duty at Shagbrook.

When I came out again, my wife had gone. She'd had the last word as always. Though untrue about my love, God knows, and giving away the motive of not being watched.

I wish, all the same, to make it plain I'm not accusing my wife of a lie in this vital interview, saying Nimmo had not sent her to pull the sheep-wool over my eyes about the Pincomb hook-up. If so, she mightn't have known it. Clever as she was, Nimmo could play on her like a piano. On her cleverness and her pride. Even her bad opinion of herself. Building her up as a noble free soul and knocking her down again as a light woman.

But though very reluctant, the position was now definite— I had no course but to write to the agent telling him to put the Cottage on the market, and to Nimmo, I wouldn't be responsible for his papers there because the place would be shut up and then sold, due to our separation.

# 21

THE row about the buses was the first charge against me in the Pincomb case. What are the true facts, as they came out after? Nimmo wanting the third address quickly, advertised for Thursday morning, saying anniversary of sister's death. Though Shagbrook people say she died on a Wednesday night in November.

Protests from Shagbrook residents, vicar of Battwell and several leading magistrates claiming Nimmo, as chairman of Emergency, no right make subversive speeches. Drew attention Chief Constable previous address on Saturday, April 24th, as printed and distributed.

Copy of this speech already in our files with note of Chief Constable's query and Frant's answer to lie low for moment in view Nimmo's local influence all parties.

Conveyed magistrates' Chief Constable's warning to Nimmo and received personal note from Bootham requesting private meeting clear up difficulties. Offering assurances.

Answered not aware of difficulties. Matter quite simple. Nimmo aware danger of inflaming opinion. Meanwhile Nimmo, seeing transport freeze on 4th and fearing flop at Shagbrook, applies Strike Committee for bus permits on ground of religious service.

Strike Committee Lilmouth, about half Communist, refused flat, Strike Committee Tarbiton, mostly Wesleyans, agreed and said good idea. Would advise strikers attend. Proposed local secretary read from Bible, after prayer.

But Lilmouth and Tarbiton Bolshies threatened to picket roads. Bootham wires, "Urgent, confidential. Appeal protection. Challenge relig. freedom. Suggest immediate round-table conference. Lord Nimmo, T.U. Sec. Tarbiton strike. See Lilmouth Chief Constable. Bootham."

Chief Constable answers by post there is no precedent to supersede ordinary courses official action. To me personally, "What bloody business has Boothie got to do with it?"

At same time Nimmo sends my wife to Pincomb, and they strike some kind of bargain, nobody knows what except Nimmo, Pincomb and my wife, and none of them cares one damn about the truth. So nobody will ever know it.

I say Tuesday, May 4th, first day of strike, was complete freeze transport. Nothing moving. My niece Sally was stopped in her car on the way to the Town Hall and walked two miles carrying about a forty-pound bag of supplies. Also being five months gone. It was because of this condition she'd taken on job of canteen at Town Hall for volunteer workers and specials.

I may say her husband and Nimmo had both tried to stop her. Said she should be independent of party politics, meaning she should play with both sides. But Sally, as I say, is an honest girl—and growing up. I saw a lot of her these days. She used to bring me up my coffee to the office. And when I told her she mustn't go carrying heavy bags through the streets, apart from a chance of trouble with some commie lout, she said, "Well, uncle, it's my job." I took to Sally. I was pleased when people saw the likeness between us. Sally being a Latter through her mother. But what I say is, the good stuff is there, everywhere, if we give it a chance.

After that first day, I got Sally quarters at the Slapton Arms in Tarbiton. This suited us both. She was away from the politics at Battwell Manor and I had a responsible person to see my men got hot food when they needed it. I also arranged for a guard in her car to bring in supplies.

But on Wednesday already, the worst of the freeze was over. People were going about in own carts picking up friends, cars taking passengers, and first volunteers out with buses. All very quiet and no opposition except some abuse and threats in Lilmouth.

Thursday morning, more volunteers, a few trains and some stone-throwing in Tarbiton, two windows broken in the Lilmouth bus.

With a view to this situation, I took a couple of men and

142

went round by moor road to Shagbrook. No sign of trouble on road and as it was raining, hoped this would keep the crowds down. But found biggest crowd yet, round Shagbrook chapel, about twice as many as last time. Estimated over thousand. Nimmo talking from back of cart drawn up to the wall of the graveyard. I understand his sister buried by wall on inside. Whole graveyard jammed with people standing everywhere on graves and wall which had been pushed down in two more places.

Nimmo accompanied by seven persons, seated in cart. I recognized Sir Henry Bootham, Countess of Lilmouth, Bob Smithers, Strike Committee Chairman, Rev. William Moon, of Mizpah chapel, Tarbiton, and Colonel Kilmain of Queensport Unemployed Centre.

Nimmo turning about and shouting at top of his voice, but owing to rain and wind not possible hear more than few words here and there.

Crowd very quiet and attentive. Chiefly strikers in Sunday clothes. As one of my men said, nothing much else for 'em to do. Also church attendance gone up last Sunday even in Tarbiton, as in war.

Some of crowd had paper with address printed, as first time. This having run out being passed from hand to hand. I sent one of the men to get a copy. He failed to do so as on approaching members of the crowd, they recognized him as special and refused to give up paper. This was first sign noted of local bad feeling against specials due to Communist propaganda. I therefore sent man to cart to obtain a copy.

This he duly did, with some difficulty, by approaching from behind and obtaining Bootham's attention by means of pulling coat. Bootham at once, as soon as he understood what was wanted, descended from cart and proposed to bring paper in person. My man, Rimmer, carrying out his orders, procured paper and brought it to me pronto.

I needn't quote this third Shagbrook address. All three have been published since. But I maintain I was quite justified in taking exception to the words, at that time, addressed to a mob engaged in revolutionary action.

"My friends, make no doubt, as a freeman of England, I stand for revolution, the everlasting revolution. I am with you against the oppressor, whatever guise he wear. My friends, we meet to-day on ground sacred to the cause, I say the holy cause, of liberty, and sacred especially to my heart, at a moment most terribly fraught with destiny—yes, a day that will stand in history as a turning point, a crisis in the fate of the world. For you, my friends, Englishmen, freemen of the West, are entrusted with a fearful responsibility, not only for the destiny of England, but of Europe, and the whole earth. Be in no doubt—you are the masters—power has passed to your hands. And your wrongs are deep and perpetual, you would be perfectly justified if you used that power to tear the present scheme of things apart, to destroy for ever a society which had turned a deaf ear to your legitimate complaint, and a blind eye from your gross and patient sufferings."

I'd only got this far when Bootham came up. And I asked him at once what difference there was between this stuff and

144

the Communist manifesto. "What I want to know is how far Nimmo is actually hooked up with the Bolshies. How did he get this bus permit out of Pincomb? Why shouldn't I tell Whitehall he's double-crossing his own Emergency Committee?"

Bootham, very polite to the dangerous lunatic Latter, just said he saw my point. Only too glad seize this opportunity at last immediate discussion all outstanding points of difficulty. Suggested we withdraw to canteen.

The canteen had just been set up by the ladies' committee for volunteer drivers. Organized in a cottage adjoining the village, opened as a reading room and bus stop in memory of Nimmo's sister Georgina. By this means the ladies' committee, that is, my wife, had undertaken to repair the Nimmo Memorial Cottage and put in a heating system and new floor at the expense of the rates, a typical Nimmo racket.

Bootham a bit blown after pushing through crowd. I said sorry for his distress but hadn't much time for talk—had to get on with my job seeing roads kept open. But he asked for five minutes and we went into canteen. Place was occupied by lady volunteer in charge, Miss Slocomb, of the Lilmouth Slocombs, a very fine girl. She procured us a corner in the back room, among the stores. We sat on packing-cases and used kitchen chair for table.

I pointed out if anyone made a speech like this, I'd have to arrest him. And I told him the Divisional Chief was thinking already of reporting some of Nimmo's games to Whitehall. Bootham looked as if agreed all the way. The perfect stooge and secretary. Said that passage had a bad look and feared others worse, but ought to consider whole picture. Strong feelings of working class, with revolutionary tendency. Necessary to go along with that feeling—make them feel you were sympathetic with their grievance—and give them hope of improvement. Great point was for someone to get a commanding postion—and Nimmo bid fair to take this lead. Once in the lead, of course, he could also guide. And all had to admit Nimmo had proved his powers of leadership—and guidance. It wasn't too much to say he was a political genius —and genius was something irreplaceable—invaluable—wherever you found it.

I said I'd heard all this before. I didn't doubt Nimmo was a first-class gas squirt and clack merchant. In that kind of leadership, he was right in front. But what did it lead to— revolution—smash.

"Let's admit that there may be a revolution. There are all the symptoms. But what does that mean—all the more we should need the experienced leader. All the more, I say."

This gave me the first big surprise about Sir Henry Bootham. I said to myself, "My God, is that what he's made of—stooge all through—nothing but stooge."

"A revolution," he said then, warming to the noble work of giving himself away, "is pretty much what you make it."

"When you come to animal grab, it's who's the quickest monkey on the cork."

Bootham now grew still more confidential. "It's not quite that. I think you'll agree with me, Latter, from your own

African experience, that government is largely handling people —picking them and managing them."

"Honest people to do an honest job," I said. "Then you can leave 'em to it."

Bootham thought a bit and took another line. "Will you forgive me if I make a personal confession. I've known our friend for nearly thirty years and I know him pretty well. And if you know him—you can—well—handle him. It's a question of catching him in the mood—and getting an angle—the right word at the psychological moment. In some ways, as I think you realize, Nimmo is extraordinarily simple—his reactions are those of a child. His conceit, for instance; no flattery is too much for him—he really believes he is ten times cleverer and wiser than other people. He really believes that God has given him a special mandate to save Britain—yes, and the world."

I say Fat Boy Bootham had considerably opened my eyes. In fact, I'd said to myself I'd better lie low and let it come. But this last effort was a bit too much. I saw the chap was as rotten as the rest. I said, "Hallo, hallo, I thought you were Nimmo's man."

This gave him a shock. He was quick enough to see his mistake. He took another look at me out of the tops of his eyes and said very carefully, "You misunderstand me. I have the very highest admiration for Nimmo—I think him a unique person and probably indispensable to the country at this moment. But for that very reason I am trying to take a clear view of his character—as it is. We have to remember, Latter, that we are

147

dealing with an old man—old for his age—and one who has lived for thirty years in a very special atmosphere. A man who has had power—especially the extraordinary power of the popular speaker—the mob orator, if you like—well, naturally, it has certain effects on the character—it gives a man a certain detachment from what we might call conventional standards. He's apt to look upon us ordinary mortals as pawns in the game—he hasn't time, you might say, for our little susceptibilities—he tends even to forget them. As in your own case—a most shocking one—a really disgraceful thing."

He waited for me to agree but I said nothing this time. I was wondering how far the chap would go.

"And yet, as you perceive, it has given you, in this crisis, a very important, perhaps decisive position in relation to our friend's political future. The case of Parnell is not of course a parallel, but it is near enough—if you and I cared to act together—"

"It's nice of you," I said, "Fat Boy. But I don't think I can play in that yard." And as for handling our friend, as he called him, I had no time to waste and I was going to report direct to Chief Constable and ask for a ruling on sedition. Otherwise I should have to consider *my* position.

Bootham jumped a bit when I called him Fat Boy. He saw he'd got in wrong. But he was not to be put off. He began to sweat and moan. He hoped I wouldn't take any precipitate action. Give him an hour. He'd get in touch with Nimmo as soon as the address was over and come direct to the Town Hall. He promised every satisfaction.

148

I record this proposal, though hard to believe, without comment on present state of common honesty, not to say loyalty
in politics.

I paid no attention to Bootham's request. The reason why
third Shagbrook address was not reported that morning was because I failed to get to Town Hall. I hadn't got half-way before
a patrolman came along on a motor bike to tell me there was a
Communist road block at East Tarbiton, on the main road, that
is, it would stop the Shagbrook buses on their way back.

# 22

THE East Tarbiton bus incident has been greatly exaggerated.
I shouldn't refer to it at all if it didn't cast important evidence
on the Nimmo policy of double-cross. It is simply a lie buses
were set on fire and volunteers murdered. This may have happened in London but it is nothing but a slur on the decent people
of East Tarbiton. The absence of newspapers started all sorts of
rumours but this was the worst. I got to the place as soon as
anyone and saw the thing from the start. I found only one bus,
in the road opposite Potter's back gate, partly crashed against a
lamp-post. The road had been blocked with scaffold poles taken
from Clay's timber yard, and the driver had come upon it unexpectedly and taken the pavement. The driver, volunteer, was
standing by the wall—young university man in a tweed coat. He
was looking embarrassed. Two young fellows had opened the

150

bonnet of the bus and were knocking out bits of the engine. About twenty-five passengers, mostly women, standing on the verge looking on, and another twenty or thirty, men, women and children, all ages, and locals, gathered behind. Two chaps on guard to see none of them went round the corner to warn the next bus. Some of the young women were arguing with him saying they had to get home to get their husbands' dinners and they wouldn't tell tales. One old woman was screaming at some fellow called Tom, telling him she recognized him and she'd tell the police he was there. But most of them were looking on patiently or chatting together as if it was all in the usual way, nothing to worry about.

Fellows on guard and putting engine out of commission, all young but all sorts. One I recognized as a chemist's son from Tarbiton, one of the sellers for the Communist paper. Another was a nice young lad who used to be in and out of the Yacht Club on racing days, and sometimes got a job as crew. He was laughing and shouting, having a fine time of it. But the one who seemed to be directing operations was a stranger. He was a young chap in a grey suit and open shirt, with a pill-box hat. He was giving the orders—walking up and down with his cap over one ear and a cigarette in his mouth, pointing with a little crooked stick he had to show where he wanted his sentries. Cutting the hell of a dash. His day of glory. They weren't paying a lot of attention to him. Sometimes he got in among them and pushed them about. Even then they were not too ready. But when they turned on him he went quite mad and yelled and waved his arms—you would have said he was off his head.

151

And then they gave way and he went back to his swagger parade.

Everything very quiet, like Sunday morning. The people looking on were so quiet you could hear the fellows hitting the engine with their hammers and somebody giving directions. But more people were coming up all the time to watch, and just then another bus came round the corner and put its brakes on in a hurry. It stopped only about a foot from the barrier and the driver looked pretty scared. Then he turned and shouted something at the gang. One of them yelled back, "Scab," and some of the crowd muttered, as if they agreed with this. The chap in the pill-box hat got on the bus and ordered the passengers off— some of the women protested and argued, but they got off. The driver, a tall chap, probably a student, sat where he was and no one interfered with him. Going down with the ship.

When this busload joined the rest there were about a hundred in the crowd, altogether, and it was beginning to make a certain amount of noise. Two or three people were talking loudly, one was the same old woman who had been screaming before, she seemed a bit hysterical—and two or three of the men were giving their opinions pretty loudly. A few people were agreeing with both—most were as quiet as ever and looked as patient as a lot of sheep.

It's charged against me from the first I acted with too much precipitation. I say each time I saved serious trouble. I realize any of your tame good-willers, seeing that crowd, would have said, quite honestly, it was a lot of very nice, quiet, reasonable people, about fifty miles from any idea of making trouble, much

152

less revolutionary action. And they would have been right about seventy per cent. But they would have been quite wrong about the rest and the rest were enough to do all the arson and murder any Communist would wish for. The lunatic fringe. The minority that makes all the trouble in the world, swindles, robberies, murders, and revolutions. It's an old tale. "The people were quiet till the cops came." Of course they begin quiet. Quieter than usual because two-thirds don't know what to do next and the other third is watching if it's safe to start the looting.

But I'd seen such crowds before, in Africa. I knew they were ready for anything. They'd been shaken up. They'd been turned suddenly out of their usual rut. They were all saying to themselves, "Something's going on. This strike we've heard of is really a big thing. It's stopped our market bus."

I'd seen a crowd like that in Africa and just as quiet, quieter, turn into a dangerous mob in about two minutes. A woman began to scream and some fellow shouted, "Kill the whites." A crowd like that anywhere has got a certain number of crackpots—half-loonies who are fed up with life and go about all the time wanting to yell and smash things. The same in England and Africa. Only the African is a little quicker to get crazy and then goes off with a bigger bang.

The most dangerous crowd is the quietest. Till it blows up. Till the detonator goes off. I know such crowds and I know the moment when you have to take action. It arrived with the second bus, about three minutes after I arrived. I therefore went up to the fellow in the pill-box, and said, "I give you five minutes to clear the road. If it's not done within five minutes

153

I'll run you in." He turned round and said, "I'm not taking orders from any bloody Fascist. I've got twenty men and you can bugger off or it will be worse for you." I said that in that case I should be obliged to take him in charge. And I told him to come along. Several of his men had come up and now began jostling in, and uttering threats. I did not want a struggle so I went off to telephone from a fish shop at the corner and called up reinforcements of six men.

The crowd had watched all this and were making a little more noise. It's the usual process. The excitable elements began to recognize each other and get together—one group of about ten, men and women, formed in the road, and others came from all parts to join it. The fellow in the pill-box went and talked to it, explaining the situation according to his ideas.

Another dozen were waiting for me when I came out from the shop. They gave way but followed me and one of them, a boy of about fifteen, called out, "Go on—bash him—the specials are worse than the coppers."

This was the new racket—stirring up feeling against the specials, saying that they were worse than the regular police, calling them the White Guard. The Communists wanted to make up to the police and get them on their side in the revolution.

The crowd following me and the crowd in the road then came together, and several of the younger men took up the boy's cry, "Bash the specials. What's he doing here? Bloody Fascist," and so on.

This hostile attitude of the crowd can be testified by inde-

154

pendent witnesses, including Sir Henry Bootham, who arrived just before in his car and was duly held up. He was much surprised and alarmed by the demonstration and I advised him to leave his car and retire by a side road. This, however, he refused to do, on account of an urgent message from Nimmo. I said it could wait—this was no time for talk. He answered, no, it was urgent. Because it concerned the great need of avoiding any provocation to extremists while situation so delicate. I said I fully understood this and begged him to keep out of the way. I also noted Nimmo's anxiety to keep in with his Communist friends.

# 23

I HAD had Pincomb under my eye for some time, pushing about in the crowd. He is easily recognized, being very tall and thin with a red face and a scar on his nose. I knew him well from seeing him on his box in the market-place and also once or twice at the Cottage. Nimmo had been getting up relations with him for at least a year. And my wife charming him in the same game. Idea was to get him on the Unemployment Committee but Pincomb wasn't having any. He looks a quiet sort of chap, used to be a schoolmaster. Really the worst kind of thug, the cool kind. He gave me a nod, but kept his hands in his pockets, and asked me what I was going to do. I said, "Get reinforcements, arrest the fellow in the hat and clear the road. And I advise you to keep out of it." "I came to help if I could."

Communists don't help the police unless it suits their racket.

156

I thought quickly and said, "Is that because you guaranteed the buses?" I didn't say "for your friend Nimmo to preach revolution."

But Pincomb answered at once, "I told Nimmo I wouldn't stop his buses either way. That is, I told Mrs. Nimmo—beg pardon, Mrs. Latter."

I may point out I had every reason to resent his gratuitous insult intended to provoke trouble, but I knew my duty and carried out orders just conveyed even though by unofficial sources, that is, Bootham, to avoid trouble with Communists. I therefore showed no sign of indignation and simply answered that if he made the promise, he'd better do something to carry it out. And the following conversation took place:

PINCOMB: "I didn't undertake to keep the main road clear. But I'll do what I can."

LATTER: "They're your men."

PINCOMB: "Some. But most of 'em not. All sorts from strikers to youngsters out for the lark."

LATTER: "What about the leader?"

PINCOMB: "Name of Brock, clerk at Frant's."

LATTER: "In the Party?"

PINCOMB: "No, he only wants the strike to win. His father is a miner. And he's specially keen to get Potter's men out. A lot of 'em come from Battwell by bus."

LATTER: "I give you ten minutes. And they've got to clear the road."

PINCOMB: "I'll do my best but I have my doubts about the

latter point. You can't treat 'em like bad little boys." "What else are they?" "They're fed up with the mess that society has got into. I believe you agree with 'em." "I can't discuss your politics." "Wait a moment and I'll see what I can do."

He went over and talked to Brock. Meanwhile the crowd, that is, the excitable and political elements, including the dotties and the boys, got more and more noisy. Fellows, hearing the noise, came running out of side streets. Some of them, the older quieter ones, stopped some way off to watch, but the ones who liked a noise and those who wanted trouble joined in. Especially the boys about eighteeen.

The fact was at this incident in East Tarbiton, which has been called the beginning of the trouble, I didn't act too soon but too late. I should have had my reinforcements up at once and arrested Brock before the crowd knew what was happening. Especially before the cranky and Bolshy elements in the crowd had got to recognize each other and come together in a group.

It is true, as Pincomb said, this group was not all Communists. A lot were simply village people fed up because they couldn't do their shopping. But village people are the same everywhere—quiet enough to meet, and ready to tear the world down over something that wouldn't worry a townsman more than a wet day.

Some of the women were screaming at me to know how they were going to get their men's dinners if I couldn't keep the buses running. I asked them, had they heard there was a strike on, and one old woman screamed back at me, "What's that got to do with me and my shopping? Strike, strike, strike—it's all you men can say." Several other women called out, "That's it," and "You tell him, Mrs. Biggs." Most of them, even the quiet old grandmamas, seemed to agree with her, and about eight of them began at me all together about the prices in the market, the rents, the state of the main Lilmouth road, and about half-time at some local works. I thought one young woman would scratch my face. Because her husband had been out of work for a year and her roof was leaking. I said all this was not my fault, but she went on shrieking that she'd had enough.

Pincomb was still arguing with Brock. I think he was as glad as I was when two buses came along together, and one of them brought my reinforcements and the women got into the other. But the important thing was these buses coming abreast down the road broke up the crowd and drove it on the pavements. And before the more violent group could come together again, my men were pulling down the barrier and the village women were off to market.

Brock blew a whistle and took his gang away. Pincomb came over to me where I was standing with my men on the pavement, also certain persons who had taken refuge with me against the locals, still very excited.

As soon as Pincomb reported to me, one of the women called out, "You get off to Moscow. We don't want any German spies around here interfering with the strike."

Bootham, who had been fussing considerably during the whole incident, now came forward to reprove the woman, but

159

she screamed back at him, "Don't you talk to me, you beetle—I lost my husband on the Somme."

Pincomb answered it was no good talking to fools and I told one of my men to move the woman on. Bootham now shook hands warmly with Pincomb and congratulated him on his truly statesmanlike action. He also offered him police protection. Pincomb laughed at this and said, "No, Sir Henry, it's a good idea of yours but you can't catch this bird with cheese. What would my credit be worth among the workers if I accepted police protection?" "But, Mr. Pincomb, your action to-day in avoiding violence is far more creditable and perhaps, in the long run, more advantageous to your party."

But Pincomb went on laughing at him. "No, Sir Henry. Nor birdseed. And don't let Lord Nimmo think I'm eating out of his hand either. I acted on party orders to-day, that's all."

"I can assure you, Mr. Pincomb, that Nord Nimmo feels the deepest sympathy for the workers in the present crisis."

"Lord Nimmo is a rich man and is entitled to feel a lot of sympathy. But what is he going to do about it?"

I said, "You don't deny, Pincomb, you're out to make all the bad feeling and trouble possible in order to smash up everything and bring about a revolution?"

Bootham looked quite frightened at this plain speaking to Nimmo's Communist friend and said quickly it was hardly a fair question. "I don't think Mr. Pincomb can be expected to answer a question like that."

But Pincomb answered at once of course he wanted a revolution. "I should think any sensible man who saw the present

160

state of Europe would want one. It's about the foulest mess in history. And it's dying of its own filth. But so are a few millions of people who can't help themselves. Don't you think it would be a good idea to help some of the filth down the drain and clear the air a bit?"

I said nothing to this and my men had finished their job. So I returned to Headquarters. But I left two men to keep an eye on the gate at Potter's. I had taken note of Pincomb's remark about Potter's. Also about a bargain with Nimmo through my wife. I at once dispatched note, to Lord Nimmo, to know exactly where I stood with Bolshies, in case of serious trouble. This note is numbered 6 in documents submitted to court in first enquiry.

Confidential                                          Town Hall, Tarbiton.
                                                              6/5/26.
Dear Lord Nimmo,
    I understand from William Pincomb, Communist leader, that there is some understanding between you and him relating to transport and also other matters of a confidential and private nature; therefore not disclosed to the police, but known only to yourself, Mrs. Latter and him.
    I beg to point out irregular nature of such relations between the chairman of the Emergency Committee, responsible for law and order, and a deliberate agitator like this man who is only out to make trouble by any means available, and will stick at nothing for this purpose.
    This puts myself, as being under oath to support the law, in an intolerable position and I beg to have the matter cleared up as soon as possible.
                    I am, sir,
                        Your obedient servant,
                            J. V. LATTER (Captain retd.).

161

Notice this letter was marked confidential. But I have evidence it was communicated at once both to Bootham and my wife. Also that the bargain between Nord Nimmo and Pincomb was fixed up by my wife on the 3rd May, as admitted by my wife to me personally on the 6th. Also that this bargain was to sacrifice Potter's and the livelihood of three hundred families to the Bolshies in exchange for Bolshy support to Nimmo.

# 24

On that evening, May 6th, I was sitting in the Water Boy about
half-past seven o'clock when the barman came to tell me my
wife was waiting in garden. This surprised me considering her
talk of separation, but I decided it was my duty to see her on
official grounds. Owing to new information on Pincomb affair.
I should say things had moved fast in this matter, Potter's
had been out since the day before. The men couldn't face the
pickets which jammed all doors and pushed them about. These
pickets were mostly strangers and Bolshies. Old Cooke, who
lived opposite, came in that morning and told us. "The Guvnor
says if Potter's closes now, it'll close for good. He's pretty
well bust."

Cooke is sixty-four and he'd been working in the shops at
Potter's for fifty-two years, a first-class craftsman. Potter's

163

never fires a man who can work. They have some of seventy in the carpenter's shop. Old Sir Thomas has them on piece rates. Potter's is one of the old family firms—they made whalers for the Trafalgar fleet. And motor patrol boats for the Channel in the last war. They keep up-to-date. But they made a mistake in extending too much during the war. Put too much capital in the new machine shops. And got left. The slump nearly finished them, like Behrman's the blockmakers and motor parts who did go broke and was taken over by Winfield. But Winfield let them carry on. He probably bought it only to keep it out of Frant's hands.

The men knew very well that Potter's, like Behrman's, was in debt to the banks and it was touch and go whether they could hold on. And the very next morning after the bus incident Pincomb moved in to attack. Set mass pickets at five o'clock to block the gates. Complaints poured into the office from six on. And I put the case to H.Q. at once. But my report crossed a memo from the Watch Committee reminding me of policy as laid down, not to interfere with local pickets unless they offered actual violence. There was a note to me personally in Nimmo's hand, dated from London. "My dear Jim, may I congratulate you most warmly on the handling of the bus affair. I had a full report by phone from a most unexpected and impartial source. Your courage, coolness, patience and discretion are beyond all praise. And I hope to get suitable recognition for them. Your old affectionate friend, Chester."

I took this to mean: (1) Let the Strike Committee and the

164

Bolshies do what they like to Potter's. It's a small firm and doesn't count much, either for political influence or votes. (2) If you are a good boy and play our game, we'll see you get a nice little gong, like the Obey Brass Eagerly.

Potter's men had a meeting that night and voted against a strike. But there was a good deal of interruption, and someone threw squibs about. When I went round to the Water Boy about half-past six with Varney, I found the argument still going on. Some of the younger tougher chaps had fought the pickets and wanted to get up a shock troop to break through. Some others were all for the strike. This is where I got definite information about the bargain with Pincomb. The man Williams, whom I propose to call as witness, was standing in middle of floor, saying Potter's ought to strike. Williams is a draughtsman, and had a good education. He admits he was employed spare time at Communists' H.Q. And he had been telling Potter's men from the beginning it was no good their expecting help from Frant, Nimmo had written Potter's off and told Pincomb to go ahead and smash it, because anyhow it would be good for Frant's business if Potter's did go smash.

I went to the quiet end of the room with my friends and didn't attend to the speechifying. But I heard something about the specials and Varney told me there was new story going round, that Potter's wasn't getting protection because I had family money in Frant's.

I said this was just another lie put out to discredit the specials. I paid little attention to it because it was nothing to some of the lies. And when people couldn't print lies, they talked them. It seemed if they hadn't got news, they had to make it.

I didn't notice this propaganda had much effect. I may say there was no disorder in East Tarbiton up to this time, except what was caused by strangers and Bolshevists brought in for the purpose.

Even this lie about the specials being used for capitalist purposes to ruin Potter's, had little effect. Several people round confirmed what Varney said but they were quite apologetic about mentioning it to me. The papers are full of how good and steady the British people were under the greatest provocation and all the efforts by big mouths on the make and the commies to stir them up to violence. I agree. I can't speak too highly of the poor devils, what they call the common British people. It should be uncommon. And don't think they didn't understand what was going on or didn't feel it. It was eating their hearts out. And down there in East Tarbiton when Potter's was being sold up because London couldn't care less, it was too small for these great statesmen, the people themselves knew all sides of it as well as any professor adding up the figures to show how cheap the battle was won.

It was in the Water Boy that night a young woman gave me the right word. She was looking for her brother and came over to our table to speak to old Cooke. I don't suppose she was more than twenty but she looked forty. Grey face and her bones sticking out. I asked her, was her husband out of work? "More than a year," she said, and the trouble was if Potter's

166

closed there wouldn't be more work in the place for her father. He was the only one with a job. Young Williams began to explain unless the workers hung together they couldn't get anywhere—the only way to fight capitalism was the strike. But she asked him what difference it would make to the strike if Potter's went on. "I'm not talking about Frant's, Frant's can stand a strike. But this will finish Potter's off, and finish off the lot of us, too. Except you at Frant's. Father's got no complaint against Potter's. He got good pay, and if Potter's shuts down, he'll be done for. He's sixty-four. How can he get another job at sixty-four with all them young chaps wanting work?"

She looked at Cooke as if to ask him for support, but he said nothing. As the argument got hotter, the older chaps went quieter. They didn't believe in argument.

Williams said no doubt it was hard on some of the old fellows. "But so it is in a war. Some get wounded and some come through." "You're going to come through all right," she said, "anyone can see that." "That's personal," said Williams. "There's no need to get personal. Trouble with you women is you can't stick to the point."

Old Cooke didn't seem to hear all this but now he waked up and said to me, "It's the war."

"What about the war?" said Williams.

"It's the war started it all. All you young chaps looking for trouble. You say you want a fair deal for the workers but what you really want is war. You don't like it quiet any more. Like it is around here. So you come in and make a war."

Then all the young fellows came crowding round. They were

**167**

laughing at the old man. "Go on, Daddy Cooke," said one, "tell us some more." "I'm telling you," he said, "you young chaps like a fight. If you can't get booze or girls, then you want to get up a row. So you say everybody's the same—everybody's out for himself. According to you one man's as bad as another."

"Hear, hear, Daddy, only some are worse."

"All I say is that I've been working for Potter's for more than fifty years and I don't regret a year of them. Because you could feel you were doing a good job and the job would be appreciated."

A young barmaid, Polly, who was going round collecting glasses and answering orders, came in with some bread and cheese and put it in the middle of the next table. She said quietly, "Don't talk to 'em, grandy, a lot of Frant's boys. They don't know anything and they don't want to know. What do they care?" "Here, missy," said one of them, "do you mean me?" And they all started laughing at the girl.

"Yes, I mean you—I mean the whole lot of you." She suddenly blew up and began shouting at them. "You dirty low scum."

"Come on, Poll," said one, taking her by the skirt. "You're a nice girl. You wouldn't hurt my feelings, would you?" And another got her by the arm. So she shouted to let her go and started fighting and screaming, and the old man got up and pushed one of them and about three of them turned on him and knocked him down and walked on him.

It all started so quickly he was on the floor before we could get out of our chairs. And when we sailed in to do something

168

about it, the young fellows all ran out in a crowd and scattered down the back lanes. All we could do was pick the old man up and prop him in a chair. His face was running blood but he kept on saying to leave him alone. "It's all right, gentlemen. I'm all right."

The first woman brought a basin and sponge to wash his face. She was quite calm and seemed just the same as before, only a bit greyer and thinner. "Never mind him," she said. "He doesn't like to be noticed. He doesn't want to have anyone do anything for him. And it's all my fault. I started it. And everybody knows it anyhow."

I asked what they knew and she said what they knew was they didn't know anything really. Because you couldn't believe any of 'em.

# 25

AND it's another deliberate damned lie I planned to confront my wife with Williams and prove her a liar. What happened was the following. I helped to take old Cooke to the door when he insisted he would go by himself with his daughter. This was about 18.50 hours. I was standing near door watching Cooke across the road when young Williams came up behind and said, "Excuse me, Captain—about me being a liar."

When I turned there were a lot of Williams' gang, young commies from Frant's, closing in, and I saw it was a put-up job—he was out to make trouble. I thought also he was tight but understand a teetotaller—type that only gets drunk on gas. I said I hadn't called him a liar, but he answered I'd been accusing him of telling lies about the Nimmo deal. And he'd been there. Then he turned to his crowd and began to put out the usual story about the capitalist plot.

I told him Potter's men would get the same protection as any others going about their lawful occasions, and warned him to be careful what he said.

Some of his crowd muttered at this, but I pushed through back to my seat at my usual table by the back window on the garden. I may say during whole strike I was never offered personal violence in Tarbiton district. This was about 19.00 hours and I stayed at table with Varney till I received my wife's message. This was at 19.30.

I then went straight to my wife who was standing in the darkest corner near the house where some bushes kept off the light of the windows.

It was a chilly damp evening and no one else was in the garden except a couple of lads at the riverside doing something to a boat. When I came out from the house my wife came to me. I said, "Hullo, this is a funny place to come," and she said she'd been to the Town Hall but they wouldn't let her in. And she said she supposed I wasn't very keen to see her.

My wife spoke as if she were laughing at something, as if we'd never had a cross word in the world. It was the voice she always used after a row, when she wanted to make up, to apologize. You may be surprised she should come to make up to me after all that had happened. But I was not. This was the tone she always used after a row that would have floored any other woman.

I told her I was glad to see her, and had no idea of avoiding her. The fact was, of course, there had been so many spies and maniacs prowling about the Town Hall we had had to put on a guard.

I told her this but she said only, "Still you don't want to see me, do you? You're furious with me."

I said no, I wasn't furious. So if she had anything important to say, we ought to get to it at once. As it was getting late and I had to go back on duty.

"You could not love me, dear, so much, loved you not duty more."

This was an old jibe about a letter I'd written her from school about Colonel Lovelace's great poem I'd just discovered. The most beautiful and true of all poems. And ever since whenever she was in this mood of baiting me she would bring it up simply to provoke me to some word or action I'd be sorry for.

Yet she knew as well I did that when I wrote that letter as a schoolboy of fourteen who loved her with all his soul and explained what it meant as the master had explained to him, she'd said she would never forget it, and would stop cheating and stealing from that day, in case I couldn't go on loving her. And though she didn't stop, she meant it. At ten years she didn't laugh at an idea because it was true and fine. It was only after thirty years of Nimmo and London society, she found anything comic in a word like duty and could use it to make a fool of her husband. It was easy for her to make me feel like

172

a prig—that's a regular established woman's trick to make a man lose his temper.

I said I wasn't talking sentiment, but just the fact. It happened to be a fact I had a job to do.

But she went on amusing herself, "You said duty before and you looked duty at me. Yes, you're furious—and getting more furious all the time. You'd like to hit me. Well, why not, darling? If it relieves the atmosphere."

"I'm sorry, but I don't just feel like it. And I'm not at all furious."

"If you're not furious, why don't you come home to the Cottage? I promise not to be nice to you. I'll sleep in the nursery."

I explained I was on night duty from eight o'clock, and stayed on the phone which was plugged straight to my office. And even during the day, I was not supposed to leave Tarbiton except on a sudden emergency.

"Do you really hate me so terribly? I'm not really a politico, you know. I'm really nothing. Poor Aunt Latter is turning in her grave to hear me say that, but the Latter half of me never grew up. It's you who are the politico—you take it all so seriously."

I said things seemed to me pretty serious at the moment with a general strike putting the whole country into danger. But she said it had been in danger as long as she could remember. And nothing ever happened to it. She was still laughing, and then suddenly she put her arm round my neck and cried that the serious thing for her was our quarrel. How could we be so stupid?

However, just at this moment, there was a kind of embarrassed cough behind and we both looked round and I said, "What's that?" Whereupon Williams suddenly came out from the shadow of the bushes and began to talk again about me calling him a liar.

I suspected him of listening to our talk and accused him of it. But he said no, he had only come to vindicate himself. Then he began to apologize to my wife. "I'm sorry, Mrs. Latter, I'm sure I don't want to make trouble but, of course, I don't like being called a liar either. I've got my character to think of which is important for a man in my position who's got to earn everything for himself."

My wife didn't seem to understand all this. She had pulled up her coat collar again as if to hide her face. She asked Williams who he was. "Well," he said, "I was in Mr. Pincomb's office when you came about the buses being stopped and about the picketing."

"No one was in the office," she said.

"But perhaps Pincomb had put Mister Williams at the keyhole," I said. And there was obviously something in this because Williams denied it. "There's only a plaster-board partition," he said, "you couldn't help hearing."

"And that's what you were there for," I said.

"There was nothing whatever about Potter's," my wife said.

"No, mam," said Williams, now getting much more polite, "but it was mentioned that it wouldn't make much difference if

174

the strike was complete at the little firms too. It's down in writing."

"Lord Nimmo certainly never wrote anything of the sort," she said, and now she was very much in the grand style.

"Perhaps not, but we had a note in our files of what you said he agreed to."

My wife hesitated a moment and then in a careless way she said that Mr. Pincomb may have said something about bringing out the small firms along the dockside. He had talked a great deal about the whole situation. But there was no understanding by Lord Nimmo, and no bargain. Lord Nimmo wouldn't dream of such a thing.

Williams said if I wanted any more proof, he would get two other witnesses to speak. But I told him it was unnecessary and I didn't want to hear any more from him. He then went off and I told my wife I was sorry to go, but it was nearly eight and it was time for me to be on duty.

She asked me if I believed Williams, that she had been making a bargain with the Communists. I said I didn't know what to believe. But she must realize that, in my position, as being in charge of the specials, I had to know where I stood.

I then took her to her car. She seemed very thoughtful. She suddenly asked me if I had put Williams there on purpose. I said no, and I much resented such a charge. I had had no suspicion of her being in this plot about Potter's.

She said it wasn't a plot. But she got into the car and drove away at once.

# 26

I'M accused of being suspicious and cranky. Look at the facts as now revealed. My wife left at 19.55, ostensibly for home but actually to the Tarbiton Hotel where she had a conference with Bootham. Bootham had been in touch with London during the afternoon and knew Nimmo had succeeded in obtaining a private conference with the Prime Minister; also he had received a précis of my ultimatum, confidential though it was, from the Committee secretary, who handled my files.

The heat was on all round. Sir Thomas had the same news about Nimmo in London. He agreed with Bootham it was important. But in a different way. He thought it the worst kind of news. I found him in the office when I came back from the Water Boy. He'd refused to leave a message—he couldn't trust anyone who had anything to do with the Committee. He'd been waiting two hours to see me and get some line on the facts, anything at all he could rely on. What was going on? Was there any law left in England or were we really sold out to the Bolshies?

He'd brought two shop managers with him, so no one at the yard could say he hadn't understood. "Look here, Jim," he said, "the Watch Committee has asked me to shut down for to-morrow in case my men start fighting the pickets, and when I rang up Nimmo, this fellow Bootham answers and says Nimmo appeals to me as a patriotic citizen with a sense of duty. I say what about next day—could I ever open again—what about the mass picketing and assaults on my men, and they just go on about difficulties of the situation. They're telling me—"

The old man was flustered and excited. He'd had threats to set fire to his place and didn't know where he was. He'd lost his confidence. He suddenly jumped round on me, "For God's sake, Jim, what's behind all this—who's doing it to us?"

Thomas Potter is one of my oldest friends, and one of the finest types of employer. Knows all his men personally and takes a personal interest in them and their families. In fact that was the chief trouble with the firm now. He'd been keeping open for the sake of his men and working at a loss when smart business men would have sold out when they saw the slump coming. But after two hundred years, a firm like Potter's doesn't sell out.

Potter is seventy-six at least but still a strong man. Now he looked more than his age, his cheeks were purple, his eyes were red. He went puffing round the office muttering to himself and every minute he'd stop and stare at me as if I was in the plot to keep him in the dark and knock him out from behind.

177

"There's only about a hundred commies in the whole of Tarbiton," he said, "but it seems they're running the place. What's happening in London, Jim? Is it true the Guards were out yesterday? Is it true Nimmo's in with Lloyd George to get up a national government?"

I told him there were lots of such rumours flying about but most of them were lies. As for the government, it had a good grip and plenty in hand.

I didn't say I couldn't be sure they would have the common guts to use their power. I didn't say things were slipping. Because I had to do my job which was to back up the government, including our precious Watch Committee.

"I see," he said, popping his eyes at me again. He looked as if he was going to have a stroke. "You're not telling—or do you tell me to close?"

I said I was afraid I couldn't advise.

"Are you giving me protection?"

I said so far as I was concerned my job was to give protection to all citizens while going about their lawful affairs and I'd already taken measures against mass picketing and intimidation. But the Watch Committee was my boss and had the last word.

"If I shut, even for a week, it means being late on the only paying contract I've got and they'd jump at a chance to break it. People are looking for any excuse to get out of contracts these days."

"I know—it's the same with half a dozen of the smaller firms round here."

"But why do they ask me to close and not Fingleton's at

178

Queensport? No trouble at Fingleton's with pickets. No trouble allowed."

I said the commies hadn't made trouble at Queensport. Their method was to concentrate on each objective in turn.

The old man suddenly came up and took me by the button. There were tears in his eyes. "Jim, I've known you all your life. And it's not only me—you know very well if we shut, half East Tarbiton will be on the dole—and no chance of another job for years. Men who've been with me thirty and forty years. But suppose I carry on and they burn me out—it would be easy enough with my timber stocks and wooden roofs. Do you think I should risk it?" And then, seeing I couldn't advise him, he began again, "What's behind it all, Jim? What's going on— really going on? What is a man to believe?"

And I couldn't tell him what was behind it all was a lot of crooks playing for position—a mass of faking and dodging, lies and cowardice. If I had, I'd have deserved to be kicked out, just a little before the Watch Committee got round to it. Nimmo had pushed me in the job to close my mouth and it worked like a charm. It split me off even from my old friend Potter.

He gave it up and turned to his men. "What's the good. We shouldn't have come. You told me and I didn't believe it. All right. I was wrong and you were right. They're all in it together. And they won't tell." And he waddled off without another word or look for me.

And I couldn't have sworn we weren't all in it together. Wasn't it pretty likely, to say the least, there was some connec tion between my wife's sudden approach and Nimmo's games in

London and the Watch Committee taking sides against Potter's.

Actually during this interview with Potter I was rung up three times. Once by Bootham, wanted to see me on most urgent business. I said I was engaged. Once by a typist from somewhere saying Lord Nimmo would call through at ten, that is 22.00 hours; and again by Bootham to say he was coming round and he was sure I would see him as he came at Mrs. Latter's personal request. And he rang off before I could say no. But I thought it queer to find my wife, who hated Bootham, sending him to see me on our private difficulties. Unless the whole thing was worked by Nimmo on his new line.

Bootham was actually waiting in the hall when I went out with the Potter party. He had a pass, of course, but he wanted to see me alone. I took him into the Mayor's parlour which we used for a night office.

I own I had taken a strong dislike to this man since his giveaway remarks about Nimmo, whom he owed everything to. I knew him then for just another rat in the sewer and I daresay he felt it. He was in his most oily state on this occasion, and began with a lot of compliments about my fine job on the day before over the bus trouble. I said oh, but what was his business?

He gave me a long rigmarole about the critical state of tension due to mistrust, and said he had a proposal to make for an immediate settlement, satisfactory to all parties concerned.

He then put his brief-case on the table and produced a paper in duplicate. "I have Lord Nimmo's authority to say that he will agree to all these terms." And he read them out to me.

180

Firstly, Lord Nimmo would agree never to visit Palm Cottage except by invitation or permit from Captain Latter. Secondly, all papers, files and memoranda, now at Palm Cottage, including any letters written to him by Lord Nimmo's late wife, should be handed over to him intact. Thirdly, Nimmo undertook not to see Mrs. Latter except at times agreed by me and in my presence or in that of some third person approved by me.

Fourthly, the terms of this settlement being agreed by both parties, Captain Latter undertakes not to proceed against Lord Nimmo in any manner likely to cause prejudice to his good name.

I said it was a nice-looking paper but he could take it away again. I told him I didn't quite see eye to eye with his views on matrimony. I didn't think husbands and wives ought to need political bumf, even if signed in duplicate, to keep their marriage straight. No doubt he had other ideas, but there it was. Each of us made our own bed and how we kept the lumps out of it and the wives in seemed to me very much our own private affair.

This was a pretty broad hint because it was well known his own marriage was not going too well. Sally and he were scarcely on speaking terms since her taking on the job at the specials' canteen. He understood me and turned a bit red. But Fat Boy had not been thirty years in politics for nothing. He had the hide of a rhino. And he went straight on. No doubt, he said, his suggestion was a trifle unconventional, but not so much as I supposed. Ask any lawyer. And as for his venturing on so delicate a matter, he would not have dreamt of it without my wife's

181

approval. In fact, she had accompanied him that evening to the Hotel and was now outside in his car, waiting to be summoned. And then, before I could say what I thought about this funny game, he went out of the room and in three or four minutes came back with my wife.

She was laughing when she came in and her first words were, "This isn't my idea, you know, Jim, but Sir Harry loves a conference."

"Bootham has just told me it was your suggestion."

"Not the signing. I knew you wouldn't like that. Or do you?" She looked at me a moment and said, "I'll sign it if you like."

"If you need to sign such a thing," I said, "it proves it's no good."

"I quite agree," she said. "But still I think you'd like me to sign it, because then you can really feel safe with me. Have you got a pen, Sir Harry?"

Then she sat down and signed the paper, though still half laughing, and handed it to me—I gave it to Bootham saying that it was his affair. I refer to the matter only because the paper has since been put into court as Document No. 8, and it has been noticed I did not sign. I wish to say the reason was not because I was set against any kind of reconciliation, but because I considered the whole proceeding wrong. It simply drags down marriage into politics or business. Which, in this case, I had good reason to think was its actual purpose.

182

# 27

BOOTHAM at once left with paper but when I held the door for
my wife, she stopped and asked me what kind of accommodation I had in this dreary place. I said I slept or rather dossed in
my office which was quite good enough on what was equivalent
to active service. She said all the same she was sure she could
make me more comfortable and she would like to see the place.
I said she could see it to-morrow. "But Jim, it's my duty to see,
as your wife. I don't really think you can keep me out."

This from the woman who'd said two days before that we
must separate. But I didn't remind her of the fact, she knew it
very well. That's why she was laughing.

"Nina," I said, "you don't want to climb up four storeys to
a dirty attic, just in order to tell me something about my work-

183

ing arrangements and then climb down again. And you won't be allowed out unless I come down with you."

"Yes, I must see. I ought to have come before. It's really disgraceful—but there, I haven't been a very good wife, have I?"

This was her apology, and she gave it to me as if it was a good joke. But even though, as I say, I had every reason to suspect its purpose as due to ulterior motives, I gave way. I say a man is a cur who throws a woman's apology in her face and I couldn't do it. I said if she wanted to see my room she could certainly come up, but she must not complain if the place was a mess. It was a billet, and not the Ritz.

I was sleeping in fact on the floor on a couple of mattresses sent over from the hotel. But as soon as my wife saw this arrangement, she said it was very nice. If we put them side by side, we should be quite comfortable. I said I was sorry but she couldn't stay, women weren't allowed in the place except service women on duty. But she answered, laughing, "So you won't forgive me." I said it was nothing to do with our private differences, it was a rule.

But she paid no attention to this. She said she knew I wouldn't forgive her, and she didn't deserve it. She had behaved very badly, she was a bad woman, it was only my goodness had saved her from being a very unhappy one. But we had been happy—she had made me happy sometimes, hadn't she? She said all this in the same amused way and sat down beside me and put her arm round my neck, kissing me and then looking to see the effect. As if consoling a child that has lost its temper.

184

"Nimmo and Bootham," I said. "They've got it all worked out."

Then at last she frowned and said, "How stupid all that is— when we were so happy—when we can still be so happy. He's gone and he won't come back. And it was all nonsense what happened. You forget how old he is, poor old man. Really nothing happened. Though I hated it because I was afraid it would upset you." And then she took me in her arms and began to tell me how she loved me, and how terrible these days had been without me—days and especially the night. She hadn't been able to sleep.

I had known of course all along what all this meant. And lawyers can talk about condonation which was no doubt just what Nimmo-Bootham was after. But I'm not ashamed my wife, as they say, had her way with me. I say again the man is a brute who holds off from a woman who only wants to make her peace with him. But I wasn't taken in. I wasn't surprised when at six in the morning when the alarm clock went off for reveille, I heard her say she had a confession to make, she had talked with Pincomb about the buses. I asked her if she had done any more jobs for Nimmo in the last two days, but she answered she was sick of politics. After all, the only point of politics was to make people happy and now we were happy again, why trouble about them.

"I didn't raise the question."

"But you are thinking all sorts of questions. No, Jim, you don't really love me or trust me. You think I came here to-night on some secret plan, and just played with you, like a street woman. You make it all disgusting—a nasty thing. But what can I do, Jim? If you won't believe what I say, I must try something else. And once it was so sweet—anything we could imagine was simply a way of saying I love you. It was all true and good. And it's still true for me."

She went on like this for a long time, until the special came to knock on my door in case the alarm had not waked me. Luckily he only knocked and did not come in. I dressed and told her she must go too as the room would be needed for the office. Then she burst out suddenly, "You think I'm going behind your back all the time but I've never done so in all my life. Everything—everything is so that we can go on being happy together. But you don't believe a word I say—you don't trust me."

"Why do you harp so much on trusting you? I've trusted you again and again."

"No, never, never, never. If you really loved and trusted me, you would never even wonder what I was doing. You would be absolutely sure all the time that I was true and loyal— you would never dream that I could really betray you."

I didn't say in that case I should have to be a great fool.

But she saw what I was thinking and went on, "No, that *wouldn't* be stupid in you—it would be simply because you loved me."

"People in love can be fools too."

"Of course they can—but they don't spoil everything. They make it a happy thing as it ought to be. They're not afraid of being really in love."

186

I said nothing more about this because I saw she was excited. But when I got up to dress, I told her about my information. I said I wasn't afraid of being deceived by her so much as being wangled into a false position by Nimmo and Bootham. And I wouldn't ask her if they had told her she must make it up with me because it wasn't a fair question. "I think that precious pair have got some hold over you," I said, "and perhaps when this crisis is over and they've grabbed what they want, they'll let you alone and we can start again."

This didn't satisfy her. She said, "Only start again." But before she went away, she kissed me and said, "Can you believe something? They *did* want me to make it up. Of course. And it *does* suit them to get rid of this horrible quarrel. But that's not why I came. I came because I simply hate quarrelling—and, after all, I always do come. You always win in the end."

This wasn't true. She knew it wasn't true. But it was said to please me and I knew though I couldn't trust this woman a yard, yet she was truly fond of me, she did truly wish to make me happy. She was still the gentlest, the kindest, the cleverest woman I'd ever known.

And I said to myself, even if I could not trust her, I never had really trusted her and she was still the first woman, the first person in the world for me, the only one who had ever given me any happiness in this mean dirty world. And so I was glad to think we had started again and could forget the past.

# 28

HAVING now definite proof of hook-up between Nimmo and Pincomb I took immediate steps to let his lordship know it and ask for definite instructions *re* picketing. I informed him I could not be responsible for order unless strongest measures taken to control position at Potter's. Also to prevent further seditious meetings in neighbourhood of docks. Lord Nimmo replied immediately by phone approving again of my bus action and saying I had full powers to arrest agents of sedition.

I asked again for confirmation in writing, and received none. This caused no surprise to police authorities or myself because we understood Nimmo, though now courting Whitehall, was not going to commit himself against the left until he had got his price out of the government.

I was therefore in a very difficult position. I want to remind court these were critical days of strike. Tanks were out in London, and there was a sudden increase in every kind of violence, propaganda, libels and rumours. Strike committees everywhere were more pernickety, as viz. this received by me on morning of 7th: Document No. 10. "Mr. John Costan, Chairman Tarbiton Joint Strike Committee to Chief Constable, Tarbiton, for immediate attention Captain Latter. *re* visit of Major Brightman to S.S. *Dantzic* on 6th inst.

1. We understand that Fascist leader Brightman on the 5th instant visited strike-breakers at present accommodated on S.S. *Dantzic,* moored opposite No. 1 quay, who addressed them on Fascist policy.
2. Our representative, Mr. Wilkins, was refused permission on the 4th instant to visit the S.S. *Dantzic* and he was informed by Captain Latter that no visitors were allowed, except on a pass signed by himself; and that such passes were issued only to relations of strike-breakers on urgent private affairs.
3. Nevertheless Captain Latter issued a pass to the Fascist leader who then gave a Fascist address.
4. We protest in the gravest manner against this political action by Captain Latter and the special police and we are at once withdrawing our vigilants from the dockside as we can't be responsible for order in the docks while Fascists are allowed free entry and ingress.

Yours truly,"

I answered at once Brightman had no pass and no right to

189

visit *Dantzic* where disciplinary action would be taken against parties concerned. Also Brightman was not a Fascist and had spoken up for the unemployed. See copy.

I want to say this answer wasn't the usual official dodgem. It was the truth.

I didn't know about Brightman's action till next day when I paid my regular visit to the ship to see if all was well. The ship was moored in the channel, owing to threats from dockers to murder volunteers. For the same reason volunteers were not permitted outside the docks during the day or out of the ship after dark. As on the sixth, I was unable to see the men before their return on land, I therefore proceeded by boat. I rowed myself out in a dinghy, accompanied by three passengers, the ship's cook, a young man joining for the first time, and Lady Bootham, my niece, who was accustomed to take out stores for the canteen.

The ship's cook, a baker in private life, then mentioned Brightman's speech. He thought it too far to the left and asked if Brightman was going over to the commies. Lady Bootham at once said no, the Major was simply trying to get out a sensible plan for after the strike.

I said at once, "Has Brightman been on the *Dantzic?*" My niece said, "Yes, last night." I said, "What was Dakers doing?" Dakers being in charge and having strict orders to admit no visitors without a pass. And the following conversation took place:

LADY B: "He was in bed with 'flu."

CAPT. LATTER: "Why wasn't I told?"

LADY B: "Well, uncle, we didn't think it would matter."

CAPT. LATTER: "Who didn't think what wouldn't matter?"

LADY B: "Some of us on the *Dantzic* didn't think it would matter having Major Brightman on board for a drink."

CAPT. LATTER: "You mean he came by invitation?"

LADY B: "Yes, we asked him."

CAPT. LATTER: "Who are we?"

LADY B: "A lot of us. We were just talking on deck and someone said Major Brightman would like to give us a call and tell us about his plans, and we all thought it a very good idea."

I said nothing more then. I saw my niece was quite ready to argue the point. As I said, she is a young woman with lots of guts and not afraid of anybody. Also much worried about politics and a bit turned against Nimmo, not to speak of her mother.

I was quite aware she had been seeing a lot of Brightman. He was always dropping into the hotel and talking to the volunteers billeted there, bus drivers, ambulance men and what not. We couldn't keep him out of the hotel because of the law, the hotel having a licence.

I say I didn't start an argument with my niece on the boat, in front of the cook and the recruit. But when I got on deck, I asked for the names of those who had sent for Brightman. I said there was a serious breach of rules which could cause a lot of trouble if known.

It was now pretty dark and not much light on deck from

cabin windows. Most of the young fellows had come out and stood about the hatch combings. They knew me pretty well even in five days and we were on good terms, though not my type. These were nearly all students from different colleges and most of them, being after the war-wave, against soldiers.

I stood under the bridge and said I wanted to know who had asked Brightman on board. Someone in the dark at once answered, "What for?"

"Because it looks like a piece of dirty work. He waited till Mr. Dakers went sick before breaking the rule."

"Well, sir, we wanted to know what he had to say."

"It doesn't matter what he said. What matters is he's not allowed in here without a pass."

"But why, sir?"

And someone said from the back, "Because it's an order, you mug. Signed J. V. Latter, Capt." This was a joke. But no one laughed. And I said at once, "Excuse me, but I'm not doing army work here. I'm on a civilian job. And as a civilian and special policeman I'm not allowed to take sides. Nor my men. Nor you either. Which I am trying to carry out."

I want to say these students were a decent set of fellows, and doing first-class work. Also conscientious. I'd been sent for already because some dock clerk wanted them to sort champagne cases and they said this wasn't an essential foodstuff. They said they'd volunteered only to prevent starvation of people in the towns and that didn't include wines. I said they were right, and the champagne was left where it was.

192

Also when I congratulated them on doing twenty per cent more work per hour than the regular dockers they answered it was the dockers' life job and a holiday for them. This was fair and more than fair.

They were some of the best and knew how to jump to it, but always asking why this, why that, and was it right to do this or that. As now.

"Yes, sir," said another young fellow in front, in a green jersey which was, I was told, an Oxford fashion. "But we weren't taking sides. We just wanted to find out what he had to say. And he didn't talk Fascism. He talked about the bad state of the country and the need for a completely new set-up, including a workers' charter."

I said of course they were free Englishmen and at liberty to join up with Brightman if they liked but not while volunteers in my charge. I stated if they wanted to leave the job, they could do so. And go over to Brightman at Lilmouth. That was none of my business. But while here, I was responsible for them not taking sides in the strike but only carrying on essential public services for the sake of non-combatants, hospitals, women and children.

One of them asked me then if I'd ever heard Major Bright man's plans.

"No, I don't know his plans. But all the plans are the same, including the Communist plans."

"How do you make that out, sir?"

"They all promise the earth done to a turn on a silver plate by some talky boy who's never cooked up anything yet but a stink."

But they didn't like this. They said, all the same, ideas were important. And the old ideas didn't seem much good. They had brought them a terrible war, and now millions of unemployed and great misery all through the world.

I said, yes, that was so. No one knew it better than I did. And I had my own ideas on the cause of the trouble. But they must excuse me talking politics, especially as I believed politics was the nigger in the wood-pile.

The young fellow in the green jersey then asked me if I knew Major Brightman was of the same opinion and wanted a new kind of assembly instead of parliament.

I said I did not know it. But I believed in the constitution. The trouble was not institutions but the people who worked them. The difference between a good regiment and a bad regiment was not the King's Regs. which was the same for both, but the colonel, officers and men and what they thought right. I then said I expected the men who had asked Brightman on board to give their names to Mr. Dakers, and took my leave.

I may say the whole crowd accompanied me to the side and gave me a cheer as I rowed away. Also six names were sent in, which I fined one day's pay.

I was not surprised by these students' attitude, having had some experience. Students at universities, especially Oxford, get in among a lot of ideas which starts them thinking ideas are all that matter instead of men. But I was a good deal surprised when my niece came back at me again, as soon as we were alone in the boat.

"I didn't think you would mind about labels," she said to me. "But perhaps you just have to pretend."

# 29

I SAW at once the girl had caught something and I had better be careful. I am very fond of my niece who has been almost like a daughter to me. A bit strongheaded but always polite. I said therefore of course I understood her friends on board were interested in ideas, but I had certain orders to carry out. It was my job.

"But at least I think you could be fair."

"What have I done that isn't fair?"

She said at once, "I mean calling Major Brightman a Fascist as if that was enough to prove he wasn't worth anything. And you admit you've never listened to him or read anything by him."

I said that was true but I thought I had a pretty good idea

of his line. He wanted a revolution. And so did the Communists.

"But uncle dear, do forgive me, but revolution is such a vague word. And you do say you want things changed. Don't you think if we change things, we ought to have a plan?"

"My dear Sal," I said, "plans are two a penny. What we want are men—a few honest men."

"But why are you so sure Major Brightman is not honest?"

"I'm not sure—I just don't like the looks of him or his little ways, or his gang or his paper. The paper is the worst."

"I'm sorry about that because I'm afraid I thought the last number rather good, with the manifesto about a new England."

I remembered the girl's condition, and girls carrying their first are often a bit erratic. So I said only, "Why, Sal, I thought you were a Liberal."

"Oh, uncle, all these old labels. Do they matter any more? Do they even represent anything? The whole world is breaking up in every direction and people still talk of Liberals and Conservatives and Labour and Communists. They might as well try to put labels on a lot of broken glass after a bomb has gone off."

I asked her if this was something out of Brightman's paper.

She didn't answer this. But she said she thought I didn't realize how people's minds had changed about these old party tickets and how people felt, especially young people. The volunteers on the *Dantzic* were nearly all in agreement with her. They all thought the old muddled England was finished and that a new plan was necessary.

197

"Brightman's plan?"

"No," she said, "some of them are for the Fabian plan and some for the Communists. What they all want is a real plan of some kind."

As I say, the girl was not herself. So I didn't say all this talk of plans was an old tale. There's always been plenty of plans all my life. The trouble was to choose. I said only I hoped she wouldn't fall for Major Brightman.

"I'm awfully sorry," she said, "but I've promised to help with the paper. Major Brightman is very keen for an article on the volunteers as a social service. And I felt it was something I really knew something about. And I said, too, I'd go to his rally in the Town Square to-morrow to speak about volunteering service generally, how important it is to the state. It's so near I can easily be back for duty at four."

I at once saw the danger of this. Not only owing to family connections with me but connecting volunteers with the Brightman movement. But I was well aware the girl wasn't a Latter for nothing, being obstinate too according to her age. So I said of course I wouldn't interfere with her political ideas, I would only ask her not to take any definite action till the strike was over.

She answered this was impossible because the article was already in Brightman's hands and she had promised to attend rally.

"Didn't you recollect my order no one employed in Town Hall to take part in political action during emergency?"

198

"Yes, but is the canteen under the specials? I thought it was under the Canteen Committee."

"It's for the specials. Brightman will give it out you represent the specials and so will the commies."

"Then I'm afraid I won't be able to come to the Town Hall any more or the canteen either."

I said no more then. But about an hour later the girl came up to the office where I was about to turn in, and said she couldn't go to bed while she felt she had upset me. She hated to give me more worries when goodness knows I had enough.

I don't hesitate to say I was much moved by this visit and so was she. She said some more very nice things about how much she had liked helping me at the canteen, and if I absosolutely forbade her to go to the rally, she'd get out of it at all costs.

"I'd no idea you'd mind so much. And if you like I'll try to get that article back, though really I think you'd approve of it. It's simply about doing one's duty to the country and not always talking about your rights and seeing how much you can get out of it. And I do think, uncle, it does need saying now when people are so lost. And the poor old government doesn't seem to have had the faintest new idea in the last fifty years but just goes fumbling on in the old way."

I could see she thought I was an old fumbler myself who hadn't learnt anything in the last fifty years. It was no good arguing with her. But I have to admit I should have taken her at her word and forbidden her to attend Brightman's rally, which afterwards caused so much trouble.

I say I admit I did not take the necessary steps in this case because of the girl's state of mind and not wishing to take advantage of her very decent act in offering to break her promise to Brightman. Which I knew would cause her much distress being quite as proud as her mother and much straighter. She was in fact about the straightest girl I've ever known.

# 30

I say I was surprised at my niece, a good solid Liberal, turning
even half Fascist. And the volunteers, good solid responsible
fellows who were really saving the country, going soft towards
common or garden plan-merchants like Brightman, Pincomb
and the rest. But when I looked round in the next two days, I
got used to this kind of surprise. The fact was people were
getting rattled. The country looked calm enough—calmer than
at the start, and if there were a few more incidents, they weren't
even known to most. I heard them at H.Q. only through official
sources. But the general atmosphere was getting charged up all
the time, and now it began to crackle a bit. A lot of minds
were melting like neapolitan ices at a gymkhana when thunder's
coming on, going soft at the edges and the colours running
a bit. The white getting in the red, the red into the white, and
the green all over the plate.

You could expect Brightman to shift a little on the plate, he was playing politics all the time. When I read his manifesto it had quite a new line of sympathy for the strikers. Also a plan for industry to abolish unemployment. Works councils to run factories, limitation of profits, free doctoring for all, and abolition of public schools. All this was simply time-serving, taking advantage, bum-suckery for the mob, in case it came out on top. What I mean by melting is the way decent honest ordinary people began to slide about in their ideas for the first time in their lives.

I don't mean everyone was going left because they thought the left was winning. Quite the other way. A lot like my niece were going Fascist. Raby, a chap who had been against every-thing for years, even the war, now came out everywhere about guild socialism which was simply Mussolini with a coat of paint. Some of my specials thought nationalization was the answer. Lots more officials to push more people about.

Old Penrose, chairman of the bench, suddenly told me if it wasn't for the King, he'd go over to the strikers. Because he had come to the conclusion we couldn't go on with such unem-ployment and poverty, and he'd been shocked by the attitude of some fellow magistrates. But he trusted the King to see there were no reprisals on the poor. This from an old Tory farming his own home farm and owning another thousand acres. But what really waked me up was our vicar, Shermer. He came along to ask for a guard on the church. Shermer was the man who refused my wife communion, after the Nimmo divorce. And I took that badly and stopped going myself. I just went to matins. But he'd given a fine sermon on the first Sunday of strike, on the Christian Society, and I said to myself, "He's all right—a decent spike. And I'm beginning to see what he means about hard cases making bad law. My God, I am. When I see the young thugs pleading bad nerves and let off with a warning so they can go and beat up another poor old woman in the street."

Shermer had been in Lilmouth and seen a row. A bus was attacked and some passengers and the driver cut with broken windows. A lot of blood on the road and the water-cart men had not only gone on strike, they'd taken out some essential pieces of their machines. People seeing a lot of blood for the first time shy like young horses. Shermer had got a shock. He's a plump, rosy little chap, with a blue jaw, but he looked quite yellow about the gills when he came into the office, and his waistcoat was hanging on him. I told him I hadn't a man to spare but I considered the churches pretty safe. He cheered up at once. His waistcoat bulged out like a spinnaker on the home leg. "Of course the Communists are a very small element in the situation."

"Yes," I said, "like the bullet in a gun or a tumour on the brain."

This knocked him back again. His watch-chain fell in a bit. "They are certainly very active and determined—they know what they want."

"That's it, vicar, and they all pull together. They've got discipline—they're not afraid to shoot their own men as well as the enemy. It gives them a lot of steam."

203

At this his waistcoat got so hollow I thought to hear his navel pop inside out.

"I'm told they're a strong influence in some of the largest unions," he said.

"They run 'em," I said.

At this he cheered up again. About half-way. Watch-chain peeped out again between the wrinkles. His navel was back in its crater. And he said with deep thoughtfulness, "We have to remember that Communism has a strong moral appeal. Indeed, the early Christians practised community of goods. Christ even laid it down for the apostles."

"He didn't say the state should own the lot including the apostles and give it leave to crush a man's balls to teach him not to believe in God."

"No, no," he muttered, "no, indeed. Do they do that? No, it's a bad business—one can't compromise with such devils." And you could see him jelling before your eyes—deciding to sell his balls dearly for the church. At any rate, the spikes. And I've no doubt he would. His guts weren't all in his waistcoat. The point was even vicar began to go soft at the edges, in the middle of the week. As for old Digweed, the Fore Street grocer who'd been called names in the street, and young Palto, the chemist, they were in such a hurry to get on the band wagon that as soon as they heard of the Strike Committee complaint against me they dashed round to the Town Hall to sign an appeal for condign punishment on police and specials for their Fascist sympathies, before there was any appeal to sign. Digweed told me in so many words the government had

204

forfeited his confidence and he understood the Communist atrocities in Russia had been greatly exaggerated. Besides, Communism in a civilized country like England would be quite a different thing. It might put the taxes up a bit but it would not be necessarily anti-bourgeois, and it would at any rate put the workers in their place. No more strikes and no more go-slows. As for Palto, he assured me scientists were the aristocracy of the Soviet Union, which had had the sense to assess the importance of research at its true value.

Both of them were in such a nice liquid state you could have poured them into moulds and frozen them into Buddhists or Hindus supposing the Tibetans or Indians had occupied Lilmouth in force.

The heat softened up the soft sweets and hardened up the hard cakes. We had letters every day asking for troops. Meaning shooting. Being an old Nigerian Service man I was all against troops. See my Luga pamphlet, The Daylight Press, 1922, price 7/6, chapter 9. Starting line 13. "The present policy of the Colonial Office to lay down trunk roads through the Luga farms, has already produced very serious repercussions on an unspoilt people strongly attached to their homeland. I protested at the time against this policy (see my memo. from Dutchi, No. 218-43 of 1917) and I now understand the ferment in Lugaland has begun, engineers have been molested and a patrol of troops is demanded. I hereby state such a patrol would be a betrayal of our whole tradition in Nigeria and a crime against the good name of Britain for honest trusteeship of African interests. The calling in of troops destroys all confidence between a political officer and his people and sets back his work for years.

"I have been a soldier and do not hesitate to say about half patrols could be avoided by use of more political officers and attending to their advice, being the men on the spot."

I put in this document because of charge against me of militarism. I want to say when troops were finally summoned to Tarbiton, it was not by suggestion of Chief Constable or myself. But due entirely to very dangerous situation due to continued weakness of Watch Committee where several councillors had begun to slide. Like Penrose to the left and two I shall not name to the shoot-'em-down brigade.

# 31

I BEG to bring this point to notice of court owing to hostile
attitude of certain elements in Watch Committee at this date
against my personal character, leading to failure of essential
support at the crisis of 8th–10th.

I said Communists had been libelling me and Nimmo from
the start both by whispering campaign and speeches, saying I
was bought by Nimmo and both of us represented the capitalists,
being crypto-Fascists. They repeated this libel on morning of
7th with details due to Brightman incident. Also circulated it
among specials in a leaflet. That morning, two members of the
Watch Committee sent for me in confidence and asked if I had
seen the leaflet, saying it was a serious libel. I said yes, but what
of it?

"We have had representations about it. People consider it
is time some action was taken, through a solicitor."

I said such action would only bring out a lot more lies and dirt which would do no good to anybody.

But they answered in a solemn way it was a matter of public confidence in a public servant—also of common morality.

I said again this libel was a private matter and if they considered my character too much damaged for my job they'd better sack me.

This stopped them, and they said they hadn't meant that. But they didn't apologize. And when I pointed this out, they said only they considered me mistaken in my attitude. I did not realize the very grave nature of the libel and its effect on my reputation.

I said, thank you, yes. I was quite aware of all this and did not give one damn.

I may say here I was not completely frank with these councillors X and Y. I shall now tell the whole truth. When I saw the hotted-up libel on 7th I at once proposed to take action and went, that same day, to lawyer Clint.

But he advised me strongly to keep out of court, on the grounds Nimmo had recently settled certain sums on my wife and also presented her with expensive jewels. He showed me his insurance list of nine thousand pounds' worth deposited at the bank. "And it looks very much as if our Communist friends know something about it," he said.

I had heard nothing of these jewels. But I couldn't admit it to Clint as I was now reconciled with my wife and considered I owed it to her to give her first chance of explanation, if any.

So I said the jewels were a private question which might easily be explained, but would be settled between Nimmo and me.

The following conversation then took place, in these words:

LAWYER CLINT: "Lord Nimmo gave Mrs. Latter a settlement only three months ago. You'll agree that would be a rather awkward fact if it came out in court. And, as I say, some of these arrangements do seem to have leaked out as they are apt to do when prominent persons are concerned. Even clerks know Nimmo's name and are apt to talk if they notice that he is giving large sums to lady friends."

CAPTAIN LATTER: "I don't know anything about rats and their talk and care less. I'm used to it. All I know is my wife and I are now reconciled and I don't proposed to go back on it."

LAWYER CLINT: "The question is what a jury will believe."

CAPTAIN LATTER: "You mean will they take my oath? I know nothing of any settlements and did my job without fear or favour."

LAWYER CLINT: "It's a bit tricky in the circumstances."

CAPTAIN LATTER: "You mean the commies will get away with this deliberate political lie simply because the jury won't take my word against theirs?"

LAWYER CLINT: "We have to allow for that possibility."

CAPTAIN LATTER: "What is the good of your precious laws if they can't distinguish between an honest man and the biggest known liars playing the dirtiest kind of political racket ever seen anywhere?"

209

LAWYER CLINT: "I'm afraid the law is human and so are juries, very human. Not to speak of judges."

CAPTAIN LATTER: "I've heard that pretty often from lawyers, but what does it mean? Simply that justice is all for the crooks and liars. Ask any policeman. And you can ask yourself why this country is in its present state of corruption and chaos."

Lawyer Clint didn't answer this. He thought I was just another village natural who didn't know his arse from a hole in the ground. That's what experts think all the time—that's what they said when Galileo ventured to suggest the earth went round the sun. They said he was an ignorant fool and also a goddam nuisance. They were in the job of telling people the truth—they were trained in it and no one else was supposed to open his mouth. The same in politics.

When I told the governor of serious danger in Lugaland I was slapped down. When I told Watch Committee on morning of 8th that serious riot might occur unless strong display of force to prevent any gathering near Chapel Road and Potter's main entrance, I was informed no need of special precautions. And what was happening in committee was a split vote between the two councillors who wanted to put me out on account of loss of confidence in my character and old Penrose plus Frant pointing out how difficult it would be to get rid of me on the grounds available and also that Nimmo wouldn't stand for it. Nimmo and Winfield being away. Frant never wanted to go on record for strong action, being born rabbit and millionaire. Penrose had melted to the left. And the two shoot-'em-down

210

councillors were not going to take advice from a man whose reputation was public mud, besides being quite ready to let him get a brick on the head and so remove him from his job and clear Tarbiton from the contamination of his presence.

I am credibly informed one of the councillors said afterwards, "If the commies really make a riot so much the better because we can get tanks."

# 32

On 8th morning I had first warning serious trouble when Potter's closed owing intimidation. Then discovered Strike Committee had withdrawn labour Vigilants due to Brightman incident and also Brightman rally in Town Square. These Vigilants had done first-class work keeping order along docks. Although no fraternization with specials, there was a good understanding due to confidence between Strike Committee and myself.

This now being at end the Vigilants were withdrawn without notice and before I could get reinforcements to Potter's, my two men there were pushed on one side and the gates were blocked by concerted rush from back lanes.

I reported at once this serious danger of allowing strikers and commies to get away with this success. But Watch Committee answered could not grant special protection.

I was not surprised, therefore, on morning of 10th to find repeated mass intimidation and only a handful of Potter's men got through.

Position, therefore, on morning 10th May was as follows:

1. Vigilants still withdrawn from patrol on Potter's quay and main gates owing to Costan-Latter correspondence as per schedule.

    This correspondence now continued by letter from Strike Committee quoting Lady Bootham's letter in Brightman's paper *New Worlds for Old* and accusing Watch Committee breaking pact to keep volunteers clear of political action. Letter received 10.30 hours. Answered by express on bicycle. Lady Bootham removed from duty. No acknowledgement Strike Committee.

2. Meeting summoned by strikers and commies at Chapel Road within fifty yards of Potter's main gates. Report this meeting to be addressed by Pincomb in person.

3. Warning from Chief Constable, Lilmouth, to Chief Constable, Tarbiton, Lilmouth gang on way to meeting. This gang being responsible for riot Lilmouth on 4th when four buses burnt and private cars wrecked.

4. Brightman rally in Town Square 11 A.M. billed to march along Potter's quay in deliberate challenge to Strikers' meeting.

5. Police retained on usual duties and six specials only detailed to watch meeting.

Notice Pincomb's meetings usually in afternoon or evening

213

but this one billed for 10.30 hours. This idea was to get up feeling against Potter's and attack Potter's men leaving works at 12.

All police and specials were perfectly aware situation was highly dangerous and Watch Committee had let them down. When I detailed Sergeant Varney for duty, being my steadiest man, he said, "It seems we're for it, Cap." I said we'd been in tighter spots. He said, "They say some of the committee would like a little bloodshed so as to bring in the tanks."

I'd heard this too through Miss Willis, Committee secretary, but I considered it confidential, also not confirmed and bad for morale. Therefore said this was one of their cantonment yarns.

Varney said, "Well, they might be right. I daresay they've got some information—and that Lilmouth lot are getting a bit big for their boots."

The porter who was standing by said he didn't see why we should get our teeth knocked out because old so-and-so the draper and so-and-so the coal-man had gone savage.

But Varney only said Councillor X the draper was all right. He'd played bowls with him and there was nothing wrong with him except his nerves.

I may say none of the specials or police to my knowledge were affected in their duty by melting of ideas due to heat of strike. Being ordinary decent fellows who had volunteered for service in the ranks, they were not the type to change their notions of right because of sales-talk by humbuggers and a few stones through a window here and there.

Although they knew they were for it on this occasion, they

214

did not complain when they got the order, only made the usual jokes any old soldier has heard when going over the top.

"Give me bricks every time—you can see 'em coming."

"Not with the back of your head."

"But you won't know anything about that one."

"I'd rather the Huns—they only use machine guns, grenades and poison gas."

"Well, we're going to have lots of poison gas before they gather up the remains."

I say I picked my best men for this duty and you couldn't find better in the Guards. I also decided to accompany them to scene of action, and see it through with them, being the critical day.

On arrival at Chapel Road, I took up position under chapel wall where flanks covered by buttresses and also inconspicuous from observation. According to my orders from Nimmo's committee to avoid all provocation.

At this time already some hundreds gathering in side-streets, but no disorder. These people chiefly young men with nothing else to do.

This meeting at the old chapel which caused all the violence and damage has been described in court. What witnesses didn't bring out is it was perfectly quiet and in hand till Pincomb's speech. Even the Lilmouth gang gave no trouble till then. They left their buses down the street, marched up in military formation and stood to one side during the first speech, by Colonel Kilmain of the Unemployment Centre.

I understand Colonel Kilmain had been requested by Pincomb

to lead off, and consented provided free to say what he liked. He made appeal for peace, brotherhood, abolition of armed forces, Christian sharing, and also spoke of natural manures and wholemeal bread. In this case he was undoubtedly used as a front by the commies, because before he had finished, Pincomb suddenly appeared on opposite side of road, speaking from back of car. The crowd then turned round to listen to Pincomb and Kilmain concluded.

This trick left me and my men at some distance from speaker. Pincomb at once incited the crowd to march on Potter's and bring out the men. Although, as I say, there were only about a dozen had got through in spite of intimidation.

I gave immediate order for Pincomb's arrest and began to push through crowd with my men. But at same moment the Lilmouth crowd attacked with sticks and also a large force of Frant's strikers came in behind. These last broke into the yard of the Case Is Altered public house where they found a number of empty bottles and began to throw them at my party.

Being now surrounded on all sides it was absolutely necessary not to break formation. We were therefore a good mark. I may say not a man wavered although all understood extreme danger. As Sergeant Varney said to me, "This looks like it was it."

He also requested me to stand in the middle as not being so much exposed. These brave men then placed themselves round me to which I attribute I escaped all serious injury. I mention this as showing these good men still had confidence in my command in spite of the attacks on my character.

216

Three of my men were down in the first five minutes, of whom Rankin is permanently injured and Sergeant Varney is still in hospital. After Varney fell with his face cut open, the mob pushed us off our feet and trampled the three men on the ground. But all were now injured with broken glass, stones, or bricks.

I do not hesitate to say our whole party owe their lives to the arrival of police reinforcements brought in by Chief Constable on his own authority.

But such was the fury of the mob that having effected this rescue, the police withdrew from dock area and telephoned for reinforcements.

The reinforcements were actually refused by Watch Committee which ordered evacuation of Chapel Road and Potter's quay. With the result of immediate violent attack on Potter's, penetration of works both by main gate and the back wall, assaults on workmen there and extensive damage to machinery and stores.

I say the refusal of Watch Committee to take notice of my warnings on 8th, refusal of special precautions on 10th, and withdrawal of police at 13.00 hours, from dock area, in order to patrol Fore Street and protect shops, produced a situation of the highest danger. All elements were present for the forces of disorder to take over our town. Which would have happened that night if not for the magnificent action of special constable Maufe in arresting Pincomb.

What are the facts:

*at* 11.00 *hours:* Pincomb addressed meeting, urging immediate taking over of Potter's by strikers.

*at* 11.20: Attack by Lilmouth gang, Frant's men on specials.

*at* 11.35: Arrival of police. Removal of wounded specials.

*at* 12.10: Withdrawal of police to patrol shopping district, suburbs.

*at* 13.00 *hours:* Arrival of Communist parties summoned from Lilmouth, Queensport. Large revolutionary forces gathering both in Tarbiton and Lilmouth dock areas, intending immediate attack on the police station, Town Hall, etc., and prepared to use all violence. At 20.00 hours the situation was in official communiqué as highly menacing. Watch Committee appealed for troops.

*at* 23.00 *hours:* Tarbiton and Lilmouth as peaceful as a Sunday evening and troops request cancelled.

What brought about this complete change? The arrest of Communist leaders at Lilmouth and Tarbiton, especially the courage of my man Maufe in arrest of most active leader Pincomb.

Notice Maufe was alone when he tackled this dangerous criminal, who had two guards with him. He challenged him in the dock area close to his own H.Q. and at once closed. Pincomb and the two guards put up a most determined resistance and Maufe is a small man. He was obliged to use his truncheon and even then the prisoner would certainly have escaped if it had not been for the arrival of the patrol.

I have already expressed my serious regret for injuries received by Pincomb. What I wish to point out is he brought them on himself, and all my men had been hurt and three very seriously wounded that afternoon while doing their duty to maintain law and order. They were brutally attacked with stones and bottles and unable to defend themselves. Sergeant Varney is still in hospital, Rankin had his jaw smashed and is permanently affected. If Pincomb got a knock on the head it was entirely his own fault, due to resisting arrest. The vicious libels on the specials and the persecution of Maufe personally were simply a political racket. It is a disgrace to the law they were allowed, it is a proof of how far the rot has gone through the so-called leaders of this nation that they have had the effect we see.

I hereby state, in the most solemn manner, as a man answering for his life, that the action by John Maufe, on May ten, saved untold violence, arson and bloodshed, at a most critical moment, not only for the South-West Division but the whole country. And what is his reward? To be had up and tried—to be ruined. But of course he is a poor man. He had no party behind him. He is expendable.

I charge a country where deliberate libel and abuse bought and paid for can frighten the responsible authorities out of doing their plain duty is nothing but a fraud and can only be despised by its own citizens. Which is sooner or later the end of that country however it may blow itself out with its own wind, about its own righteousness.

# 33

IF you want heroes, I say Maufe is the finest kind. He wasn't looking for medals. If he'd been crippled for life, like Rankin, he'd have got nothing to make up for it. He went out and did this brave thing only because it was his duty.

I saw him next morning when he came from the hospital where they'd been dressing a cut he got in the chapel riot. Maufe is a quiet young fellow. When I congratulated him, he said only, "Well, sir, I had a hunch I'd find the chap round about Drake Lane and there he was. I'm sorry I had to hit him but he was getting away."

I excused him from work, but he said he was quite fit, and we were so short of men I let him go on patrol.

Of course the commies at once put in a complaint of unprovoked criminal assault; they said Pincomb was dying. They always make a complaint; it's a rule. But two hours later the Watch Committee suspended Maufe from all his duties. Didn't even ask for his defence. I couldn't believe this wicked action till confirmed by Chief Constable. I immediately protested in strongest terms to Watch Committee and phoned Nimmo in London.

I was informed from London Lord Nimmo was engaged on important business. I said my business was of very highest priority as affecting extreme injustice to public servant and also threat to discipline and loyalty of special police, not to speak of encouragement to all forces of subversion.

I was told impossible to disturb Lord Nimmo who was in conference with Prime Minister. This message sent at 13.20 hours should also be noted in view of fact Nimmo had actually left London when I telephoned, having given instructions not to disclose movements. This fact refutes the typical insinuations I knew of his presence in Tarbiton when I left office. The fact is just the reverse.

What happened was this, as supported by my witnesses. Failing to receive satisfaction from Nimmo or Watch Committee, in case of Maufe suspension and slur on all my men, I placed my resignation in hands of committee.

It's true I then left my office, but this was entirely in the best interests of the service. On reporting my resignation to the Watch Committee I pointed out the absolute necessity, in present very dangerous crisis, of continuity in command and proposed my deputy should take over job as from that moment.

The Chief Constable strongly agreed with this view, as see record, and I handed over the office to Brigadier Manning as from 22.00, on 11th instant.

Having then actually nowhere to sleep at Town Hall, I left for home, that is, Palm Cottage.

# 34

I say Nimmo, according to the office hand-out, was in London. I was therefore surprised on reaching my house to find a small car parked in lane which I recognized as his. It was one he used for secretaries and servants, also when he didn't want to be recognized.

I left my own car at top of lane and approached by kitchen garden. I had still no idea Nimmo himself could dare to be present in the house. My idea was he had sent Grant with a message, or to fetch papers. As house was in darkness on lower storey but the upper still lighted, I concluded my wife was going to bed, entered the house with my own key, and made direct for bedroom.

The stairs are old and creak badly, as I came up I heard a noise at door of bedroom, concluded my wife had heard my approach, and called her name. There was no answer and when I came to landing I found bedroom bolted on inside. I thought quickly and tried the dressing-room door alongside. It opened and I went in. As I did so I nearly ran into my wife. Coming from bedroom. The dressing-room was dark and my wife was only a dark shape with a white patch for a face. But I knew the shape of the patch. She shrank back against the wall between the bed and dressing-table, thinking not to be seen.

I had now realized Nimmo might be inside. I could not believe this but thought if it was true, it was time to get the whole thing straight and no more lying and dodging. I therefore locked the dressing-room door behind me, put the key in my pocket and made for bedroom. This involved passing close to my wife but I did not speak because I could not do so. I say I realized she was up to something and I was ashamed of finding her out. How can a man say to his wife, "I believe you're a whore." My wife said love is trust and I say marriage is trust or it is nothing. I did not speak to her that night because I was ashamed for her and saw she was in great fear. I saw I did not know how rotten she was, I did not know any truth about her at all. That's why I passed her in silence and not from spite or cruelty to the poor creature. God is my witness I never wished, I could not wish to make her suffer.

When I went into the bedroom, it seemed to be quite empty. Then I noticed Nimmo's little yellow phial of heart medicine on the bedside cupboard and also a brandy bottle half-empty, and tooth-glass half-full. And when I came round the foot of the bed I saw Nimmo's head down between the pillows. He was lying right down the middle, stiff and straight, with his eyes closed. For a moment I thought he was a corpse laid out. The cheeks were grey and shrunk, fallen right in. But when I looked close I could see the pulse beating quick in the big vein next his forehead. He was putting on another act. And I said, "Good evening." He opened his eyes and whispered, "Who is it? Where am I?" I said Jim Latter, and my wife's bed.

"Is that you, my dear fellow? Something happened. Yes, I fainted—just outside. They brought me into the house. I'd just come from the train. Fearfully tired. And I had an attack. So they put me to bed. Is Nina here? But no—she went for the doctor."

I didn't ask why anyone should carry a fainting man upstairs to put him in my bed. I didn't say he was telling a damned silly lie. A man in my kind of jam finds out things. I'd found out how silly the clever ones can be, they think they can get away with everything. I said to myself, "This clever old man is universally acknowledged to be about the cleverest wangler in the country—and see what a fool he makes of himself."

He'd closed his eyes again. I said the reason I was there was I'd resigned from the specials on account of the action against Maufe. Nimmo made no answer to this. He was thinking it over. After a pretty long minute, he made up his mind and said in a wondering voice, as if he still didn't know exactly where he was. "Oh, yes, Jim! Just the man I was looking for. What was it? Yes—Clint. I had a note. You were asking about the trustee investments."

I didn't answer him. I didn't want to talk about investments.

225

That is, the money he'd spent on Nina. It wasn't a thing you could talk about. You can't talk money to the man who's bought your wife.

"I rather wish," he said, "you'd come to me direct. I'm not blaming you, of course, for—what shall I say—a certain secretiveness in my direction. It leads to misunderstanding. For instance, about old odds and ends of Nina's, relics of the past— I believe she keeps them at the bank as they're not quite suitable for the local dinner party, and I certainly told Clint to keep you informed about any changes in the trustee stocks."

"Or the eight thousand pounds' worth of Frant shares you transferred to her three months ago. On top of the diamond and emerald collar at the bank since last Christmas."

This stopped him a moment. He opened one eye again about a sixteenth of an inch and took a long look at me. "Yes," I said, "I've found out a lot of funny things in the last week or so. And don't blame Clint. He was only doing his job trying to stop me bringing a libel action against the commie paper for calling me a kept man. He thinks I'd lose it. Everyone would take it for granted I'd been kept for years. In fact, I'm not sure myself it isn't the truth."

Something, a stud or a small coin, fell down in the dressing-room and startled me so much I forgot what I was going to say next. And Nimmo in the bed jerked up his head and stared at the dressing-room door with a very queer expression. I suppose he'd thought Nina had made her getaway, he hadn't realized I'd been too quick for her. It certainly gave him a shock. He turned red.

This careless movement of Nimmo's had turned back the sheet and showed something white just under his chin. I came up to the bed, pulled off the clothes and found he was fully dressed in white shirt, wing collar, frock-coat and patent leather button boots. But before I could say this was a funny dress for a sick man to be put to bed in, he jumped up and shouted at me, "What you are is a fool. That's what you are. A fool and a fool and a fool. An everlasting unlimited goddam wooden-headed fool. And I've had enough of your pistol waving. I'm sick of the whole lot of you. For God's sake make a finish. Go away—or shoot. Of course we didn't tell you anything. Because we knew you'd get it all wrong, because you are our biggest headache. Because you are a kept man. Because you have to be kept by people with some glimmer of common sapience—kept or you'd starve. Now shoot, you kept ass, you hanger-on. Shoot —shoot—shoot." And he actually planted himself in front of me as if I were a firing party. "Go on, get it over and give me a little peace."

I give these words because they show how Nimmo really believed. And how he turned things round in his mind. Because he really meant what he said. He'd really lost his temper. He was shaking all over, his face was all out of shape and blotched like a bad apple. I saw the real Nimmo, a miserable old wreck fairly coming to bits with his own putrescence. A canting mummy who talked of liberty and believed in swindling the people. A living lie who'd ended by lying himself into looking-glass land. And from that moment I began to be sorry for the old crook, thrown out on his neck.

But he was still full of spit and spite. He went on screaming like a wild cat in a trap. "Shoot—shoot—you bloody parasite. God damn your silly soul. Shoot and give me some peace. Vindicate what you call your precious honour and go to Hell."

"My honour is my own affair," I said, "and you needn't strike these attitudes, I haven't got a gun. I didn't expect to find you here to-night. I was actually foolish enough to take your word for it that you wouldn't come here again."

"I came here to-night because of your idiotic proceedings in Tarbiton. Because as soon as I turn my back you proceed to murder the only man in the district who knows how to keep the really dangerous elements in hand. I came to save what I can of decency and fair dealing while there may be time to avoid a general crash."

He was now out of breath and by the time he'd blown off this last tale, he was obliged to sit down on the bed. He looked so queer I thought he would faint and offered him the brandy bottle. But he waved it away—like a peevish baby.

I said this yarn about Pincomb was new. Just now he'd been fainting in the road. He took this quite calmly, and said in a complaining voice, "I was fainting when I came—after ten hours in the train and the third night without taking off my clothes. After a week of continuous struggle to get some sense into a horde of imbecile officials, or anything at all out of the drivelling old women who call themselves Labour's council of action. I wonder I'm not dead."

He looked up and stared at me—he'd forgotten me already—in the memory of his cruel wrongs. Then he reached out for the

228

tooth-glass and took a swig of the brandy. This made him cough, and coughing made him angry again. "You people down here don't know what it's like—you can't imagine what I've been through," he said. "On one side a lot of rabbits in a cold sweat and on the other a pack of raging maniacs determined to commit suicide and take the country with them. Labour terrified of its own power and Tories foaming for revenge on the starving poor who've given them a fright."

He was now quite flushed and his voice got stronger. He suddenly caught my arm—he was always grabbing or jabbing people he talked to. To show we're all friends together. "I tell you, Jim, a madhouse. And who is master in this asylum—this raging chaos of pot-bellied union fools and raving paranoiacs. I went to see the P.M. and he had gone to bed. Not to be disturbed on any account. Nor would he see me this morning. That is to say, he dodged. And why," he jumped up, "why, Jim, why won't he see me? Because I'd tell him the truth—that the country is slipping into revolution, a revolution it doesn't even want. That nothing can save it now but a national government of all parties. A new government. For this is war. War for the soul of England—the very heart of liberal Europe. And we are ready. Lloyd George will serve. I will serve. In any capacity. We do not demand guarantees. This is not a time for haggling. And always remember this, if we threw in our weight with the workers, we could tell the Tories to get out, we could toss them into the Thames. And make such a revolution the world has never seen—it would transform history—and who would dare to say we were not justified? We have been flouted and ignored

—the men who brought this country through the agony of the war—the most tremendous, the most bloody in the history of man. Our experience is despised, by the miserable pettifoggers and time-servers who are paltering with a crisis equally beyond their imagination and their powers."

# 35

HE might have been on a platform. He was waving his hands, puffing his chest, beating the dust out of his frock-coat, fairly delirious at the notion of this little game, of playing the traitor. He was furious when, at this moment, there was a loud knock on the door. He rushed at it as if he would bite it. "Who's that —is that you, Grant? What are you doing here now? I told you to go to the hotel."

"Yes, sir, but Sir Harry—"

And then Bootham's voice came from the garden below the window. We went over and there was Fat Boy standing among the laurels and turning up his face in the moon. Nimmo made a lordly gesture to open the window and I obliged the old cripple. He shouted down, "What in God's name are you doing there, Harry?"

Fat Boy, who seemed in distress, apologized for his presence but said that he had been surprised to hear that Chester was at the Cottage, after their recent arrangement.

"Arrangement," Nimmo shouted at him, "what arrangement? I don't know what you're talking about. And neither I should think does Jim Latter—here beside me. Aren't I allowed to talk to a friend for five minutes? Go away—go away—right away." He banged down the window himself and turned to me. "His arrangements! Another office boy and file-pusher. And he thinks he runs me. That booby. As if I hadn't had enough of them in town. My dear old friend," he laid his hand on my shoulder, "you know the type. You too have had to fight the anonymous horde of minute scribblers of Whitehall in the cause of flesh and blood. For agonized and bewildered humanity. You know what it is to be pestered to death by gnats and fleas—you can understand what I have suffered these days. You have been patient with me, Jim. I lost my temper just now. I used unpardonable language, and you behaved, as you always do, with the most noble courtesy. Ah Jim, they say I am a revolutionary, an anarchist. But there is no man in Europe who has a deeper appreciation of what it means to the world that there is still such a thing as a gentleman. I wonder if you realize the pleasure it is to me only to be with you—to come out of that raging chaos of low fears and mean calculation into the company of one who is incapable of both."

I said all this was very kind but I was still wondering just exactly what had been going on that night, in my house.

"You have every right to know," he said, "and I propose

232

immediately to satisfy you. I came, as I said, about the urgent matter of Maufe. I only reached Tarbiton at seven to find out that a file was missing—the Pincomb file—a confidential file. And I telephoned Nina to know if I could come over for a few minutes to examine my papers here—I thought I might be able to supply certain urgent necessary information from my own notes. Now Jim, my secretary, the committee secretary, Miss Willis, was present—fortunately—when I made this request. She sleeps at the Hall. And I must beg—I must insist—that you should come with me now to confirm the fact."

I saw this was simply another lie. In fact, as he spoke, he turned towards the dressing-room and raised his voice. He was giving Nina a line. And now he said loudly, "Perhaps Nina would drive us. I really can't stand another hour of Grant."

He was looking at me all the time and I daresay he saw what I thought of such a scheme, at this time of night; for he went on quickly, "My dear Jim, I own that your feelings are justi-fied but I think we both owe something to Nina's. It was my fault to come—at least let me clear her."

"She's through that door," I said, "if you want to see her."

"Through the door!" affecting great surprise. But at this mo-ment Nina herself came into the doorway.

I said I supposed she'd heard Nimmo's story about a phone call but I wasn't asking her whether it was true or not. As for going to Tarbiton, twenty-four miles, at this time of night, that was up to her also. She could do as she liked. Nina didn't an-swer but came forward a little into the light. She looked very strange, I had never seen her so small-looking, thin and white.

Her cheeks were as white as chalk. But of course she was wearing no make-up. I noticed now she was in her night-dress and had my Sunday overcoat on top of it. I suppose she'd snatched it off the hook on the door to cover her white gown.

"So you'll come," Nimmo said, and he began to apologize to her for this suggestion, but she must see that it was only fair to Jim—as well as herself—to remove any possible suspicion. Nina made no answer. But she went into a corner and began to dress under the coat. We went outside to wait for her. We did not speak again because of Grant's presence, who stood beside us the whole time.

My first idea had been to let the pair go off together. I said to myself, "What's the point of this elaborate nonsense. Why should I hold myself out for a fool. Let them go off alone and if she has the nerve to come back, I'll think again. But that's all."

But as I stood at the door when they went out, Nimmo turned and said, "You're coming, Jim. It's no good our going without you."

"I don't see the point," I said. "I've heard your tale—no doubt you can back it up. It doesn't mean anything either way."

Nimmo waved his hands in despair. And then turned to my wife as much as to say, "It's up to you." She hesitated a moment and then touched my sleeve. She didn't speak but it was obvious she wanted me to go. Because her clever Nimmo had a plan.

And I wasn't going to argue with her. I didn't care even to look at the poor creature caught in such a situation.

# 36

So we went to the cars, and at Nimmo's suggestion, Grant drove us all. The object was to prevent me being alone with Nina in my own car till the evidence had been arranged. But what did I care? I sat next Nina on the back seat but I did not speak to her nor she to me. What was there to say? For either of us?

The car park at the Town Hall for cars on emergency duty was opposite the Hall main door on the other side of the road. At the moment we arrived there was a military convoy passing —troops were usually moved by night during the strike. The lorries were passing at fixed intervals, and we crossed the road all together, Nimmo, my wife, myself and Grant, at the first gap. We went up the steps in a group, though my wife was beside me I did not look at her for the same reason I could not speak to her, it would have embarrassed us both. And at the top of the steps I was listening to Nimmo asking the porter whether Miss Willis, the secretary, was still up. And noticing the porter's surprise. Obviously, I thought, it wasn't very likely Miss Willis would be up after midnight. This was why I didn't know what had happened when I heard Grant's shout and realized my wife had disappeared from my side. According to Grant, when actually under the entrance arch, she stopped dead. He said afterwards it was as if she had come up against a door that wasn't there. Then she turned round, rushed down the steps and threw herself in front of the troop carriers.

The first I saw of her was falling between the carrier which had swerved across the road, and the wall of the post office beyond. Neither could we reach her for several minutes—the road was barred by the carrier, the troops who had jumped down to help, and Grant and the police. The latter, with the lorry driver, lifted her and carried her past us into the Hall. The special on duty, as night messenger, who had been sleeping on a couch just inside the door, had already called up a nurse from the first-aid station in the main waiting-room. This woman, an old army nurse who had volunteered for the emergency, treated us all like defaulters, even Nimmo. She cut short his enquiries, and turned us all out of the room. She opened a moment later and called me over, only to tell me my wife wanted to apologize to the lorry driver and to say she was entirely to blame for the accident.

I asked the nurse if she was badly hurt, but the woman answered sharply it was impossible to tell. She had sent for a doctor and meanwhile the patient must be kept absolutely quiet.

I carried out this order. But what I was wondering was, why

**236**

did she stop? Why did she turn back? Why did she give up after bringing me along to hear more explanations? What had gone wrong? And as I came back up the steps I asked the porter if Miss Willis had been there at all that day. He said, "Oh, yes." "Was she here when Lord Nimmo called before?" "Lord Nimmo hasn't been here before, sir. Miss Willis was trying to find where he was all afternoon to phone him a wire from London. But no one knew where he was after he left London this morning."

"Where's Miss Willis now?" I asked the man.

"In bed, sir, in the basement with the canteen ladies."

"When did she go to bed?"

"About half an hour ago, sir."

"But you're sure she didn't get Lord Nimmo on the phone?"

"Yes, sir. She left orders to call her if any news of his lordship came through."

So, I thought, Nimmo's yarn about a phone call to Nina from the Town Hall was a complete lie.

I saw the porter looking at me in a queer way. He was wondering at my questions. And just then the special came to ask if I would go to Lord Nimmo at once. He'd been asking for me.

The last I'd seen of Nimmo he was being pushed out of the waiting-room like something for the dustbin. And he'd looked like an old rag, folding in the middle. I thought he might have passed out in some corner and went at once. But I found him just inside the door, sitting on the special's bed with his head in his hands. Grant had just given him a drink of brandy and was standing by with a flask in one hand and the cup in the other.

A middle-aged woman, partly dressed and wearing a rain-coat, whom I took for one of the typists, was fussing behind. She had some papers in her hand and was trying to make up her mind to make Nimmo look at them. One of the police constables, the special and a girl from the canteen, stood round with sympathetic expressions. Wherever Nimmo went in those days he gathered a court.

Nimmo had lost his head from the beginning. As we turned and saw my wife fall, he gave a shriek like a woman and then almost spat in my face. "You've murdered her at last." All the way, while she was being carried into the Hall, he kept hopping round me, spluttering and gasping. Seeing him now bent down, I remembered his fainting fit in the garden and asked him if he was all right. He looked up and said, "That was a bad moment, Jim. How is she now?"

I said I didn't know. The doctor hadn't come yet and the nurse would tell me nothing. Nimmo suddenly noticed Grant and the rest standing round and waved his arms at them. "Go away, people—go away. *I'm* not in danger of my life. For God's sake let me alone." At this Grant did actually withdraw a few steps, and the others retreated into the porter's lodge. Nimmo said to me in a low voice, "Have we killed her between us? Don't tell me it's my fault. I know that too well. I am guilty before her and before you and before God. Whatever happens, I shall never see her again." He gave a kind of sob and seemed to fall into himself. I was afraid he would roll off the bed and caught hold of him. Grant started forward. But all at once, he jumped up and fairly shouted at Grant, "Let me alone, Grant.

Why can nobody let me alone for two minutes?" Then took my arm and said, "Thank God you're here, Jim. How long is this doctor going to be? Come, let's get away from these jackals." And we walked down the corridor, past the waiting-room door.

# 37

LET me say, in the first moments after that attempt, when I stood in the passage pushed out by the nurse, I felt bitter against my wife. I was sure she would die and it broke my heart. But I was angry against her. I knew what the parsons meant when they said suicide was a crime against God. It was as if a man should desert the colours. Here Nina had done a great wrong and run away from it, made a complete getaway. I didn't want her to suffer but I wanted her to know what she had done and stand up to it. "Yes," I said to myself, "the church is right. Suicide is a wicked thing—it's treachery. Nina has dodged again —she's run away for the last time. You can't do anything with dodgers like that. They really are good for nothing."

But when that porter spoke to me and I knew for certain Nimmo was lying, wangling still, I had such a flash of joy I

240

never forgot. For standing there where my wife had stood not ten minutes before I knew why she'd turned back from the door and thrown herself under the lorry. She could not pass that door into the lies inside, more wangles, more tricks. She was through with lies. I said in my heart, "She had the truth in her soul—she was ready to die for it."

I remembered Nimmo's speech that first minute and I knew what he meant. I say a man in my kind of jam finds out things all the time. They simply come at him. Not only about people, about himself too. I found out now I'd done a cruel thing when I thought I was so patient in that car—a cruel thing in just doing nothing and saying nothing. And every step along that corridor was a prayer I shouldn't be punished for that cruelty. I was in terror my wife would die.

All this time, Nimmo was hanging on my arm, bumping into me, looking up at me, appealing to me. You would have said I was his dearest, his closest. Except of course Nina. "How did it happen, Jim?" he babbled. "What were we doing? We should have known how she felt. She was so quiet. And then, we know our Nina. She has so little endurance of pressure or any kind of tension. Let's admit it, she's a woman who can't bear much unhappiness. And why should she? When she can charm it away so easily—ah, she was our master for years. And she made us love our servitude."

I'd heard all this before. Nimmo had always talked Nina to me. Even in the days of his glory when he asked me to his grand dinner parties, he liked nothing better than to get me in a corner and talk Nina to me—her beauty, her charm, her taste, her tact, her intuition—the woman he had stolen from me. Even at that time when he was plotting with my family and my creditors to drive me out of England for good, so that I should never be able to come near Nina again, he sent me newspaper cuttings about her parties and told me where to find her photograph in the society papers.

At first I used to think he played these tricks out of spite, just to rub it into me he was the winner. But when I came back to England, and visited his house, I found out how wrong I was. He was all over me. Because I had loved Nina, because I loved her still. He actually invited me one afternoon to see her being tried on, with some new frocks, so that I might admire her figure. I suggested this was hardly proper, Nina herself might object, but he blew up. "Damn it, Jim, you don't think I don't know what Nina has been to you. Why this hypocrisy now? True, Nina may object. She is very conventional in some ways, as you know. But if I'm there too she'll be agreeable enough."

I refused to enter into this cockeyed scheme. It was a bit too strong for my stomach. But it was typical of Nimmo. The truth was Nina was a kind of miracle to him. He'd never been with a woman before his marriage, and he'd had the luck to hit upon one who exactly suited him, who got over all his queer ideas about what was right and what wasn't right. Who showed him how to enjoy life. And so cleverly, so gradually, she never frightened him. Nimmo, as anyone could see from the beginning, was built for a good time. Full of blood and bounce, a bit hairy at the heels but any amount of go. Straining at the bit, bursting at the buttons. And Nina worked him loose. People

242

think he was puritanical, all against the rich. But no one ever enjoyed splashing money about more, and Nina was just the woman to teach him how to do it. No one enjoyed more cutting a dash, giving a party, showing off a pretty wife.

He got on this theme now, how Nina had devoted herself to his career and put up with his boring evangelical friends. And we made two calls at the porter's lodge for brandy. I wouldn't agree that Nimmo in his last years was drunk night and day, but he certainly liked brandy. The excuse was his heart. But I doubt if this was his reason. Neither was he drunk now. No more, that is, than usual—with his own words and his own affairs. If he hung on my arm, it was because I was Jim, who knew and loved his Nina. Talking to me was like having his dear. He kept pressing against me, hooking my arm into his side, falling over my feet. "Thank God you were here, Jim. The only man I can talk to who isn't thinking all the time how he can use me, to get him a job or push along his favourite fad."

# 38

AND it was true the old man was letting himself go. He forgot his old lies. Bits of truth came trickling out of the babble. "And how she loves the simplest pleasure. What a joy to give her things—that collar, her Christmas present, she said it was too much. Good God, how could anything be too much for Nina who gave us life itself."

Every time we came near the vestibule he would ask the special for news of the doctor—Kilbie was out on some night call on the moor. Twice he went to the first-aid room to be turned away again by the boot-faced nurse. Each time he cursed her for a jack-in-office, a spoilt spinster, and each time he came back to me more jittery, and more leaky.

"Let us admit it, Jim, poor Harry—your Fat Boy—has some reason to be fussy about that impulsive youth, his ancient mas-

ter. I give a handle to misunderstanding—I forget the letter of
the law in pursuing the spirit of a nobler dispensation. I should
not have trespassed so far even upon your hospitality. I am a
man too little regarding of public fame, too warm, too hasty
to play a part before public opinion—yes, even to give that consideration to its prejudices—its reasonable prejudices—required
by accepted social understanding, much less by common pru-
dence. I have a horror of hypocrisy, Jim—which has led me too
often into conduct that seems needlessly insensitive to the feelings of others."

He pressed my arm and looked into my face to see how I
took this gambit.

"You know me, Jim, perhaps better than I do myself. Perhaps better than anyone except Nina, who knows us both too
well—too well. How often she has saved me from follies—from
making unnecessary enemies, from neglecting faithful friends,"
another pressure to show I was included or perhaps at that moment he really did think of me as a friend. A man like Nimmo
—top brass for forty years—gets so much into the air he simply
forgets what common, low, ordinary, human people are like and
what they mean by common ordinary words.

"Yes," he said, "when things go well with me, I am tempted
to something like arrogance. I am too impatient of the time-
serving rabble. I expose myself to humiliations, as in this very
week—among the tin-pot gods of the new dispensation. I was
brought up in a rougher, franker world, among greater men—
men of faith and power. I learnt to swim upon the storm, from
crest to trough, now exulting in the foam, now struggling for

life in the shadow. How terrible the darkness of those gulfs. Yes, in adversity I fall too easily into dejection. Sometimes even my faith has left me. I have said to myself indeed, 'God is mighty and never to be mocked.' I have said it but it no longer struck an echo in the soul. The life of my life did not rise to the trumpet. I tell you, Jim, as Nina could tell you, there were moments of the war when I was very close to breaking. The world thought me bronze, but Nina saw the poor shivering human creature and warmed him back to hope—to that life of the spirit, that deeper than faith without which hope and God himself, are but words, wind. And why not, Jim? Is not her faith a deeper thing? For her there was neither victory nor defeat, only the immediate task, a broken soul—it was in my darkest hours that her tenderness, her patience, her trust, relit the spark and raised the dying flame. What on earth do you want? For God's sake go away, go—go." This was to the woman in the mackintosh who had followed us down the corridor. A snarl that made her jump a yard. "Where was I, Jim?" "You were getting Nina to raise the dying flame," I said. "But there's no gas at the Cottage."

He looked at me. He knew what I meant, but he didn't care. I doubt if a slap in the face would have stopped the flow. He had to let pour out to someone. "Ah, Jim," he said, pressing my arm hard, "my dear old friend, you too have known the cruelty of things. I tell you there was a time this afternoon when I touched bottom. No words can tell the blackness of that despair. I have said and written often enough that it is a fearful thing to see and know by daily experience the ways of politics—the

246

destinies of millions in the hands of fools and power-grabbers, men so crass in mean ambition that, my dear Jim, they treated me like a fourth-rate clerk out of a job. Without a character. Not merely the pipe-smoking higgler we call Prime Minister, but the petty bourgeois zanies who represent the twenty million workers of this unhappy land. The end is not yet, Jim, of this fearful crisis, but I tremble. As I came from that crawling train to-day I asked how many of us would survive next week—how much of the England we love and know. I was at the lowest ebb. And let me admit it—the lights of your house above were too much for my weakness. I told Grant to stop in the lane while I went in for a moment. My dear boy, as God is my witness, I meant only a moment. I went to tell her only that whatever happened to the country and to me, I could not despair of humanity. For I had known her spirit. My hopes were ashes but I should die in peace. My soul could rest upon the goodness of God, who gave her to the world with her woman's heart."

All this was Nimmo to the life on his get-together line. Even bits from speeches. And a third story about what had taken him into the Cottage. I couldn't trouble to point it out—I had other things to think of. But I couldn't get away from the old man. He hung on to me like a life-buoy in a short sea. I was glad when at last Miss Willis turned up. I'd seen her in action before and knew she if anyone could deal with Nimmo.

She'd waited to dress herself in full office uniform, complete with pince-nez and powdered nose, puce on purple, like a sloe dipped in sugar. She marched up to Nimmo as if she were going to stick him and jabbed a telegram at him like a bayonet. It was in his hand before he realized what was happening. "What's this?" he quacked. "What's this?"

"A wire from London. Priority—at four o'clock this afternoon," said Miss Willis. Her voice was like a bone-saw. "And I promised you'd get it."

"Hallo—hallo," he said, looking sideways at her. But she kept on glaring at him and he read the thing. Miss Willis is what you call a good secretary—she knows so much about Nimmo, he can't put her down.

"No," he said, snapping like a mud turtle, "the answer is no. They wouldn't see me when I went to see them and that was three days ago. Tell 'em I'm in bed and can't be disturbed. Wait a minute. What does the fellow say?" He took back the wire and read it again. "No, I'd better phone him. Excuse me a moment, Jim. It's from the Labour side about a proposal I made last week—and I must at least be polite."

I didn't ask him if his weakness on picketing, and the suspension of Maufe, had anything to do with this private canoodle with what he called the Labour side. After the Prime Minister had thrown him out. I wasn't interested any more. Besides, before I could even say yes, he was hopping upstairs like a goat, beating the secretary and Grant by about one step in two. I went outside to walk in the square. Nice cool breeze off the sea. Moon sailing along in a windy sky. I found the tears on my face. Nimmo had said one true thing. My soul could rest on goodness —just one little bit of it—Nina hadn't been able to face that lie.

# 39

THE doctor came at last and my wife was at once carried to hospital for X-ray and a possible operation. She was then unconscious and I saw nothing as they carried her past in the stretcher but her face, as white and lovely as a marble on a tomb. I knew then what it was to feel like a murderer. "If she dies," I said, "then I am a murderer. And I deserve to die for it. As I shall die. For the world will be a grave to me."

And I made a promise to God if she lived, I should never again show her that hardness which so much affected her. I said to myself as I myself had been a sinful man, so I should forgive. I said what I'd known for forty years though I wouldn't admit it, this woman was more weak than wicked. As Nimmo had said, she loved happiness and so she hated to say no to any crook. She had been spoilt from the beginning. And I wrote to her then and there in the hospital waiting-room, on the back of an admittance form. I thought she might die without recovering consciousness, but still I had to ask her pardon. I said this was the time when our life together began again. Because our old lives were done for—we could not begin again the old way if we tried. So let us go away together, away from the lies she had hated, and this place that had such evil memories for both of us. Away from the Cottage which we couldn't afford any more anyhow. Because she would understand I couldn't live on Nimmo's money. Nor could I pay Robert's school bills. But some of the finest and truest men and women I'd ever known in the world had never gone to school at all, and earned their keep and kept their families simply by their own work, and as for Europe and its so-called civilization, they didn't know what it meant and cared less. And if they had known it they would simply have asked why all the people went to so much trouble to make life complicated and what had they got out of it. They would have thought Europe wasn't a very happy place to live in, and Europeans were simply an unlucky lot of people who'd taken a wrong turning somewhere and walked right off the proper natural road into every kind of trouble.

I said the older I got the more I was sure my Luga pagans, so despised by the smart fellows in pin-stripes, were the happiest people in the world and lived the best and truest lives. At least before we brought our disease to them and taught them the grab and bunco game. And even now they were a few thousand years better stuff. I couldn't ask her to come to Africa with me because she mightn't be able to stand the climate but I hoped she would agree to come to some quiet country far from any town where we could live as God meant, under God's own sky, by our own work, and forget tea parties and politics and never see a newspaper again.

I hadn't meant to write about Africa or the Lugas because how could I ask my wife to go to Africa with me. Away from her shops and concerts and cocktail parties, her week-ends in London and her trips to Paris and Cannes. All at once was too much. It would frighten the poor girl out of her wits. She'd think I really had gone mad. But then I thought, "It's what has to be done. No other way is even possible, for a clean new start. And am I going to start this new life with a wangle? Am I going to play about with her, cat and mouse? I'd rather she said no right away. I'd rather we broke up." So I gave her the whole tale, and I said if she didn't like the idea, and I couldn't expect it, then I'd clear out by myself. Out of the country. Out of Europe. For the humbuggery was eating me.

I gave this letter to a probationer, a girl who knew me, to deliver it as soon as my wife was fit to read it. And the girl took it because she was sorry for me, she thought Nina was dying. The surgeon had just come and was to operate in a few minutes.

That operation saved my wife from bleeding to death with internal injuries. But by so little, she wasn't out of danger for a fortnight. And in that fortnight all visitors, even husbands, were barred. Or perhaps I should say, especially this husband. For when the nurses knew she was not actually dying, they took a different angle towards Jim Latter. They went in for the gen-

251

eral view he was one of those dangerous freaks who don't always shout yes even when really important people pull the string. I saw it in the eyes of that very probationer who had taken my note on that fearful night of suspense. She was a nice young thing, daughter of the Vicar at Queensport. I'd known her from the time she was born. I'd given her her first lesson in dinghy sailing—she was one of the best.

But the strike was over, the Pincomb case was up before the magistrates, Maufe was in the dock, and the newspapers were out again to report all the juicy bits. Like these questions (by Mr. B., smart young lawyer who was trying for the council on the Radical ticket), "You say you had instructions to arrest Mr. Pincomb whenever and wherever you found him?"

MAUFE: "Yes, sir."

LAWYER: "Who gave you these instructions?"

MAUFE: "Captain Latter, sir."

LAWYER: "Did Captain Latter tell you to pay no attention to the Watch Committee because they were run by a lot of Communists."

MAUFE: "Oh no, sir."

LAWYER: "Did he say to you that the strikers had been knocking the specials about and it was time they got their own back?"

MAUFE: "No, sir."

LAWYER: "Six specials had been injured on the day before."

MAUFE: "Yes, sir."

252

LAWYER: "I put it to you there was great resentment among the specials on account of these injuries and Captain Latter told you to go after prominent Labour men."

MAUFE: "He said to arrest Pincomb because of his speech."

LAWYER: "Did he instruct you at the same time to go up to Mr. Pincomb walking alone in the street and smash his skull with your truncheon?"

MAUFE: "Pincomb wasn't alone—he—"

LAWYER: "Answer my question."

MAUFE: "No, sir—I was simply instructed to make the arrest."

LAWYER: "Did you say so before you fractured Pincomb's skull?"

MAUFE: "He tried to get away."

LAWYER: "Two witnesses have sworn that you struck him without warning."

MAUFE: "But they're commies—"

LAWYER: "Are you suggesting these two very respectable men are committing perjury?"

MAUFE: "Well, they're telling lies."

Of course the lawyer made a fine tale of this, and also of Pincomb's injuries.

Poor old Varney's evidence didn't do us any good either. He was in the Workhouse Infirmary and the magistrates took his evidence at the bedside.

But when our lawyer referred to his good service during the

253

strike, their man brought out that even before the Chapel Road
riot he had been accused of brutality against the unemployed
and turned out of his job at the Unemployed Centre.

Lawyer: "Is it true, Sergeant, you were turned out of your
job for brutality to an unemployed youth?"

Varney: "I turned out a lad for being drunk and using bad
language."

Lawyer: "The Unemployment Association took the view you
were unfit for your post because of your attitude to the unemployed."

Varney: "I resigned."

Lawyer: "Just in time—according to my information."

And Varney didn't know how to contradict him. He was a
smart chap, that lawyer, and worth his commie pay.

But what was the real truth, the truth he turned into a lie?
That vote against Varney at the Centre, worked by the commies
at the beginning of the strike, had been referred back by the Unemployed Centres Association. They knew very well the work
he'd done—they knew he was a man of the highest character and
guts who could be relied on to do his duty, without fear or
favour.

But so did the commies and they meant to get him. They
set on about a dozen young oafs to make the Centre impossible
for anyone but commies and when Varney turned them out,
they washed their faces and put on collars and went in a deputation to Kilmain. Said Sergeant Varney was prejudiced against

young democracy, didn't understand their problems, had no Christian charity. They made Kilmain cry.

And he came down to Tarbiton hot-foot and told Varney he was sorry but somehow he had failed to get on with the younger element and this unpopularity with so important a part of the community was a serious handicap to progress and a threat to the whole future of the good work. He advised him to resign for the sake of the Centre so dear to them both.

Otherwise he kicked him out and at the time of this case, Varney had neither a job nor a home. Old Mrs. Varney was in the workhouse on the female side and God knows how Margaret was feeding the children. Potter's was closed for good and half the mothers in town were looking for jobs to scrub at sixpence an hour.

Varney wasn't bitter, he only told the truth about the trouble at the Centre, and the Communists' determination to close Potter's and make all the misery they could in the town. But the truth itself was bitter, and the lawyer had only to say it proved strong feeling in the local specials. And then of course he kept on referring to Varney as "this ex-soldier."

An ex-soldier in peace-time is always a bloodthirsty blackguard. The end of it was Maufe was remanded in custody to await medical report on Pincomb. But it was pretty obvious he would be convicted of unjustified violence or even sent for trial, and we were already preparing for an appeal.

# 40

WHY didn't I leave the Pincomb case alone? I wasn't called as
a witness. Both sides were afraid of what I might say. By this
time everyone who didn't know me said I was a mad dog; and
a man of the lowest character. Communists, Fascists, old Tories,
young Labour, they were all on the same game. Brightman had
an article in his paper referring to the Communist libel and asking why it hadn't been taken to court.

I didn't read any of these rags, whether they were national
fly-catchers or international poison-shooters. It was my niece
Sally brought the Brightman thing to me. She was shocked.
She said a man like Brightman would never do such a thing
to one for whom he had such a regard as myself. It must be a
mistake by some subordinate. And she proposed we should go
together and see him.

So we went along to the olde Englishe headquarters. But I made my niece stay in the car in case of an argument.

Olde Englishe lawn nicely shaved by motor. A couple of squads at drill. No uniform. Brightman lot never had a uniform—except they went in for open shirts. Democratic. But they'd taken a tip from the vigilants and given in to arm-bands. And they had a first-class drill sergeant in charge.

I found the hero in the hall standing among his generals like Napoleon at Austerlitz. And he'd got to look a good deal bigger in the last few days. Due to sticking his chest out and throwing up his jaw. And probably cork lifts in his shoes.

He took two steps forward to receive me as laid down for an emperor receiving a king, shook hands for thirty seconds and said, "I've been waiting for you, Latter. You and I need each other."

"The hell you do," I said. "Then what about that article in your rag?"

"I have followed your work with the greatest admiration," he said, weighing his words out for posterity. "You are one of the few men in the country who has the courage to stand up against the forces that are tearing Europe apart. Magnificent effort. But quite hopeless—you'll get nowhere."

"What I want to know," I said, "is where you're getting."

"This is the age of the group, the union, the party," he said. "The only way a man can make himself felt is in alliance with others of like mind. And what is the difference between our aims? In all important objects we are identical. We want to clear

257

out the gang of parasites that have fastened on the country—
we want an honest Press—"

I said, yes, and what about the article in his own Press?

But he went on about our common aims till I had to say I
wasn't any kind of Fascist, even the sort that called itself democratic. I was a Liberal and I stood for freedom and all I wanted
was some honest men in politics. "All that's wrong with this poor
old country is the men who've got hold of it—the gang of hot
air politicocks who came in with the Press millionaires and the
gold bugs to wangle the world, and steal the government. And
I don't see your silly show doing any better. You've got a different lie for a different mob, that's all. The dirt is the same."
As see the last issue of his dirty rag.

Brightman then said he had seen the article and approved it.
And if I was so interested in the morality of public men he was
surprised I wanted to hide the most glaring scandal of modern
times, he meant the Nimmo scandal. Especially as he was credibly informed Nimmo was now deserting even his own dis-
credited party and intended to sell himself, at the highest possible price, to Labour.

"And you didn't mind dragging my wife—not to speak of
myself—in the dirt to do it," I said. "Do you know, Brightman,
I always knew you weren't a gentleman, but I did think you
were a gent. Down to the neck. You had the idea if not the feeling. But I see I was wrong. And I offer you my sincere apologies."

"As for gentlemen," he said, sticking out his chest a little further and trying to look like Napoleon. But bringing off some-

thing between the old firm and Mme. Tussaud's. "I'm not engaged in a drawing-room comedy but a fight for life in which I don't propose to tie my hands with the petty etiquette of small beer provincials. And as for gents, Latter, I wonder if even a gent can afford to lie down under the names of ponce and pimp."

I hit him then and five of his thugs threw me into the road and walked on me. And I said, "Thank you very much." For I knew I'd been a fool. A fool, a fool and a fool. Like Nimmo said to me. For I'd been taking it three weeks and I knew something.

Sally Bootham was calling names as she got out of the car to give battle for her dear uncle. But being about as wide as the door, she was hampered, and the young guard laughed at her. So I told her to give me a hand while I got the cricks out of my back, and drive me home.

The whole affair was a considerable surprise to the young lady. She was quite red in the face. She said it was an outrage. She hadn't known such things could happen in England. And Brightman was not the man she took him for. He was a bad man who had deserted Liberal principles. She said so all the way home and offered me her warmest sympathy. And she urged me to take strong measures against these blackguards.

But I said strong measures were no good in politics. What you wanted was a whopping popular lie and I hadn't got one. I hadn't even got a small yarn. Whereas Brightman had so many yarns he could throw them away on mad dogs like myself.

Sally said I wasn't mad. But it didn't come out pop. She hesitated forty seconds. An honest girl. And when I said, "Well, look at this expedition—to a modern political hero on the make." She didn't answer that one.

I didn't ask her where Brightman got the little extra information for his article, the bit about me forgiving my wife. Whether from Sally in a trance—that is, during the strike—or from some other cell. He'd got 'em everywhere, small but active. And I didn't ask why those newspapers, what they call national papers, had pictures of me being shot down Brightman's steps. From his own publicity department.

Of course I was news. The hounds had been on the scent for years. Now they were warming up to the kill. They called themselves anti-Fascists, but they took Brightman's hand-outs.

And the smartest of them, the biggest Tory daily of the lot, ran a paragraph about Brome, in the same number. She'd broken Nimmo's car windows again and they'd put her in an asylum. Idea was that Brome and me were a pair.

They didn't say so. They left libel to the commie and Fascist rags, peddling their filth to a few thousand. They only shouted it to millions in big headlines—they only gave the mob a wink and a push in the ribs, knowing the mob would be wise. To a lie they knew was a lie.

They know what Nimmo is. They know what I am. They know Brome is a crazy woman. They know I'm telling the truth. And why do they hide the truth, shout this libel meant to make out I'm a lunatic? Because they hate me? No. It's because it builds up the yarn, the excitement, and sells more papers.

A fool and a fool and a fool. For I knew it wasn't what they

260

said about you. It was what you knew about yourself. Like I'd said to Nimmo.

A wooden-headed God-damned bloody fool. The very time those up-and-coming boys were rubbing my face in a fresh turd, I'd got Nina's answer in my pocket. Written in pencil the first day they'd let her see my letter. Saying she'd go with me anywhere. She only wanted to be with me again. "You say you want to start again but you've no idea how much I want to do just that. And to get away from the place, from the people, even from the poor old Cottage where we have been so happy. (But perhaps it's because of that happiness I'd hate to see it again because it *was* the old happiness and now it can only be in the way.) I just long for an entirely completely new life, even to the chairs and tables—and as for Africa, I always did love the sun. I am going to be perfectly well again in quite a short time, and nothing will make me better quicker than to know you're waiting for me and that you really do want me still."

It was because of this letter I went to stop Brightman's mouth. I saw the publicity coming. On Nina too. But was a fool because what I did brought more publicity. Once the hounds are on you, you can't dodge 'em. If you turn to fight, they roll you over, with your face in a turd. When Nina came out of hospital, there were cameramen on the doorstep. I didn't take her home, because I knew they'd be waiting there too. We never wanted to see Palm Cottage again and it was up for sale. We were on the run and I'd picked about the loneliest place I knew for a hide-out. Fisherman's cottage in a cove under Staple Head, called Rockpit. There's only one path to that bay, a dangerous

261

track down the side of the cliff. We got tnere by dodging from a taxi into a lorry, from the lorry into a bread van. The pack thrown off that time. We wanted peace for a week. We were sick of the rackets and the ramps.

Sick of the gimme game, the grab boys, the bunkum and spoof. But we found pretty quick in England you can't get out of it. Perhaps not in Europe. It's soaked into everything. It's crept into the last cracks. It's a bug that floats about in the air. It's a web that's tied up people's lives till even their private thoughts are stuck up ready to be eaten by the spider.

That first evening we thought we'd got away. We thought we'd thrown off the pack. But next morning when we were lying in the sun, a cameraman walked out from behind a rock.

I chased him with stones, but he got his picture. Me looking like a cretin in a fit—as I got up to hide my wife. And still he was too quick. Nina's thin white face with her great eyes, looking as terrified as a child who's seen a ghost, went all round the world. It was a great success. It made a lot of money for that sportsman, and all the others said he'd deserved it. He'd bought our landlord for five pounds. A decent old chap but he had a daughter with T.B. A daughter he loved. He sold the woman I loved for the girl he loved. And Nimmo tells you God is love. Nimmo's god. A god that doesn't need any principles, that doesn't need to keep his word. A god in the love racket, turning out hot stuff for the papers.

# 41

A KIND friend who didn't give his name sent us a bundle of three papers and when Nina saw them, she asked me to take her away that moment, why couldn't we go to Africa at once, now that I had a job?

In fact, I'd been offered two jobs in Africa, one in Kenya to go on a farm with an old friend; and the other to act as assistant manager at a tin-working project in Nigeria on the plateau. Kenya was better pay and more what I was after, as having to do with the land and the production of food, but I was strongly attracted by the second proposition, as there was a lot of Luga labour on the mine and I should be among old friends. The plateau too would be a reasonably good climate even for Robert. I had therefore written to know if there was any farm attached to the manager's accommodation at the mine, or if not, whether some suitable land could be provided, where labour was also available. And I was awaiting an answer.

But Nina now said it wasn't necessary to wait. The farm did not matter, nothing mattered but getting out of England at once.

I'd never seen her in such a state of mind. She was, on the whole, a plucky girl, allowing for an occasional fit of nerves, or charming attitudes, when she pretended to be frightened of cows or guns. But now she was really terrified.

It's true she was not yet strong after that crash. She was thin and she could not sleep. She did not like me to be out of her sight, and unluckily, after the first week, I had to be running to and fro a good deal to keep our side up to the mark. I'd soon found if you want a case like this to get anything like justice you've got to make a noise like a first-class battle. You've got to be such a goddam nuisance your friends will run a mile to keep away from you. And all this just to let people know an innocent man is being framed on a political racket.

The papers wouldn't print my letters. Even so, the case was *sub judice*. *Sub* is a good word for squashed under the weight of the racket. The law racket. And when I called on the law, the lawyers weren't at home. I wasn't allowed to see counsel. I got out a leaflet and put it in letter-boxes with my own hands. And some people read it because I got answers. From working men who knew a dirty job when they saw one. From the broken-hearted old tradesmen, late of Potter's, who had seen what happens to the weak and friendless in this happy land of freedom.

But I daren't leave my wife more than the inside of a day.

When the case was coming on and it turned out I'd have to spend a day in London with my lawyer, to see the counsel for the defence, that is, two nights away, she had a weeping fit that frightened me. I'd never seen her cry before. I told her if I had to go away again she must come too. And to hell with the cameramen and the papers. We'd have to get tough to them. We'd have to learn to use them, for if the Maufe case went wrong, we must go for an appeal. And that would mean all the publicity we could find. For in this swindlers' world, publicity is king.

But she couldn't face it. She was a sick woman still. And I hadn't been away twenty-four hours before I had a letter.

"I did go to bed early, according to orders—but then I'm rather afraid I got up again. In fact it rather seems as if I can't sleep anywhere except in your presence—a rather close presence. This happened before, you remember, when I was nine years old. Or don't you remember? (But I see already this letter is going to be a nuisance and I'm not going to post it—I'll write to please myself.)

"You said yesterday I was the most precious thing you had and I'm living on trying to live on that now. The only disadvantage of it as a diet is that it's all holes—I simply don't believe it. I believe you were simply being kind to my headache and trying to build up my morale (why I should object to this when I love being spoilt seems rather mad. But not so mad after all when the truth is so important. After all you can never trust a christian *being* christian to be quite honest and what I'm longing for is the *true* truth—I mean the *real true everlasting cross my heart rock-bottom truth* that you can go to sleep on even all alone at three in the morning with the wind making a noise outside like a very small and discouraged damned soul just managing not to scream under the red-hot pokers in case of annoying the devil in charge and small slow waves falling on your brain drop after drop like a Chinese torture—every one is *deliberately* slower than the last and hurts more when it does hit you.)

"You seem so enormously disappeared already—as if you'd simply dived out of the world and time had closed over you already. Not even a bubble. An absolutely solid wall of nothing. I'm imagining you as hard as I can at this moment but you refuse to turn into anything more substantial than a rather bad photograph and a voice. It's so hard to keep hold of the feeling of you (I do wish I had a good recent photograph) I mean the feeling *with* you, the special feeling of hereness and nowness. (No I absolutely shan't post this—you'll say again it's a case of out of sight out of mind—and it's really the other way. You're so terrifically present when you're with me that nothing can fill the hole when you go except waiting for you to come back.)

"If only I'd asked you to write—but you would say a letter written to order is no good. But it could be wonderfully good. Even a wire. The truth is I never can quite believe you love me. Don't be angry at this, dearest Jim. Don't be furious with your too honest woman. I've never all my life quite believed that anyone could really love me (and, after all, you've often told me what a bad character I have, and of course you're quite right), and especially you, who know me so well and I've treated you so badly. And I still can't quite believe it, I mean there's something in me that keeps on saying, 'No, you'll wake up some day and find out that he's simply being kind and nice to you because he's naturally affectionate to women and because he's got such a strong sense of family duty. And because you're Robert's mother.' But I never did. Instead I waked up (or rather you generally waked me up, my dearest love, and you simply can't imagine what bliss it was) to find that you wanted me still. Yes, I must burn this letter (really and truly what you call an effusion) it will simply annoy you, and waste your time. But it's not wasting my time because time is nothing when you aren't here—just an awful gap. I fell into it to-night so I know, and really thought I'd never get out. It's simply the truth that when I look at your pillow so round and smooth (this is 3.15 A.M.) I simply can't believe you ever had your head on it. I simply can't imagine what it was like when you were here (I mean how it really was—if it was really a safe married kind of feeling). And after all there is a gap—because the new happiness is going to be different and the old is over (which is why you are so right about the Cottage. It belongs to our childhoods—love so marvellous—so agonizing—and we must break out at last from that enchanted cave.)"

I got this letter, delivered by express, about an hour before I started back to the cove. I give it here to show she admitted her bad conduct. And to show why I went back to her. Let them call me ponce and pimp—I say I had a right to condone, I had a right to forgive and to love.

# 42

I DIDN'T realize my wife would be called in the Maufe trial. But I think she'd expected it. I think that was one reason why she could not sleep when I was away; why she didn't like me out of her sight. She knew there'd been some hanky-panky. When I took a room in the Water Boy for the case, she insisted on coming with me, though the Water Boy was not exactly the sort of place she was used to and it was impossible to keep the crowd away from the door when she went in and out.

And when she got the subpœna, she only said, "I thought this would happen." I saw her nervous state and told her she needn't be afraid—I knew Nimmo had got at her—I knew about the Pincomb hook-up—all that was past and we were forgetting it.

She asked me then if I did not think Maufe had been too

rough. I said this was the tale the politicos were putting over. Because it might get them some votes. And because Maufe had only one vote and no friends. No one mentioned Pincomb and the strikers had nearly murdered six of my men, smashed up Potter's and ruined two hundred families. Because there wasn't an election in Tarbiton. The election was at Battwell and somewhere in Yorkshire where the people didn't need to know the facts even if they wanted 'em.

After this, my wife made no more reference to the case, and seemed quite calm about it even immediately before she went into the box.

I want to recall this case to the court. It is only a month old but already no one seems to bother about it. This man Maufe, one of the bravest and honestest men I ever knew, was now being put on trial on the grounds he had deliberately gone up to Pincomb and fractured his skull without warning. The case turned on whether he had used undue force, whether he had given warning and whether Pincomb had resisted arrest.

Before magistrates in first hearing, the only evidence offered was by commies or left-wingers, and great prejudice was created by fact of Pincomb's injuries, also the strike being now over, everyone had forgotten the dangerous situation of the 8th and 9th. And all the people who had been melting and sliding about between May 4th and 12th were now on the 20th quite firm again, and even a little stiffer than before.

I wrote to my niece Sally, electioneering for her husband at Battwell, and sent her the subscription list of the Defence Fund. I couldn't afford all the defence. Justice costs a lot of money.

I'd sold my saddle and Purdey guns and my last boat, but the lot only came to two hundred pounds. So the specials subscribed and the poor. Shillings and sixpences, from households where sixpence was a meal. Coppers slipped into the Maufes' letter-box when no one could see. From half-starved women who knew what the specials had done to protect their husbands and tried to save their homes.

But Sally answered she was sorry; she couldn't support Maufe's case; it was her considered opinion that violence ought to be put down. With a firm hand. And Henry quite agreed with her.

Her Henry was now holding himself out as a good deal better Liberal than his old master, who was not at all sound on principle. And the girl who had been speaking for Brightman in Tarbiton market-place not two months before was now winning votes every day for her good Liberal husband, with her honest-to-god big belly.

As for Councillor X and Y, it was libel even to suggest these gentlemen had ever wished for an excuse to call in troops, and chairman Penrose was strong for administering the law. Every-one was out for the poor victim of the wicked police.

We knew very well Maufe was an honest man telling the plain truth; also there had been independent witnesses. The trouble was to get anyone to come forward.

At the trial, we had first same evidence as at police court except Pincomb was now able to go into the box. He turned up with his head in bandages and had to have a chair. He made a big impression. Then doctor to state he had been hit with great force and was likely to lose his sight. Also that the worst blow must have been given from behind, seeing Pincomb was taller than Maufe. And then four different witnesses who swore Maufe had walked up behind Pincomb and laid him out without warning.

We had a man from London for the defence and he did his best in cross-examination. But he only brought out from Pincomb he'd made a speech on the 9th May urging the mob to smash Potter's; and Maufe had said, "Pincomb, I've got you. This is an arrest," before he hit him.

Pincomb denied he'd been seditious, or that he'd expected an arrest. That he'd gone about with bodyguards or hit at Maufe. Every time he was pressed, he put his hand to his bandages and said he couldn't remember. The doctor admitted Pincomb's skull was unusually thin but insisted he had had two or three very violent blows, especially one from behind. And of course the commies stuck to it they had made no resistance, that Maufe had jumped out suddenly and laid Pincomb out before he could even turn round.

Our man then got his turn. He didn't say much to start with, only that Pincomb had been making seditious speeches, that there was a warrant out for him and that he was arrested among his own supporters where it was difficult to find anyone bold enough to give evidence on behalf of the police. But fortunately he had such a witness. And he then called a new witness, Bell, who'd actually seen the arrest.

# 43

IT'S not true we got hold of this vital witness on information. The truth is he offered himself because of his conscience, being, I believe, a sincere Christian. His evidence was a surprise to the defence as well as prosecution, and only at one day's notice, which they accepted. But it was not very well prepared by us.

Called to the box, he turned out a little, skinny jumping-jack of a man, with all his hair on end and his eyes sticking out of his head. He kept wriggling about and tapping the ledge with his fingers. He stated he had seen Maufe approach Pincomb and told him he was arresting him. Pincomb was with a friend, a bodyguard. Maufe took hold of Pincomb's arm and Pincomb then swung at him. Maufe dodged and closed. The guard tried to trip Maufe and all three were dodging and hitting out at each other. Then a lot of Communists came running out of

272

Drake Lane, and Maufe blew his whistle and two specials came from the water-side. And the whole lot started fighting together and trying to trip each other and Pincomb fell back with his head on the kerb. That's what broke his skull.

COUNSEL FOR THE DEFENCE: "You saw Pincomb fall against the kerb?"

BELL: "Yes, he fell hard on the kerb and then the specials came up and got an ambulance and took him to the hospital."

COUNSEL: "Did you see Pincomb strike at Maufe?"

BELL: "Yes, the very first thing—he started it all."

COUNSEL: "When you say that Pincomb swung at Maufe do you mean that he actually struck him?"

BELL: "Yes, sir. He tried to knock him out but Mr. Maufe took it on the arm. Mr. Maufe is a boxer, that's why he didn't get hurt."

COUNSEL: "But afterwards the Communists came running to Pincomb's help?"

BELL: "First one of them who was standing near, and then a lot more from Drake Lane."

COUNSEL: "Maufe then blew his whistle for assistance?"

BELL: "Yes, sir. And he needed it too—the men in Drake Lane which was full of commies——"

COUNSEL: "Yes, yes. But all we want to know is that Pincomb gave the first blow and that afterwards, in the struggle, he fell on the kerb. And these are facts of your own personal observation?"

BELL: "Yes, sir."

273

COUNSEL: "Why didn't you offer this evidence at the time of the first charge in the police court?"

BELL: "I offered it right away, sir."

COUNSEL: "On the 9th?"

BELL: "No, sir, the 10th. I didn't know Mr. Maufe was in trouble till that afternoon. So seeing it didn't look fair to him, I thought I ought to do something about it."

COUNSEL: "And what did you do?"

BELL: "I went to the Town Hall and asked for Lord Nimmo himself."

COUNSEL: "Why didn't you go to the police?"

BELL: "I thought I'd better see Lord Nimmo privately—he was always very good to us Tarbiton people when on the council and parliament too. He'd always see a Tarbiton man."

COUNSEL: "Yes. So you asked for Lord Nimmo. Did you see Lord Nimmo?"

BELL: "No, sir, they took me to his secretary."

COUNSEL: "Miss Willis. What did she say?"

BELL: "First she said it didn't matter. They had enough evidence about Maufe. And as for seeing Lord Nimmo, he was very upset about the brutal action of police and all against it. I said I had a different idea and my evidence was different. She said I could do what I liked about it. I said could I write it down for Lord Nimmo, and she said I could. So I did. Two pages. And gave it to her."

COUNSEL: "Did you hear any more about this statement?"

BELL: "No, sir, not another word."

COUNSEL: "But seeing the case had gone for trial, you came and offered your evidence?"

BELL: "Yes, sir."

COUNSEL: "Did you do so entirely on your own initiative?"

BELL: "Yes, sir."

COUNSEL: "You were afraid of a serious miscarriage of justice which would lie on your conscience?"

BELL: "Yes, sir."


Counsel for prosecution then got up to cross-examine and started by asking if anyone had approached Bell to give evidence on behalf of the police.


BELL: "No, sir."

COUNSEL: "On your oath, did you come up on your own accord?"

BELL: "Yes, sir."

COUNSEL: "After waiting six weeks."

BELL: "It got on my mind, sir."

COUNSEL: "In those six weeks, did you discuss the case at all?"

BELL: "No, sir."

COUNSEL: "On your oath, you never mentioned it to anyone?"

BELL: "I may have said a word about Mr. Maufe getting a bad deal."

COUNSEL: "What sort of word? Did you read the evidence in the police court?"

BELL: "Yes, sir, in the *Gazette*."

COUNSEL: "Did you notice the question asked then about who gave the first blow?"

BELL: "Well, yes. I did."

COUNSEL: "Did you speak about this to your friends?"

BELL: "I may have said I'd seen Pincomb hit at him first."

COUNSEL: "Did you say anything about it before you'd read the evidence in the police court?"

BELL: "I told Miss Willis about it."

COUNSEL: "You're sure of that?"

BELL: "Absolutely sure, sir. It was why I went because I saw how Pincomb started it."

COUNSEL: "You mentioned the fall backwards to Miss Willis?"

BELL: "Oh, yes, sir."

COUNSEL: "Did you realize the importance of this evidence?"

BELL: "Yes, sir, that's why I went."

COUNSEL: "Why did you say nothing at the police court and wait six weeks before coming forward now?"

BELL: "I saw it was no good saying anything. They had it in for Mr. Maufe in the office. And they wouldn't give me protection either."

COUNSEL: "What do you mean, protection?"

BELL: "I asked for police protection, sir. Because I'd had my windows broken already. But Miss Willis said it was none of her business."

COUNSEL: "You had your windows broken. When was that?"

276

BELL: "On the 9th. They knew I'd seen it all. Why, they told me they'd do me in if I said anything."

COUNSEL: "Were you very much against the strikers and the strike leaders?"

BELL: "Well, I thought they would finish Tarbiton between them—if Potter's closed."

COUNSEL: "You were strongly prejudiced against Pincomb?"

But here our man objected and the judge agreed with him. The counsel then asked Bell how far he had been from the scene when he saw the arrest.

BELL: "Quite close."

COUNSEL: "What is quite close, how many yards?"

BELL: "About ten yards."

COUNSEL: "And the time was half-past nine on a dark evening . . ." and so on. I say Bell was a nervous chap. He was soon tied up and admitted he hadn't actually seen Pincomb's fist hit Maufe, because Maufe was in the way. And he might have forgotten some details, there was a lot of fighting going on.

Counsel then asked Bell about the fall, had it happened before or after Maufe hit Pincomb? Bell said again he hadn't seen Maufe hit Pincomb, he'd only noticed the fall and that was when Pincomb had got hurt. That was why he'd gone to Miss Willis.

Counsel then held up a typewritten sheet and asked if the witness recognized it.

BELL: "That's not what I gave Miss Willis."

COUNSEL: "No, it's a report you sent to the chairman of the Bench, Mr. Penrose, in the same week. Is this your signature?"

BELL: "Yes, I signed it. I thought I'd better do something after the police case went wrong."

COUNSEL: "It says nothing about a fall."

The judge asked for the paper and read it out. And it said only that Pincomb had started the fight and that Maufe had been obliged to use his truncheon in self-defence.

BELL: "I said about the first blow. I said Pincomb started it."

COUNSEL: "But nothing about a fall."

BELL: "It was a friend typed it for me and I told her to put it all in. She must have left out about the fall."

COUNSEL: "You signed it as a statement of what you were prepared to give in evidence?"

BELL: "I put down about Pincomb starting it. He went for Mr. Maufe right away and he's bigger. And two to one."

COUNSEL: "Can you swear you didn't invent the story of this fall in the last six weeks?"

BELL: "No, sir. I told Miss Willis about the fall too and I wrote about it to Lord Nimmo, and he got it too because he sent a lady to see me about it and ask me if I was sure about

Pincomb hitting at Maufe and about the fall after he tripped himself."

COUNSEL: "Who was this lady?"

BELL: "I don't know her name but she works for his lordship."

Our counsel had been whispering with Clint and now he got up and said he thought he could produce the lady.

JUDGE: "Who is she?"

COUNSEL: "Lord Nimmo's confidential secretary, Mrs. Latter."

Counsel for prosecution protested that he ought to have time to consider this new element in the case. But the judge intervened and it was agreed to call my wife on the next day and meanwhile to call any other witnesses for the defence.

We had Miss Willis next but she was a bit too clever for us. She said she remembered Bell's giving a statement but nothing about a blow or a fall. Bell had written something in the office but it couldn't be found. It hadn't been sent to Nimmo because Bell said he wouldn't give evidence in court unless he had police protection and that wasn't her business. She had told him to go to the Chief Constable and meanwhile his report was put on one side.

She denied she had said that Nimmo was all against Maufe but she considered the specials were against Nimmo because he stopped them from bashing people about.

279

Counsel put it to her that this remark showed the prejudice that Bell had complained of but she denied it. And when our man tried to make her admit she had discouraged Bell from coming forward, the judge stopped him.

# 44

THE biggest thing in this case, first to last, was prejudice. And we weren't allowed to bring it out, not as the biggest thing. It was prejudice Bell was up against. I say Bell was a brave and good man to go on at all after he'd been threatened and after he found he couldn't get any protection. He knew if he went to the police, as Miss Willis had told him, he would be forced to come into court, and then if the Watch Committee refused a guard, he'd be beaten up.

Prejudice wasn't only the biggest thing against Bell, it was the biggest thing for Pincomb. It's no good saying courts aren't affected by local feeling, especially when you can hear it through the windows making a noise like lynching. Perhaps it didn't have much effect on the judge but it certainly touched up the jury.

And what all these people couldn't remember or didn't want to remember was how nervous they'd been six weeks before. Anyone who suggested there'd been any real danger was a traitor and a bit of a funk too. Look at this from the *Tarbiton Gazette*—"What is remarkable is the immense common sense with which this foolish attempt at intimidation was received by the general population. All classes displayed the most admirable calm, and a traveller through the country at the height of the so-called revolutionary crisis would have observed nothing more unusual than a bus driver in a Harris tweed coat, or a small holder's wife taking her basket of eggs to market in a Rolls."

The idea was nothing much had happened, and anyone who reminded 'em of one or two little accidents was worse than a dog who keeps on barking at the burglar when you want to go to sleep.

And why did old England take the strike so quietly? Because they hadn't time for anything else. Because they didn't think evil—not at first. Because they're always ready to believe "These chaps may be fools—but they mean well." Because they hadn't got round to saying, "What we need is a real clean-up— of the whole gang, right and left—of all these gammoneers— all these bugs in the wall-paper," before the talky boys saw it coming—saw the red light. And got together and called off the strike. They didn't want a revolution, any more than the other talky boys with money in the funds and safe quiet jobs, with pensions, all they wanted was to get back to the quiet times of grab and tickle. I'll look after you if you'll look after me.

But we've got to tell the same lie and that takes some working out. A general understanding. Gentlemen's agreement. Keep it quiet. Keep everything quiet. Wonderfully quiet in East Tarbiton. Unemployed Centre closed. Owing to unfortunate damage in workshops since change of management. Theft of stores. Place pretty well wrecked. Unemployed standing round the streets, very quiet indeed. Not wanted at home while women clearing up. Not wanted in pubs because can't afford drink. No money to go away. No hope of work.

All nice and quiet. And the politicos running two bye-elections on the theme of "How well we did it." See how quiet everything is. Except for that old fool Potter making a fuss about his yard, writing to the papers about his craftsmen, and a reconstruction.

Poor old Potter came to see me about his reconstruction. Would Nimmo take debentures? He had to have finance at once. He'd been to all the banks that morning. "Good morning, Sir Thomas. How are things with you?" "You know how they are. I want five thousand to open again." "Sorry, but I was just going to see you about that overdraft. Head Office is worried. Most unfortunate thing—this stoppage." "I've got orders to see me through the next six months." "On half-time." "Things will improve after the holidays. Bound to." "But meanwhile you're running at a loss. Pity about Frant's offer." "What offer?" "The one you refused last year. It was a good proposition." "To wipe me out and turn Potter's into an assembly shop." "But he offered a good price. I'm afraid you won't get such a good offer now." "I don't want offers from Frant. I don't like his methods. I've got my tradesmen to think of. Some of them have been with me for fifty years."

Banker pulls a face as if to say, "The old fool—living in the past. Don't know what's happening in the world."

In fact old Tom don't know what's happened to him. He don't know he's finished, smashed, shot to pieces. But he's beginning to feel a sort of queerness in his guts. He says to me, "Potter's yard has been in Tarbiton since 1670. We made yachts for Charles II—we made boats for Nelson and Franklin. And we employ half the place. Our men stay with us all their lives. We never put a man on the shelf while there's something he can do. And we're known all over the world. Potter's boats. Ask any shipping firm from Hong Kong to Rio." "Yes," I said, "but that doesn't count with the banks. And Frant's does." "Frant is a crook." "That's libel. He's a benefactor—he makes millions. Most up-to-date mass production in the country." "My God," says Tom, "he's not going to gobble Potter's. I'll fight him to the last." "The only hope is Winfield's. If he would back you. He backed Behrman's to keep Frant out." "But Behrman's is just Winfield's. Winfield kept nothing but the name, and sacked half the men, all the old ones. It's too old at forty now, in what they call Behrman's. Winfield's just another shark." "Don't be rude about the money game, Tom. Money is power. And power is a damn nasty customer. Frant and the banks. Winfield and the banks. The unions and the banks. All hooked up at the back like a whoreshop madam on the warpath, to keep the tarts in order and put up the price to the customer." "I'll raise the thing in parliament." "They'll talk it down. It's

284

what they're paid for." "I'll go to the papers." "They're about the biggest business of the lot. And Frant is one of their biggest advertisers." "I don't care—I'm not taking this lying down." The old man was in a highly shaky state and Lady Potter was running after him everywhere to pick him up when he had another fit. "Do come home now, dear—you know what the doctor said." "Doctors. What do they know about business? Unless they've got shares in Frant's. But my God, I'll give them a surprise, the whole lot of 'em," and off he goes to think up a surprise. Next week I saw him in the bankruptcy court. That was one surprise. And then he had that stroke. That was another.

But East Tarbiton wasn't surprised. They'd seen both coming a long time. And took 'em quietly. Went to his funeral quietly. Biggest funeral in Tarbiton for fifty years, but no top-hats. Very very quiet. Crowd of about two hundred stood fifty feet off not to see the poor old widow cry. They had manners, those poor gentlemen on the dole.

But none of the magistrates except old Penrose. From the same church. Potter had insulted 'em with all that talk about being let down. Public enemy. He wouldn't keep quiet. And Jim Latter another. That nasty ex-soldier, making a ridiculous fuss about some fellow called Maufe. Just one fellow, mark you. What's more, a poor fellow. And what's still more, an absolute nobody—a greengrocer's roundsman or something like that. Not even in a union. The lowest form of animal life—an honest freeman.

# 45

I PROTESTED against dragging my wife into the case. But the police pointed out her evidence might be vital. And she herself had know it all along. And expected the subpœna. Hence her calm.

Our man began by asking her if she remembered receiving any information from Lord Nimmo about the case. And she agreed at once she had had a note from him asking her to call on various people including Bell. But she couldn't remember any details of her talk with Bell except that it was about a fight between Pincomb and Maufe.

COUNSEL: "About the fight. Do you remember anything more definite about the fight?"

MRS. LATTER: "I remember the suggestion that Mr. Pincomb had given the first blow."

286

Counsel: "And there was a violent struggle?"

Mrs. Latter: "Yes, at least I think Mr. Bell said it was violent, but I discussed it with so many other people. Everyone was talking about it."

Counsel: "Do you remember asking Bell about Pincomb's falling on the ground?"

Mrs. Latter: "I'm afraid I don't."

Counsel: "Did Lord Nimmo's letter to you mention the fall?"

Mrs. Latter: "I don't remember that either. I'm so sorry but I can't be sure of anything except the fight."

Counsel for the prosecution cross-examined and she agreed she had had letters and wires from Nimmo every day and had interviewed dozens of people for him.

Here the judge asked if she had kept the original letter from Nimmo.

Mrs. Latter: "I don't know."

Judge: "You've kept some of his letters?"

Mrs. Latter: "A few—yes."

Judge: "Where are they now?"

Mrs. Latter: "The ones I kept are at the bank. I sent them there when I left my house."

The judge made an order for bringing the letters into court and the court was adjourned for half an hour till the tip-staff

287

came back. He brought a black tin box tied up with string and sealed. Also locked, but the key was looped onto the handle by a bit of red tape.

The two lawyers opened the box and Nina went through the letters with them. She soon found the one we wanted and it was handed to the judge who read it out to the jury.

"I'm sending you a scribble from someone called Bull or Bell who says he was an eye witness of the Pincomb arrest and Pincomb hit the first blow. He's under the impression that Maufe had been unjustly treated and is obviously prepared to make trouble. I wonder, could you look into the matter? There is a lot of very bad feeling on both sides and it will be worse if there is any mismanagement at the trial. Bull's address is 14a Drake Lane, Tarbiton."

Bell's statement wasn't in the envelope and Nina explained she'd never kept anything but Nimmo's letters which she'd been advised to keep on account of their value to history. She couldn't find room for all the other papers he sent. Some of them were thick manuscripts.

Counsel asked her if this letter did not refresh her memory about Bell's statement. And she agreed she remembered getting the statement and that it described Pincomb hitting at Maufe, but she did not recollect anything about a fall.

Counsel: "Do you remember your interview with the witness?"

Mrs. Latter: "Yes, I remember seeing him at his house."

Counsel: "But nothing about the purpose of your visit?"

MRS. LATTER: "Oh, yes, it was about the fight—I just don't remember details."

COUNSEL: "But you're not prepared to contradict the witness?"

MRS. LATTER: "No, indeed."

COUNSEL: "Did you try to make him withdraw his statement about the fall?"

MRS. LATTER: "No, of course not," and then suddenly changing her mind, "I mean, I wouldn't have done such a thing. I don't really remember exactly what it was all about."

COUNSEL: "You were very busy all the time?"

MRS. LATTER: "Terribly busy."

COUNSEL: "But you found time to make a special journey to see Bell?"

MRS. LATTER: "I passed the end of Drake Lane every day on the way to the Canteen Committee."

COUNSEL: "Is it fair to suggest that you regarded Bell as a trouble-maker?"

Trying to get in the point about prejudice, which had stopped the man from coming forward for the six weeks. But the judge stopped him again.

Counsel for prosecution only asked if she had not had all kinds of problems to investigate, and of course she said yes.

COUNSEL: "You were acting as confidential secretary to Lord Nimmo and your duty was to protect him from vague or irresponsible complaints."

Our man protested against this and the judge supported him.

Afterwards Miss Willis was recalled for re-examination, but I didn't hear this. In the last part of her evidence, after the letters were brought, my wife had been obviously very nervous and when she came out of the box, she turned faint. So I took her back to the Water Boy, sent her to bed and gave her a sleeping pill. She was always addicted to such pills and had a large supply of the strongest kind. But she would not let me leave her to sleep and in fact did not sleep. She held my hand and asked me to stay close to her.

I knew these fits in my wife from childhood. She was always subject to night terrors. And I saw of course what the trouble was now. The letters. But I could not speak about them because I was pretty sure already there was some hanky-panky about Bell's report. At last she said, "I suppose you were surprised about me writing—but it was all before the accident." She always spoke of her attempt at suicide as an accident. She knew, of course, I knew it was a suicide attempt, but she did not use the word because it was a bit too crude and might have sounded as if she were reminding me of my unkindness.

I said, "Yes, I quite understand."

"I'm sending back all his letters," she said, "and I'm asking him for any of mine, if he's kept them."

"Why not tell him to burn them?"

"I'd rather he sent them back so as to be sure he hasn't kept any."

"If they're letters you don't want to come out you'd better get hold of them."

290

"Yes, I shall."

But I was surprised next afternoon when I saw a brown paper parcel on the bed labelled in Nimmo's own thick splashy handwriting. We were packing at the time to go back to the Cottage for the last days before we sailed. We had to be at the Cottage to sort out family papers and relics before the sale.

I came in from the sitting-room where I had been putting up my official papers and found Nina packing her trunk. As usual she had two trunks with her even for this affair in the witness box. I cleared my books off the dining table and my toilet things from the washstand, but I didn't touch the parcel. Nina shut the trunk and pretended not to notice the parcel. She wished me to speak of it. But I could not do so for fear she would think me suspicious.

I sent for the porter to take away the trunks. At the last moment, Nina snatched up the parcel and said, "What shall I do with this?"

"I don't mind what you do with them."

"They're my letters, you know, to Chester."

"You could throw them in the dustbin or burn them in the grate."

Nina held the parcel in her hand and looked at me anxiously —she was trying to find out how suspicious I was. She then actually put the parcel in the grate which was, of course, empty, and said, "If we got the maid to bring some paraffin—"

I agreed to this and went out, saying I would see the luggage into the car. But in a few moments Nina followed me and handed me the parcel, without a word. I put it in the back of the car, next the bank box, which had just been returned by the court officer.

And when I found the parcel and the box both on the dressing-table at the Cottage, standing side by side, I saw the thing was working up for trouble between us, and I said, "For God's sake, make up your mind about these letters. We can't lug them to Africa with us."

But she didn't answer. She couldn't make up her mind. Nothing more was said about these letters, all that day. We spent the time going through the family things. The whole lower storey of the Cottage was now arranged for the sale and we were eating in the kitchen and sleeping in the servants' rooms next the old nurseries, on the top floor. All the family things to be kept back from the sale as worthless or to be kept for Robert were piled in the attic and the attic corridor, including a mass of stuff from my old home at Brookfield. There were trunks full of papers from centuries back and twenty enormous volumes of my Aunt Latter's albums containing old newspaper cuttings. We had decided already to burn all these and most of the papers—I lit a huge bonfire in the yard for the purpose. It would therefore have been easy for Nina to burn her own small parcel, and she had plenty of opportunities to do so without my noticing the act. But in the evening when the bonfire was dying down, the parcel was still there. I pointed at it and said, "What about it?" But she seemed not to hear me.

"You don't propose to take them to Africa with us?" I said.

"No, of course not." She looked at the parcel. And then at once her mood went away. Her problem was solved. Without any talk. And now I could see what a big problem it had been, I knew the letters must be dynamite.

She said to me in quite a gay tone, "No, indeed. I don't know how we're going to get everything in as it is."

And after another moment, she said, "As for the bank box, shall I send it over to the Longwater?"

I said, as she liked.

"I want to be sure Chester gets it personally. He's very particular about his letters."

"I daresay he is."

"Would you mind if I asked him to send someone?"

I said the letters were none of my business. And this was true at that time, about half-past four o'clock. But at six, I had a phone call about the case, that Maufe had been convicted and sent to gaol for three years.

# 46

I say the news of this cruel and wicked injustice reached me at just before six o'clock. I couldn't believe it. The evidence of prejudice against the specials, the whole scandalous treatment of Bell, the attempt to choke him off and his proof, in spite of every discouragement, that Pincomb had started the fight, his coming forward in spite of threats, seemed to me absolutely conclusive and unbeatable by any word-wangler in the law trade. I telephoned Clint for confirmation.

He answered it was true. Bell had gone to pieces in the last cross-examination. Counsel had made him say he was at least fifteen yards away from the scene, that several people were in the way, that Maufe might have hit Pincomb before he fell; that he had not seen Pincomb hit the kerb but only lying on the pavement, that he had discussed the police court evidence with

specials and they had pointed out it was important to establish
the fall as cause of injury. Then the prosecution brought the
doctor back to say Pincomb's fracture could not possibly have
been caused by a fall on the kerb.

And the judge in summing up told the jury that the important
point was not who had struck the first blow but whether Maufe
had used unnecessary force. And then went into the medical
evidence on the position of Pincomb's injuries which, he said,
must be due to a blow from behind, and they'd left him permanently crippled.

Clint said, too, there had been such feeling against Maufe in
the crowd outside he'd had to be smuggled out at a back door
into the police car.

I pointed out this was a put-up job by the commies, the whole
thing from start to finish had been a put-up commie job and
they had got right away with it. They'd got at Bell—the vital
witness—the only honest one. And we wouldn't even protect
him. It wasn't surprising the poor chap had lost his nerve. He
saw what he was up against.

Clint took all this very quietly. What did it matter to him. He
wasn't going to gaol for doing his duty at the risk of his life.
His life and children weren't ruined. He paused a bit as if to
drop a flower on the grave and then remarked cheerfully we'd
been unlucky in the unusual thinness of Pincomb's skull. I said,
what about my men smashed up on 9th by Pincomb's gang at
Pincomb's direct incitement? I said we'd been unlucky in having
a set of cowards and fakers on our Watch Committee.

I told nothing of this to my wife. I admit I was in such a

state of mind I didn't like to face her with such news. I kept away, therefore, in the attic, and it wasn't till I heard a car in the drive, and recognized Nimmo's small car, driven by Grant, I went in to the bedroom. I told her Nimmo had come, did she propose to see him? She said he'd probably come for the bank box, in answer to her call. Immediately it struck me this was the last chance of getting the facts about the Pincomb plot, if there had been a plot. For I say I'd suspected from the first, even before my wife's evidence in court, Maufe had been deliberately sacrificed.

After a moment's hesitation, therefore, I told my wife what had happened, that Maufe had been convicted and his life ruined.

"And he risked his life to do a job for his country when other people were deliberately dodging any responsibility at all."

She said nothing to this. She saw there was nothing to say.

I then said that after all I should like to see the letters. "God knows," I said, "I'd hoped all that business was over, but I don't see how I can let this fearful piece of injustice go through without doing everything I can to stop it. And I can't help feeling Nimmo's letters would throw a bit more light on things —on the Potter bargain and the deal with Pincomb. Perhaps all that backstairs work don't come legally into poor Maufe's case, but it's really the most important part of it. It shows how the specials were handicapped and how Nimmo double-crossed 'em all the time."

Nina, who was sitting on the floor among piles of old letters and papers, made no answer. So I said I would not read the letters without her leave.

296

I want it to be understood I asked my wife's leave to read these letters and my wife gave it. She did not even hesitate. She said, "As you like," and went on sorting the papers into different heaps. Afterwards, as I took the box and the parcel into the opposite corner of the room under the window, she said, "Only remember it was all before the accident."

I then opened the box with the key—they hadn't sealed it again—and began to read. After a moment, my wife got up and said, "I'll tell Chester to wait—I'll keep him downstairs till you're finished." She went downstairs to the door and I heard her speaking to Nimmo. Then the car drove away and my wife and Nimmo went down the passage into the kitchen.

I had already, at a first glance, perceived the nature of this correspondence, that it was a record of the blackest kind of treachery, a crime which will always redound to the dishonour of British so-called justice. I say I knew of my wife's part in this conspiracy against the country, and against the poorest, honestest, most humble citizens of the country, as soon as I opened the bank box. That is, before my wife left the room.

But I did not stop her leaving the room. Although I was sure she would at once join Nimmo in flight, I said in my heart, "Thank God." I knew this was really a piece of cowardice, in wishing to be spared the great agony of taking justice in my own hands, but I had never so loved this poor woman as on that day. For I knew it was because of her love she could not bring herself to destroy the letters. Though asked and invited to do so many times. For she feared I would suspect her of hiding some secret from me and of not loving me truly and completely.

I need not give long extracts from these letters—only such details as show what was going on, what was the real truth.

Letter dated 5/5/26, from my wife.

"I'm afraid I had to tell Jim about the Pincomb arrangement. He had me watched and his man saw me going in at Drake Lane. Of course I told him as little as I could—but he does definitely know there was a bargain about the buses."

Letter dated 6/5/26, from Nimmo at Smith's Hotel, Mayfair.

"I never said our dear Jim wanted for intelligence—far from it—but only that he was a political idiot—as you say yourself, it's no good trying to make him understand . . .

"I would not ask you to do this for me, my darling, but there is literally no one else I can trust to keep quiet. Never say a woman can't keep secrets."

Letter dated 7th, Palm Cottage, from my wife.

"I was with Jim last night and he was at his best (I won't say nicest—I mean his most honest and fair-play's-a-jewel). He wasn't forgiving me by any means (why should he?) but he wasn't going to say any more about anything. So the Pincomb plot is, I hope, and really think, quite buried."

From Nimmo. Smith's Hotel, 9/5/26.

"I've just been on the phone about this brutal and senseless assault on Pincomb. I gather Frant thinks I'm acting too precipitately in suspending the special involved. Not a bit of it. The case is perfectly simple. No doubt Pincomb did make some effort to avoid arrest. But he then suffered violence of a nature that may actually cause his death. This is the stark truth and this is what the public will understand. The policeman is completely untouched and Pincomb unarmed, even with a stick, is permanently and perhaps fatally injured. Nothing will shake my decision. But let me know of anything in the way of comment that comes to your ears. What does your friend Winfield think? How does J. take it? I'm afraid badly. But you could get Frant or Winfield to drop a word about our great appreciation of his services and that we are recommending him for a decoration. *This must not come from me*—Winfield is probably the best intermediary—J. thinks him honest because he is rude."

Palm Cottage. No date. From my wife.

"I missed your call. But the man I mentioned in my note (the man who said he saw P. trying to escape) apparently wrote something about it, quite a long report. Miss W. has it in the office and asked what to do about it. I said to do nothing with it for the present and I've got it here for you to see—I'll send it over by Grant when you come and if you want it. I know it would only be a nuisance just now. He wanted police protection for one thing (he was quite terrified of what he called reprissels —I thought it rather a good word) and I knew you wouldn't allow that. Miss W. asked me if I'd heard any more from you about how to handle people over the suspension. I said no, but you were certainly against Maufe and I thought you were quite right. P. is conscious and a little better, but they say he may be paralyzed."

From Nimmo. 10/5/26. In pencil and dated 10 Downing St.

"I've been waiting here for two hours. They didn't actually refuse me at the door but I haven't seen anyone yet except the footman who asked me to wait, not even a secretary with the usual smooth apologies which are so much more insulting than a slap in the face . . ."

And apparently the same day, dated Smith's Hotel and written in ink this postscript:

"Don't let anyone at Tarbiton be in any illusion about the Maufe affair. It's got all the elements of a very big issue indeed. The Communists with their usual efficiency have rushed it all over the country and here in London it is already being discussed as a key case. I was asked about it to-night by a Labour man, not by any means the most bitter or prejudiced, and he said he was betting Maufe would get off scot-free—we would take care of that. But he warned me it would have the worst effect on public feeling.

"What we have to do is prove to the country and the world, at this moment, that there is still such a thing as *British* justice. That this is not yet a police state where a constable can beat up a citizen merely because he disapproves of his political opinions."

11/5/26. Smith's Hotel.

"I'm awaiting a call from Downing Street. But for the last

300

time and not for very much longer—my patience is nearly exhausted . . .

"Very lucky I moved so promptly in the Maufe case. It has had the best effect on relations here. I saw some of the Labour leaders last night at their H.Q. and I was asked if it was our intention to bring Maufe to trial. They were most comically divided between regrets that they've lost the chance of a real grievance and relief that they won't be forced to back up the Communists . . .

"Police protection—quite definitely no. This would still further prejudice our whole position in the eyes of the public. It smells of the police witness, the put-up job. It would ruin any chance we have of relieving this dangerous situation.

"Miss W. Just hint to her that it's better not to send on these communications. They only confuse the issue. And I get enough of them already from all quarters.

"I may return to-day. And I shall pray to see you, if only for a few minutes. I wonder if you ever realize how much that hope has sustained me in this valley of the shadow . . ."

There was a good deal of this in all Nimmo's letters, between his political enquiries, what people were thinking of him and his private instructions to call on so-and-so and find out if possible if he would be in favour of this or that. Would Winfield back up a proposal to start new dock works at once; would Lady Lilmouth sound her husband on the views of the Mayor of Lilmouth?

And I'd just read how Nimmo regarded my wife as water

in the desert to the dying soul when there was a knock at the door and Nimmo walked in. I was taken by surprise and simply stared at him. He saw the letter in my hand and said at once, "Ah, you're making an investigation."

I say I was surprised at this interruption. I thought Nimmo was about the bravest man I'd ever seen. But this was wrong. The truth was he was the most impudent, and also, the most conceited. He thought there was no one he couldn't talk round— nothing he couldn't explain away.

"Yes," I said, "and I've found out a lot already."

"My dear Jim," he said at once, "private letters are meant only for their recipients. If your name has sometimes been handled rather freely in my hasty notes from town, you must not take it to heart. I have heard and read some pretty strong opinions of my own character, as expressed by you, and I think you know that they have never to the slightest degree affected my old and devoted regard."

I said I wasn't in the least concerned with his remarks about my character. I'd always known he regarded me as a political idiot. That's what every crook and three-card leg in the world thought about every honest man just because he was honest and laid himself open to be swindled. But what I'd found out now was something new and much more important. That was how a brave man had been railroaded into gaol and his life ruined by a deliberate collusion between Nimmo and my wife.

"The case is over," I said, "and what you wanted has happened. You've sold Maufe to the mob. You've made an example and put yourself right with the gang of gimme-boys and commies who mean by hook or crook, but chiefly crook, to smash this country first and then take it over. The gangs you're now sucking up to. Well," I said, "there's only one answer. You run your show on publicity for the mob and that's what I've got to do. To hit the headlines in a big way. To make an example. The Maufe case is over—the poor chap is finished. You've won. But you haven't won the last move—that's with me now."

I'd got up and put myself between Nimmo and the door to the stairs. My idea was to wring his neck. But just then I saw my razor-case on the dressing-table, and I thought it would be quicker to cut his throat.

He positively grinned at me. He said, "My poor dear Jim, do you mean to snip my head off with a pair of nail scissors?"

The old trick succeeded for the moment. Though it was of course quite useless in enabling the man to escape. As I blocked the stairs. But I looked round to make sure I had my hand on the razor-case rather than the scissors. Both were in morocco. And in that second Nimmo darted through the far door into the attic and from the attic across the corridor to the servants' lavatory. Before I could catch him, he had banged and bolted the door.

He then began to yell "murder" from the window, to call for Grant, and for Nina to go away. His calling to Grant was only another trick. I'd heard Grant drive off. But his warning Nina let me know she hadn't run off. She was still somewhere in the house. However, fearing Grant might be parking in the road, as usual, and Nimmo's yells might reach him, I set to work on the lavatory door with a milking-stool and smashed the upper panels in, to get at the bolt. Nimmo was still screaming when I began. The window was a bit too high for him and he was standing holding the sill, and jumping up to the window each time to let out a yell. When I put in my arm to reach for the bolt, he turned round and tried to catch at my wrist. Then all at once, he slipped down on to the seat. I say definitely I never touched the man throughout. The bolt was a bit beyond my reach, and I was just beginning again with the stool on the more solid part of the door frame, when I heard my wife's voice.

I turned round at once and told her Nimmo was in the lavatory, and he seemed to have fainted.

She said we must get to him at once and begged me to break the lock. I said this wasn't the important thing I had to do. But she got on the stool to look in. She was very agitated and I didn't know how to explain what I meant. I didn't know how to explain to my wife when she came to me so fearlessly. I had to ask myself if I was capable of this great duty laid on me by a cruel fate.

# 47

I SAY I never loved this sweet gentle woman so much as now when I knew she had to die. Because of the rottenness. Because of the corruption. Because all loyalty was a laugh and there was no more trust. Because marriage was turned into a skin game out of a nice time by safety first. Because of the word made dirt by hypocrites and cowards. Because there was no truth or justice anywhere any more. Because of the grabbers and tapeworms who were sucking the soul out of England.

I say I couldn't explain to her in the attic and she didn't see what was in my mind. She was half-way through the nursery, going to telephone for a doctor, when I shut and locked the nursery door and said it wasn't necessary to call anyone. This was a thing between ourselves.

Then she looked closely at me and turned white, and sat

down on the bed. She began to say again I must not mind the letters. They had been written before that day of the accident.

"My darling," I said, "it isn't what you said about me—it's about the fearful thing you and Nimmo have done. Perhaps you think it wasn't very much to betray Maufe and to join in with the liars and cowards and tricksters against an honourable man, against the honour of England. But that only makes it worse—it only proves what I say, that the rottenness has gone too far."

She looked at me a moment and then she asked me if I was going to kill her. I said a great crime had been committed and how could we just pass it over. If nothing was done we should be cowards and criminals. How could we go on together living under that feeling like rats or bugs?

She interrupted to say she couldn't bear to part from me again and if I thought she deserved to die, then I must kill her. But she hoped I wouldn't hurt her. And then she begged me again to break in the lavatory door and get Nimmo out. Because she was sure he was dead and it was horrible he should be left in such a place. So great a man. Perhaps I didn't agree he was a great man but millions of people all through the world, especially poor and humble people, revered his name.

I said this was the very ramp that had rotted the world. Tickling the mob. With lies and bunkum. The Nimmo racket. Through the jabber boys. Through the Press. And rotted Nimmo too. And her.

But I knew it was no good talking to her. She kept staring at me and saying she was ready to die but she didn't quite believe we couldn't go on as before— she wanted to so much. She couldn't understand she was up against something bigger than either of us or anyone's happiness. The truth. And nothing could change it. She didn't want to understand. It was too big. I say I knew even then perhaps no one would want to understand. As happened. Look at the way the papers have handled this thing. As a sex murder. As a common adultery case. Suggesting I killed my wife because she was unfaithful and a gold digger. It is a lie she sold me. She took jewels and settlements because it was easier to take them than refuse them. Because she was afraid of poverty and she knew I'd chucked away most of my own money. Only one of them ever quoted my words at the first statement when I said I killed her for an example because it was necessary. And in the same paragraph they put the statement by the doctor I was sane and responsible for my actions. So as to make the people see their real opinion I was as mad as a hatter and didn't know what I was doing.

The papers all got together at once to smear the thing over with rottenness, to keep the people blind, to make them think there was nothing really wrong with the country.

It's a small point, but you never read anywhere that Nimmo died in a w.c. What the papers said, he was found dead at Palm Cottage after a heart attack. And his death was not unexpected, though undoubtedly accelerated by his immense patriotic exertions during the late strike.

It has been a bitter thought to me in these weeks I'm going through hell for nothing. That I killed my darling to no purpose; that this great country is so blinded and bound, so hocussed and gammoned by the bunkum boys, the smart ones, the power and money merchants, it doesn't know where it's going or what it's going there for and it's too bewildered to care.

And if it could take the truth, it wouldn't get it. When I was first gaoled, the young man, Drew, asked for an interview. I remembered him as a decent chap and I wondered if he'd got a job. So I let him come. It turned out he'd got on to a London paper. He'd done well out of that scoop I gave him. He was very pleased with life and very grateful to me, so I gave him his interview. I told him why I'd had to kill my wife, as an honourable man, and why I was glad of publicity. I told him the trouble with the country was it was run from top to bottom by men without honour, men on the grab.

And how did it come out in his paper? A description of how I looked and spoke and a lot of stuff about my devotion to my wife and my political opinions. Nothing about honour at all. I was disgusted with young Drew. I said he was in the racket. But I got a letter from him to apologize and say he himself had been surprised by that article. It had been rewritten in the office.

Why did they rewrite that article, and cut out the only important bit, the heart of it, the truth? Because they weren't selling truth. They were selling the paper. And the men who write the papers and make them up in the office, don't believe in anything but materialism, big business, jabberwocks and power-grabbers, they can't see the simplest facts; they take all this mass of lies and grab for something you can't do anything about.

They think me mad because I couldn't live like a rat. They

think me a fool who murdered the wife he loved for nothing. But it wasn't a murder I did. It was an execution. And I didn't do it for nothing. Not even if the Press have turned it into just another sex crime. I did it because I, myself, had to do it. There was no other choice for a man who wasn't prepared to live like a rat. And that poor girl understood me at last. I saw she was very frightened at the end and I tried to slip behind her, to do it before she knew. But she guessed what I meant and caught my hand and begged me not to take her by surprise.

At last we heard a car in the drive. Grant coming back for his master. I said we could not wait any more and did she want to pray. She knelt down but said she could not pray, she did not think it would help. But would I forgive her, because she had truly loved me.

I said it was for her to forgive me and I finished the thing in one stroke. She fell at once and did not struggle at all.

# JOYCE CARY

once described himself as "one of those Anglo-Irishmen whose birth land is now a foreign country." Educated in England, he took a degree in law at Oxford after abandoning a career in art. Even then he determined to be a writer, and this was one reason why, when he left Oxford, he went out to the Balkan war of 1912-13. He wanted the experience of war and was convinced that this would be the last one. Later he joined Sir Horace Plunkett's Cooperative Society in England, resigned and joined the Nigerian service. It was not until he was invalided out of the service and settled in Oxford with his wife that he started to write. For ten years he wrote and destroyed novel after novel, trying to find an idea of life satisfying to himself. His first book, *Aissa Saved,* rewritten many times, was published in 1930.

From 1930 until his death in 1957 Joyce Cary wrote constantly, books of such richness and variety as to place him securely among the most eminent novelists of the century.

# *The* UNIVERSAL *Library*